ALSO BY BARBARA D'AMATO

Hard Case

Hard Women

Hard Luck

Hard Tack

Hardball

HARD CHRISTMAS
A CAT MARSALA MYSTERY

Barbara D'Amato

SCRIBNER

NEW YORK   LONDON   TORONTO   SYDNEY   TOKYO   SINGAPORE

SCRIBNER
1230 Avenue of the Americas
New York, NY 10020

SCRIBNER and design are
trademarks of Simon & Schuster Inc.

Manufactured in the United States of America

1 3 5 7 9 10 8 6 4 2

Library of Congress Cataloging-in-Publication Data
D'Amato, Barbara.
Hard Christmas : a Cat Marsala mystery / Barbara D'Amato.
p.   cm.
1. Marsala, Cat (Fictitious character)—Fiction. 2. Private investigators—Illinois—
Chicago—Fiction. 3. Women detectives—Illinois—Chicago—Fiction. 4. Chicago
(Ill.)—Fiction.   I. Title.
PS3554.A467H34   1995
813'54—dc20
95-23254
CIP

ISBN 0-684-19687-5

ACKNOWLEDGMENTS

Several people have helped with this book.

Most of all I want to thank Doug VanderSys, of The Bookman bookstore in Grand Haven, Michigan, who is also a grower of Christmas trees. His patience with questions and follow-up questions was great, and his knowledge of books made his extra advice rich and valuable.

My thanks to:

Dirk Hoffius, Esq., of Varnum, Riddering, Schmidt, and Howlett in Grand Rapids, Michigan.

Case Hoogendoorn, Esq., of Hoogendoorn, Talbot, Davids, Godfrey & Milligan in Chicago.

Mary Swain of Grand Rapids, Michigan, for conservation advice and for information about west Michigan environmental action groups.

Jerome C. Steketee for the story of Mayor Gillis Steketee of Grand Rapids, Michigan, 1881.

The Holland Archives at Hope College in Holland, Michigan, and Jeanne Jacobson.

For those interested in the early days of Christmas tree selling, the story of Herman Scheunemann's schooner full of Christmas trees that plied Lake Michigan each December, until it foundered and sank in a winter storm in 1912, has recently been told in the children's book *The Christmas Tree Ship*, by Jeanette Winter.

HARD CHRISTMAS

• 1 •

APRIL

Two lines of dunes lay between the farm and Lake
Michigan. The breeze brought long-distance scents of
everything west of the farm. It held the smell of the lake,
the air pure from crossing a hundred miles of open water,
the damp sand smell of the shoreline, the warm, spiced
odor of the beach grasses that grew on the first line of
dunes, a bit like cinnamon or mace, but a bit like corian-
der, too.

At the second dune, the air picked up the elusive odor of
beech woods, the large, pure stands of beech that grew on
the second line of sand dunes, their bark bluish silver, their
leaves just now showing the first green of spring, tiny soft
leaves, with miniature veins. They smelled like sunshine
and lemon and a hint of something like dry eucalyptus.

And last was the tang the breeze picked up as it crossed
the farm—a hundred acres of Scotch pine, blue spruce,
and green spruce. Row on row of trees, a pine-pitch, warm
green fragrance. All year long it smelled like Christmas.

Henry DeGraaf stood on the porch and breathed in the
Michigan air. He was familiar with every nuance and
would have known from the scent that this was a west
breeze, even if he had not seen the tops of the big oaks
near the house bending slightly to the east. If the breeze

had been due south, the scent of Lake Michigan would have been replaced by the aroma of open fields and fertilizer. North would have brought the smell of horses. And east, unfortunately, the gasses of industrialization, the city, and cars. He could tell when the breeze meant rain and when it meant clearing. Now in his late seventies, he had been reading this land his entire life. He thought that the breeze would soon drop off to nothing. It had that slight dusty flavor that meant it would warm and settle as the sun reached higher in the sky.

And that meant the spray plane would come over with the aerial insecticide. The pilot wouldn't take off if there was much wind, but he was a day late already. The lilacs were in bloom, and that was the season when whitescale insects reproduced on Scotch pine. Now, while they were larvae, was the only time they could be attacked. The adults hid under impenetrable waxy scales, tightly bonded to the twigs of the trees, like miniature oyster shells. There was a window of only a few days in the spring when the young emerged as naked crawlers, and went to find their own spot to hunker down under a shell for the rest of their lives.

Henry turned back to the kitchen and poured one more cup of strong coffee. "It's almost ten, Carat," he said to his golden retriever. "Want to check that the plane can see all our numbers?"

Carat jumped up, spun in a circle, ran to the door, came back, ran to the door again, then stared at her master, wondering how he could possibly be so slow.

"I'll get my jacket." He put down the coffee on the kitchen table and gave Carat the crust of his toast. Carat had been named by Henry's granddaughter, Nell, who said that the dog's coat looked like twenty-four-carat gold. People hearing the name often thought it was Carrot, and there was enough rich orange in the gold to make the name reasonable.

Henry went to the row of pegs next to the back door. Carat ran between his legs, crossed in front of him in the doorway, and bumped him from behind at the back of the knee.

"Hey, mutt! If I fall down and break my tokus, you won't get your walk."

Carat ran in circles.

"Where's my jacket?"

The row of ten wooden pegs set into the wall held three billed caps and a Stetson, an Indiana Jones hat, a gray vest with pockets, a yellow rain slicker, and a green and brown camouflage coat Henry sometimes wore fishing. His orange quilted down vest was missing.

"Now why would anybody take that old thing?" he said to Carat. Carat didn't care. She ran to the door again, and back to Henry.

"Oh, well." Henry picked up his asthma inhaler from the table, put it in his jeans pocket, and slipped on the camo jacket. He pushed aside a large purple dinosaur that belonged to Nell. She had outgrown it four years ago, but the dog still carried it around the house. He ought to know the name of the thing, Bennie or Barney or Beanie, but he always called it Purple People Eater, after a song that had been popular years before, and Nell always laughed, so that was okay. When he stepped out the back door, Carat nearly knocked him over.

The breeze had dropped to almost nothing, but the air still held the tang of pine trees and a distinct scent of the lake.

A row of eleven red oaks, one of them large and ten gigantic, ran along the driveway, oaks that had been planted there when the land was first cleared by the early settlers.

The family story was that the first four had been found in a rough row by the first settler, Hendrik DeGraaf, and he had transplanted others into place to make a long line. If true, this would make them a hundred and fifty years old. Henry had thought of having the University of Michigan Extension Service take a core sample of one and count the rings. But he never got around to it, and he knew his underlying reason was that he was afraid it might hurt the tree, even though everybody told him it wouldn't.

Automatically, he checked the red oak leaf buds. They were still tightly closed. His grandfather had always said that when the oak buds were the size of a squirrel's ear, you could safely plant your corn. Couple of weeks yet.

Henry sauntered out across their small vegetable garden, taking care to avoid the back of the bed, where asparagus might be starting to send up spears. Time to get out the rototiller and go over the front part of the bed soon.

"Come on, Carat," Henry said, as if the dog wasn't already way out ahead of him. "Let's check the signs for the spray guy."

The fields in the area were numbered for the crop-dusting aircraft. The identifying numbers were mounted on poles high enough to clear the top of the crop itself, painted on large pieces of wood, two per pole, set in a tent shape so the aircraft could see them from either of two directions. Once in a while, though, a tree branch or a piece of paper or plastic would blow over the numbers. The plane would not spray if there was any doubt whose field it was. A spray that was necessary for one crop could sometimes kill another. There were a great many blueberry fields around here, which used different sorts of spray and a different spray schedule from the tree farms. Henry disliked pesticides, but at this point you couldn't make any money in tree farming without them.

Or even with them some of the time, he thought.

Henry hurried. He knew the plane would take off as soon as the pilot was certain the wind was down.

There was a field of Scotch pine, then a field of blue spruce on the east consisting of trees only three feet high. It was always fun walking through them. They were big enough to look like real trees, but short enough so that you felt like a medieval giant in seven-league boots striding through a forest. Their number pole was clear of debris.

Beyond were five acres of Scotch pine, which the plane would spray, two of the acres just a year past being set out. They were barely up to his knee. Generally, they looked like they were growing well enough, although in places there were signs of winter damage. There had been several falls of heavy, wet snow in late winter. It was the weight, not the cold, that was hard on evergreens. They kept their needles all winter, and this made them vulnerable. The weight of the snow broke branches and occasionally snapped larger trees in half.

Five acres of five-year-old Scotch pine came next. Their number pole was clear. Then a field of green spruce ripe for harvest for the coming Christmas. They were very uniform, all between six and seven feet tall, all conical and deep green, the perfect Christmas tree.

Henry reached the pole and saw that a hunk of black plastic trash bag had blown into the field and lay around the upper part of the pole, over the numbers. He pulled it off, crumpled it to the size of a golf ball, wadded it into his pocket, and turned to go.

Just in time, too, because he thought he heard the

plane's engine in the distance. Or maybe it was the motorbike that his neighbor's kid, Ed DeBruyn, rode.

Henry hurried to leave. He didn't want to be caught by
spray. Not that the stuff was all that deadly. It was called
an environmentally safe mix, partly botanicals, partly Or-
thene, a lower dose of the really toxic stuff than they used
to use. But with his asthma, getting caught in a cloud of
airborne crud was not a good idea.

Henry walked rapidly toward the edge of the green
spruce field, Carat sniffing around his heels.

Ahead, he saw the biplane coming in low over the
house. So the sound wasn't Ed's motorbike. Henry waved
his arms.

The trees were over his head. The pilot wouldn't see
him.

Henry had to get out of the spray path. He began to run.
He ran toward the five-year-old Scotch pines, but before
he got there, the crop duster leveled off over the small
blue spruces near the house. Gray-white vapor emerged
from the plane and trailed behind it in a conical cloud that
sank quickly to earth.

Henry ran, waving his arms at the plane.

Suddenly, he realized that he was wearing the camouflage jacket, not the bright orange vest he usually wore in
the fields. The orange vest would have been visible to the
pilot; the camo vest camouflaged him.

Henry tried to run at right angles to the descending
cloud, but it was too close. As it sank to the earth, it spread
out and rolled, over the trees and over him. It smelled terrible.

Now he didn't know whether to run, to get out of here
as fast as possible, or whether the exertion of running was
more likely to bring on the asthma. He grabbed his inhaler
out of his pocket and sucked in a breath of the medication,

just to be on the safe side, but at the same time he kept running.

He felt that first grabbing in his bronchial tubes, that first seizing up of his chest that was so familiar.

Then it got worse. He had half a breath in his lungs, but he could neither take in more air nor exhale.

The plane came slowly around, banking, surfing against the air, for another pass over the rows of trees where he stood.

Terrified now, he hurried to the edge of the field, where he might find good air. His inhaler was in his hand. He discharged more vapor into his mouth, but though he tried to breathe as he ran, very little medication actually went in.

A creek trickled through one side of the farm. Henry had left standing all the oaks, maples, and underbrush for a hundred feet back from the water's edge. He had not cut the trees there partly because it would have been harder to cultivate the slope down to the river, but also because a wooded place beyond the fields looked so beautiful. Now it beckoned to him like a godsend.

If he could make it to the woods, the oaks and maples would break the drift of the spray. Down near the water's edge the air would be pure. He was sure of it. If he could only take in enough air to get there.

His face was coated with the moist, oily spray. He couldn't exhale; he couldn't inhale. His eyes seemed to be working in strange ways. The woods, as he stumbled toward them, were dotted with little bursts of yellowish light, and odd patches of black.

But he made it. He crashed over some wild blackberry bushes that tore at his hands, but he didn't feel the scratches. Carat ran back and forth, sniffing Henry's leg, uttering little yelps of fear. She knew something was terribly wrong. Henry bumped into the trunks of several

beeches and red oaks as he caromed down to the little
creek. At the edge of the water, he fell to his knees and
tried to take another gulp of his inhaler. He couldn't get
more than a choked quarter-breath.

It just wasn't enough. The day, the trees, the gentle
whisper of the creek, all grew distant. He no longer heard
the hum of the aircraft at all. Henry knew he was dying.
His chest muscles fought the obstruction; he could feel his
ribs bending with the force of the struggle. The day was all
so black now that he just closed his eyes.

Carat whined. She darted back and forth between the
ridge and her master several times, then made up her mind.
She lay down next to him and rested her chin on his arm.

December 1847

My dear Katya,

*We are settled, if we can call it settled. I am
clearing land, little by little, and although the days
are chilly, with snow in the air, after cutting an hour
with the long saw I find I must go to the creek and
spread cool water on my face. The creek is very
beautiful as it winds past my fields, but its useful-
ness is most important now. It provided water until
we could put in the little well. I had just money
enough for an old hand pump, and this makes
Pieterke's life much easier, as she can wash the
clothes without going to the creek for each pail of
water.*

*I must cut several more good loads of wood.
Christmas is coming, and I must earn at least a little
money. We will nail up two stockings on the wall of
the cabin. No child expects more than one toy, but*

Pieternella and little Gerritt have been good children and should receive something. They help carry sticks to the woodpile. Pieternella helps her mother cook and every morning helps rake over the dirt floor of the cabin. Someone at church, I think it was Minnie VerSluis, who always thinks she knows where the best bargains can be found, told me several of the congregation are sending to Chicago for some dolls at a reasonable price. I cannot afford it unless there is a small one, very, very cheap.

And what for Gerritt? I thought I might make him a hoop, but after puzzling over it decided not. A hoop must be perfectly round to roll properly. And where would the child roll it, anyway, in this primitive land where there are no streets? And why, dear Katya, have streets when there are no carriages and nowhere to go if you had one?

I have cut quite a lot of ash and oak. If I can find someone with a horse and sledge, I can draw the logs to the village to sell and use the money to buy a small doll. My own homemade sledge has wooden runners. I load it with three large logs, cut nine feet long, then lean hard into the leather harness and pull. But I can only pull as far as the house, not all the way to the village, and of course I own no horse.

I could carve a small steam engine for Gerritt from ash wood. Ash cuts like butter. It is a wonderful wood, and will burn even when green. Or, another idea, if I can buy a piece of tin, I might make a pinwheel, like the ones I used to have as a boy in the Netherlands. My father made me one once.

I am thinking more of home as the holidays approach. When I was a child my mother took me to Amsterdam to see Sinterklaas. On Sinterklaas

*Abend we watched old Bishop Sinterklaas land in
Amsterdam from a boat, with Zwart Piet to help him
carry his bag.*

*I must keep these images out of my head. It is the
children I work for, after all, and their future.
Always the children.*

*What shall we eat on Christmas day? Nine days
out of ten we have cornmeal mush for breakfast,
corn cake for dinner, and corn bread for supper. We
burn corn for ersatz coffee. Twice I have caught a
turtle in the creek, once a big snapping turtle with a
lot of meat on it. But they are very hard to find and
dangerous. Their jaws are strong enough to snap off
a finger.*

*It is beginning to snow. They are large flakes that
come down spinning. It looks like the kind of snow
that goes on for days. The village is a half day's
walk away, so one trip in the deepening drifts for
the tin and the doll is the most I can undertake.
There will be no holiday ham, no almond paste for
cookies, not even any wheat flour. At fifty cents a
bushel—four times the price of corn—it is much too
dear. We will have to be resigned to a hard
Christmas.*

Hendrik DeGraaf

• 2 •

THANKSGIVING DAY

My aged Bronco was running well, for a change. It's temperamental. Usually it's the gas gauge that self-destructs. This has happened three times. I'm driving along, thinking everything is fine, and then I realize that in a hundred miles the needle on the gas gauge hasn't gone down. Twice I made it to a station in time. Once I had to walk.

I was northbound on U.S. 31, a highway that runs north and south through Michigan along the east shore of Lake Michigan. A few miles north of the city of Holland—population 25,000—I turned west, toward the lake. I took Thornapple Drive west about a mile through blueberry farms, not far enough to reach the shore of Lake Michigan. The fields of blueberries looked like red mist from a distance, and as I got closer, I realized that their buds, formed this fall and waiting for spring, were red and the twigs orange. I passed mailboxes with names like Debruyn, TerHorst, Vandekamp, and DenUyl. Dutch country without a doubt. And here was the driveway I had been told to watch for. A mailbox read DEGRAAF and under it 5807 THORNAPPLE.

The driveway was a long, gravel and sand two-track disappearing into fields of pines. More pines "than you can shake a stick at," as my uncle would say. The November sun was shining brightly, and the pines were many shades of green. The fields were a patchwork of different greens—the blue-green of blue spruce, the emerald green of green spruce, and a kind of rusty green on a droopier pine that I couldn't identify. They were also of many different sizes, whole square patches of tiny blue spruce, or tall green spruce, and one square field with just stumps. Seeing the trees growing in blocks like that made the difference of color and form all the more impressive.

The driveway curved right, then curved left, then ended at a large white house. My home for the next three days.

It was an old house, made of horizontal wood siding painted white. In the central portion the boards were thinner than most siding in use today, and the windows were tall and narrow. A porch ran around the three sides of the house I could see. One end of the porch had slightly wider railing uprights, and the walls there had wider siding, with windows that were broad rectangles, not vertical. A whole section had obviously been added on many years after the main house was built. The cedar shake roof was stained red. There were two chimneys made of a beautiful pink brick, one in the middle and one at the right end of the building. Smoke snaked upward from the middle one.

After I braked behind a motorcycle and turned off the car, I could hear a dog barking. By the time I'd half opened the car door, a golden retriever had his paws on the side of the car and was looking in happily through the window. This was not an attack dog, unless you meant attack by his tongue. I got out.

He was a she, and she was pleased to see me. She licked my hand, then my elbow, and wagged her tail when I took my duffel bag out of the car.

I had just slammed the door when a young girl came out of the house. She was about twelve or thirteen.

"I'm sorry!" the child said, breathlessly. "She's not supposed to jump on people. Her name is Carat, like twenty-four carat, not like, you know, beta carotene carrots. She's not particularly well trained, but she's beautiful, isn't she?"

In my experience, children meeting strangers either talk too much or maintain a rigid silence. This was one who talked. She was beautiful herself, and actually not unlike Carat. She had fine, pale gold hair and a friendly way of leaping forward, impulsive and eager, like the dog. Better trained, though.

It was late afternoon, and the sun was suddenly eaten by a bank of clouds rising from the west like a slow-motion wave from the sea. Immediately, all the warmth went out of the day. It had been just superficial, just the light of the early winter sun.

There were two other cars in the drive and one in the garage. Probably relatives' cars, since this was Thanksgiving Day.

"Aunt Marie should be back any second. Dad and everybody else is out in the barn. Except Gran. She's taking a nap. They told me to watch for you." Carat jumped on me again. "You'd better come in," the girl said. "For some reason, when she's inside the house, Carat doesn't jump on people. She thinks jumping's an outdoor game."

I had clothes and my laptop in my duffel bag, which Carat was trying to hug. She also considered my shoes very interesting. A doggy nosegay of Chicago smells.

Also, seat-belted into a child car seat in his traveling cage was my parrot, Long John Silver. He was supposed to stay with my significant other, Sam Davidian, over the weekend, but Sam is a trauma surgeon, and discovered he had to do double duty because a fellow doctor, Chad Bennett, slipped on a freshly scrubbed floor, fell onto a syringe full of tranquilizer he was about to jam into a patient, and blissed himself into next week. Or "hoist with his own petard," as Sam said. Anyway, I didn't think Sam would have enough time to take care of Long John, so I had to pack him into his carrying cage and bring him.

I got him out of the car.

"Oh, wow!" the girl said.

"His name is Long John Silver. I'm really sorry about turning up here with him. I didn't have anybody to leave him with. But he can stay out of the way in my room and he doesn't smell or anything like that."

"What is he?"

"An African gray parrot. I know he's not beautiful, but he talks up a storm." LJ is not one of those handsome blue and green or yellow and red parrots. Like all African grays, he is an ugly gunmetal color, with splashes of what look like dried blood on his back and tail.

She said, "Oh, we'd be *happy* to have him."

LJ looked at her and said, "Beauty is its own excuse for being."

She blushed. "Does he mean me?"

"Yes, he certainly seems to." Sometimes the damn bird acts like he's a whiz at making friends. Other times, he bites.

"That's not Shakespeare!" I said to LJ. "I think it's Ralph Waldo Emerson."

The girl said, "Shakespeare?"

"Oh, the fool bird thinks he only quotes Shakespeare. He lived for twenty years with an English professor who taught at Northwestern University and he never quite outgrew the experience."

Carat was sniffing the cage. She looked at LJ hungrily. The girl said, "Maybe we should go in." She and I walked up the porch steps. "I'm Cat," I said. "What's your name?"

"Oh, gee! Sorry. Nell."

"That's nice."

"My whole name is really dorkish. But you know, we just sort of forget about it. Except Gran. Gran *uses* it."

"What is it?"

"Pieternella. I mean, can you imagine going around being called that?"

I was here because I had nagged my editor, Hal Briskman. I was at a highly ambivalent point in my career, and I was trying to pitch him a different sort of story.

"Christmas trees?" he said.

"Yes. I want to write about farming. I want to do something poetic."

"Can't you get shot at again or something like that?"

"The only thing I know about getting shot at is that you don't do it on purpose."

"Cat, I don't want you to get puffed up about this, but you've become a local celebrity. Tough female reporter thing. It's taken you forever to get to this point. Don't mess it up."

"Uh—"

"You know Si Newhouse has bought the paper?"

"Yeah."

"I want to take you national. You could be a big deal."

"Why doesn't that translate to money?" I said.

"Well—"

"See, that's why I want to do something contemplative for a change. Something that's not all buckets of blood. Something with roots."

"Christmas trees? You're taking roots too literally."

"Okay, hey, who cares. Send me to do a firsthand report

on little-known beaches of the Bahamas, all expenses paid."

"Not gonna happen."

"Something more pithy? Undercover work on a Parisian art-forgery ring?"

"I said we got bought. Not that we were suddenly *Travel and Leisure*."

"In that case, I'm going to Holland, Michigan."

"Excuse me?"

"Christmas is coming."

"Really?"

"And I have a line on some people who grow Christmas trees."

"Mmmm. I have to admit, if we do one more sweet-sweet-sweet story on how to wrap a perfect present in marbleized Japanese rice paper, I'm going into a diabetic coma."

"So what I've decided would be new and fresh is this: Where do we get Christmas trees from? Some people probably think tree harvesters just go out in a woods and cut. How are they grown? How long does it take? It's gotta be a big deal. These are *trees*, after all, not poinsettias. What makes a good tree?"

"Simple. Doesn't drop its needles the first day and doesn't cost an arm and a leg."

"The president of the West Michigan Evergreen Growers Association is willing to put me up at his house." Hal brightened at this. I knew why. "Which would cut your out-of-pocket costs, huh, Hal?"

"It just might work . . ."

"So, I would appreciate it if you would cut me a check for an advance. I'll pack today and leave for west Michigan tomorrow by noon."

"Tomorrow! Tomorrow is Thanksgiving! They'll be having Thanksgiving dinner!"

"They're eating their holiday meal at noon. Something about spending the rest of the day getting ready for cutting trees in earnest on Friday. Which figures. I'm supposed to get there around three."

"Cat, in the summer west Michigan's one of the most beautiful places in the world. Beaches of pale sand, sailing, waterskiing, windsurfing. Fields of pick-your-own strawberries and blueberries. In the winter there's snow skiing and snowboarding. And climbing icebergs in the lake. But Cat, it's November now. It's the wrong time of year for west Michigan."

"It's the right time of year for a paycheck."

"Don't let a little notoriety get you uppity. I may regret this."

"Thanks, Hal. I won't forget you. I'll take you national."

I had an ulterior motive. I was saying, "Now *here's* something to be really thankful for!"

My family was going to the home of my sister-in-law and brother—my oldest brother—in Terre Haute for the holiday. But years of experience had told me that while the turkey might be eaten, I'd be the bird that got it in the neck. At these family dinners, as the only unmarried adult female, I'm fair game. My mother and sister-in-law work as a tag team.

First they decapitate me:

"You're a perfectly nice looking young woman, Catherine."

"There's nothing really especially wrong with your looks."

Then they pluck me:

"But why are you wearing those boots?"

"You know, Levi's and sweatshirts aren't the only cloth-ing they sell in the stores."

"Catherine, don't you have something a little more *fem-inine* to wear?"

"You'd look nice in a pale pink."

"Why don't you do something with your hair?"

"Is that a gray hair, Catherine? You could have a nice dark rinse put on once a week, you know. It would make all the difference."

Once a week, she says casually! I work! I'm on the go every minute. Do they think my articles write themselves automatically?

Then they stuff me:

"You'd be so much more *fulfilled* if you had a family."

"Catherine, you need a man you can share your life with."

"Give your life meaning."

"Children make life worthwhile."

This last from my sister-in-law, who seizes every oppor-tunity to explain that her preschool's best feature is that the children can stay until five P.M. And whose youngest son has now seen four different specialists in an attempt to get to the root cause of his temper tantrums. The root cause is thirty-four years old and wears pink. And has per-fectly styled hair that is all of one color, Chestnut Mochac-cino.

They'll baste me a little, of course with the best butter:

"You have very nice hair, you know. Curly black hair is so easy to style."

"I'm sure Mr. Right will come along eventually, dear."

"Yes, don't you worry, Cat."

When I go home after a family celebration, there's noth-ing left but the bare bones.

*   *   *

"Well, this is your room," Nell said softly.

"It's very nice. I appreciate your family letting me stay here." I dropped my duffel bag next to the bed. LJ's cage went on the pine nightstand. The room was plain but pleasant, the walls knotty pine, and the window looked out on ten thousand or so pine trees.

"Well, you know. It's good publicity for the tree farms—oh-oh." She clapped her hand over her mouth, then took it away and giggled. "I don't think I was supposed to say that."

"Then we won't tell."

"I'm talking kind of quietly because Gran's taking her nap. She always naps after lunch. But she's in the other wing."

"I see. This is a big house."

"Yeah. My great-grandfather was one of eleven children."

"And this was their house?"

"Yeah. His father's, too. They added extra rooms around 1900." She hesitated. "Uh. Right out here's the um, you know."

The um-you-know turned out to be the bathroom.

"Do you want to um, freshen up? Or would you like coffee? It's all ready. Or tea? Or you could go to the barn and see what they're doing."

"Coffee first. Okay?" I had already gassed up the car and visited the service station's um-you-know on my way through Holland. It's an old reporter's and trucker's motto. Keep the car full and the bladder empty, because you don't know when you'll get another chance.

LJ pouted as I stashed him on the nightstand. Yes, it's hard to pout without lips. He does it by pulling his head into his neck feathers and jamming his beak down near his heart.

The kitchen was all knotty pine, like the bedroom, and it looked and felt warm despite the thickening gloom outdoors. Nell poured coffee from a half-full Chemex into a glass beaker, nuked it in the microwave, and poured the result into a mug. She put a carton of milk on the table, next to a sugar bowl shaped like a wooden shoe.

"I'm not allowed coffee yet, you know," she said.

"Stunt your growth?" I asked, and we both laughed.

"That's what they say."

Then she stared at me. Not in a rude way. She glanced, then looked away. Got up and poured herself a glass of skimmed milk, sat down and glanced at me again.

Children make me nervous. I rarely interview children, and when I do, I perspire a lot. I have several nephews and nieces of various ages, and there are two of them I see fairly regularly, but the others seem always to be shooting rubber bands at my neck or asking me why I don't get married. In this last perfidy they are set up by their parents, and it's not their fault, but I still think it shows a lack of natural childhood perversity on their part to go along with it.

Nell, so talkative, had run out of words.

"So your family's been here a long time?" I said.

"A zillion years. You want some potato chips?"

"Yes. But I'm not going to eat any."

"Oh. Okay. I understand." She smiled tentatively.

"What grade are you in?" Boy, that was a dumb cliché question. No better than the guy in the singles bar who sidles up to you and says, "You're a Libra, right?"

She didn't seem to mind, though. She was thinking about something else, and she answered, "Seventh grade," somewhat absently. Then she said, "Dad says you're a reporter."

"That's right."

"He says you write lots of articles about stuff in Chicago and you've been on Oprah and television. He says you're an investigative reporter."

"Well, that's right. Freelance."

"What's freelance?"

"Freelance means I don't make much money. Well, technically it means I'm self-employed, not on any specific paper."

"You investigate things."

"Right."

"Like politics?"

"For my articles? Politics some. Sometimes I do profiles of individuals. What I like best is writing about how things work. I did a long story about the lottery once. That kind of thing."

"Uh-huh." She hesitated again. "Like crime?"

"Well, yeah. Crime sometimes."

"What kind of crime?"

This was a dilemma. One of the reasons talking with children makes me uneasy is that I always picture their parents in the background, not wanting the child to know a lot of stuff about what the real world is like. And me, I don't like to lie. So I'm left tongue-tied, trying to guard my words. What kind of crime? This was a well-brought-up child who lived in a rather conservative community. What was I going to say? Prostitution? Drugs? Nine-year-olds blowing each other away with plastic automatics with Day-Glo grips?

"Well, I've covered some murders," I said, figuring that she couldn't get through an evening of television without seeing several staged murders, or an evening of news without seeing a couple of real ones. I had not expected anything like her reaction.

"You have!" She upset the milk carton and caught it just

before it tipped over the edge of the table. Carat was already on her feet, lapping a couple of spilled drops off the floor. I find that dogs truly believe in the trickle-down theory of economics.

"That's very interesting," she said much more sedately. Like Emily Post might ask about attending Aunt Agatha's garden teas, she added, "Do you go to a lot of murders?"

"Well, some. It's sort of part of the job."

"Do you talk with the detectives and things like that?"

"Some. I know several police officers in Chicago."

"Do you—do they tell you how they go about solving murders?"

"Yes. Well, actually, yes. Sometimes. They like to brag as well as anybody does."

Very casually, she said, "Have you ever solved a murder yourself?"

"As a matter of fact, yes."

"So—you'd know what to look for?"

"Well, not necessarily. It depends on the circumstances."

"But you *might*."

"I might."

She had just opened her mouth to speak again when we heard the slam of a car door somewhere down the driveway. Nell jumped up as if she'd been raiding the cookie jar and said, "Oh, gee! That's Aunt Marie!"

I looked around the kitchen. We hadn't been doing anything wrong, had we?

◦ 3 ◦

Aunt Marie had pulled to a quick stop behind my Bronco, not quite spraying gravel. Her car was red, sporty, and low slung, but not a convertible. Very few people in this climate are that foolish.

She came in the back door, carrying a brown grocery bag.

"You must be the reporter," she said.

"Cat Marsala. Please call me Cat."

She put the bag on the counter and took my outstretched hand. "Marie Heidema."

Nell said, "Aunt Marie is my dad's sister."

"Big sister," Marie said, laughing. She must have meant older, not larger. She was slender and dressed in a stylish taupe pantsuit and gold chain. Her blond hair was cut in a blunt wedge that obviously would require frequent trims. This stylishness plus the sporty red car had taken me by surprise. Somehow the old farmhouse, old farm, and old Dutch community flavor had prepared me for a folksy woman with gray hair and an apron. This was a form of prejudice, of course, and I stepped on it and squashed it, mentally speaking, as soon as I recognized it. These people lived in the 1990s, not the 1890s.

Which you could also tell by looking at the kitchen. A mix of old and new. There was a large old double oven, but also a microwave. There were cast-iron and copper pots, but also a blender.

One look around would tell you that today was Thanksgiving. To an experienced eye it was obvious, even though they had thoroughly cleaned up after dinner. In the trash can were packages from stuffing mix and empty plastic bags with the words ATLANTIC BEST CRANBERRIES written on them. In a large wire basket in the sink was a mountain of potato peelings with a few onion skins as well. Nell saw me looking and said, "We save vegetable scraps for the compost pile." On one big burner of the stove a huge pot simmered slowly. In the seething broth you could see turkey bones. On the back of the sink were two discarded pop-up plastic timers, the kind that tell you when the turkey is done. If I looked in the refrigerator, I would see piled dishes of turkey meat.

"Wouldn't you think we'd have realized we needed bread for sandwiches tonight?" Marie said, taking from the bag two loaves of white, two loaves of whole wheat, and a jar of Dutch mustard made with whole mustard seeds.

She added, "We were so busy roasting the turkey—and Mother always makes three blueberry pies—I guess we thought we'd never need another meal."

Nell said, "Guess what, Aunt Marie?"

Marie smiled at her. "I can't guess."

"Cat's got a parrot."

Hastily, I said, "He's clean and quiet and I'll keep him in his cage."

She laughed. "After all this dead turkey, a live bird sounds like a real relief."

"Shall I show Cat the barn now?" Nell asked.

"Go ahead, if Cat wants."

*   *   *

We crossed the yard in the gathering dusk and entered the barn, and this time I stepped fully back into the nineteenth century.

In the center was a cast-iron potbelly stove, orange flames playing against its fireglass window. A stovepipe ran up twenty feet to a tin-faced plate in the roof, but the light was so dim up there I could only see the pewterlike reflection of the metal around the pipe.

The barn was huge, open inside except for some raised storage galleries that stretched across the ends. It was floored with nothing but the rose-tan natural sand that I had seen outside in the fields.

The air was reddish and thick with dust. The pine wood of the siding was golden with age. Near the stove, a huge man turned a whetstone with his left hand and held a pruning blade against it with his right. The metal shrieked on the stone. Although it was November and cold outside, he had his shirt off and was sweating in the glow of the stove. His skin was reddish pale. His hair was a bright yellow, springy and coarse, and the eyebrows that tangled over his eyes were yellow, too. Everything was red and gold and hot against the deep blue of the cold, darkening day outside.

Some years ago the Art Institute in Chicago had a showing of nineteenth-century paintings of English life. There was one called "The Forge" by Joseph Wright of Derby that came as near as art could to this scene. The amber glow, the red highlights, the straining muscles . . .

I felt the raw heat on my face, while my back was still cold. We are so evenly warmed and cooled, in this day and age, that the sensation was actually pleasurable. About the only similar sensation was lying on damp Lake Michigan sand on a Chicago beach while hot sun beats down on you.

All around me were dull reflections from amber, orange, and rust-red objects against a background of warm
browns. It took me a few seconds to realize there were
other people in the barn. It was a farm barn, for equipment storage, not a livestock barn, and everywhere there
were farm tools. The people were scattered among them.
Two men and a teenage boy worked on a large piece of
wheeled equipment at the far end of the barn. On the floor
near the stove another boy squatted, running a rattail file
back and forth over the teeth of a chain saw. The metal
squealed with each move. A woman sat on a pile of boxes
with a yarn bag on her lap, apparently doing nothing.

There was electric light, one bulb at each end of the
barn, though somebody had saved money by using twenty-
five-watt bulbs. As my eyes adjusted, I realized the reds and
oranges I had been seeing were reflections of the fire on farm
tools and other objects: a very old scythe, the kind Death car-
ries in *The Seventh Seal*, with a pewter-colored blade and
dark brown wood handle; an orange-painted rototiller; a hoe
with a wide blade, pierced with holes. Several shovels
whose blades were brownish with age but nevertheless
glowed with oiling, a dusty red bicycle, an old yellow rusty
bicycle, an older bicycle in parts, wooden rakes, metal
rakes, fan-shaped bamboo rakes with springy teeth, wide
steel rakes with rigid teeth, curved saws, bow saws, crosscut
saws, pruning saws, hacksaws, a four-foot-long curved saw
with large shark teeth and crumbling wood handle, a gaso-
line-powered lawn mower, and a reel-type lawn mower,
the kind that you push, that had once been painted red.

The air smelled of hot metal, oil, male sweat, pine, and
wet earth.

A slender man in back noticed me first. He came walking forward, and the big man looked up from the whetstone. He stepped in front of the thinner man.

"Is this Ms. Marsala?" the bigger man said, in a boom-ing voice. "Sorry to be so informal!" He picked up a red plaid flannel shirt and shrugged into it as he walked to-ward me. He had only got it on, not buttoned, when he reached me. Thrusting out his hand, he said, "Henry DeGraaf. Call me Hank."

The shirt hung there, open, giving me a large view of muscular chest with ginger-colored hairs. He squeezed my hand. Still talking, he started to button his shirt.

"Glad to have you visit."

"Well, I appreciate—"

"Reason we're working on Thanksgiving Day, we start cutting tomorrow. Growers Association rules, you don't cut blue spruce until Thanksgiving. The week of Thanks-giving, actually, but we always start the day after. Blue spruce drop their needles if you cut 'em too soon. Scotch pine you can start cutting the last week of October. People know our trees. Know they're fresh. Makes a difference; there's a reputation in the market to maintain."

And with that, suddenly I was snapped fully back into the last years of the twentieth century. Where else would you get precisely that Chamber of Commerce tone?

Nell seized the hand of man who had noticed me first. The others had come over to be introduced, too. Nell said, "This is my father, John DeGraaf, Cat. And my Aunt Jennifer—"

"My wife, Jennifer," Hank boomed, riding right over Nell's soft voice. Jennifer got up off the boxes and limply shook my hand. "And my brother, John. John is Nell's fa-ther. My son Don." He waved his hand at a boy of about fourteen. "And my son Dan. My oldest boy, Calvin, isn't here today."

Dan looked about sixteen.

I noticed he said "my oldest boy," even though his wife

was standing right there and he could have said "our oldest boy," unless the oldest son wasn't hers. But my take on Hank was that he said "my" about pretty much everything.

"And this is Luis Montoya, my gang boss."

John, Don, and Dan were all blonds, in varying ways, with that pinkish, vulnerable-looking skin. They didn't look exactly alike, but you'd have no trouble recognizing them as relatives. Luis, on the other hand, was medium height, stocky, and the color of pine wood. His hair was black and straight. He held out a hand, shook mine firmly but without trying to mangle my fingers as Hank had. "Good to meet you," he said. By my guess he was nineteen or twenty years old.

For Hank this was enough in the way of introductions. He turned his back to Luis and said to me, "I wish it was still daylight. There's nothing as beautiful as the farm this time of year. Blue spruce are the most beautiful trees in the world. We use the absolute top strains. Get our seedlings from growers in Colorado we've used for decades. I mean, no expense is spared to give the customer the very best tree money can buy—"

As he talked I noticed Nell, who was standing over near the bicycles, roll her eyes up. Luis walked over to her and they started talking softly.

"—best blue color, too," Hank said. "Green spruce is good, and a lot of people like it for a Christmas tree because they feel the deep green color is more traditional. But either one has that spruce character—sharp upright growth, dense needles, branches set close together."

"I did a little reading before I left Chicago," I said, feeling that Chicago was pretty far away right now. "They said the most popular tree was Scotch pine."

"Oh, well. It probably is the biggest seller. It's cheaper to produce. Grows faster."

"Don't you grow Scotch pine?"

"Well, actually we do. You have to produce what people want. And Scotch pine, you know, the needles hang on longer. But it's not as beautiful a tree, if you ask me."

In a way I had asked him.

"We're just trying the new Frazer fir, too. I'll show you all of them tomorrow," he said. "You can be the judge."

"Wonderful."

He picked up the tool he'd been sharpening. It was a pruner with handles five feet long. I said, "Do you cut the trees with that?"

"No, no. This is to lop off branches at the bottom, so the tree can go in the baler. But it's a beautifully constructed tool, isn't it?"

"Beautiful."

"This is an anvil-type pruner. The scissor type—you know, where two blades slide past each other like scissors?—doesn't work as well, because if you prune a heavy branch the blades can spring. Ruins the pruner. This one, see"—he closed it with a sharp snick-chunk, like a guillotine—"the single blade comes down on a flat strike plate. Doesn't spring. And just look at the quality of that steel."

"Uh-huh." The blade gleamed from his attention to it with the whetstone. Something about it didn't look right to Hank, however. He ran his finger over the sharp edge, then worked the jaws back and forth. He turned and saw Luis, still chatting with Nell.

"Hey, Lu! Get me the 3-in-One oil. And quit gabbing. We got work to do."

· 4 ·

At this time of year in Michigan, the sun is down by five-fifteen and it is totally dark by five-thirty. Nell, her father, John, and I crossed the yard to the house as the dusk thickened. Luis roared away down the driveway on his Yamaha motorcycle, bundled in gloves, helmet, and parka to protect him from the cold, and Hank, after thoroughly damping down the fire in the potbelly stove, closed up the barn, and with his wife, Jennifer, and their two boys, got into an old pickup truck, yelled good night, and drove away.

"They don't live here, then?" I asked.

John said, "No. They live near Zeeland."

"How far is that?"

"Oh, less than ten miles. Eight maybe."

"But wasn't Hank the person who invited me to stay here?"

"Yes."

"But he doesn't live here himself."

John and Nell exchanged a glance. That's our Hank, was the message. "He suggested it," John said, "and Mom thought it was a good idea. You shouldn't think you're not welcome. You know, we do this cutting every year, year after year. Having you here will make it more interesting."

"Well, thanks. You make me feel better. Do you all make your living from the trees?"

"Oh, lord no!" John was astonished, but too polite to laugh at my question. Quite different from his brother, he was softer spoken, less hearty but more friendly, much less beefy looking. He was apparently the slender version of the DeGraafs, and resembled his stylish sister Marie. "You'd have to have thousands of acres to actually make a living doing trees. And then you'd be subject to every market swing. Weyerhauser tried it on a huge scale several years ago, and failed. It's practically impossible to manage."

We stood now on the wraparound porch, looking back over the fields.

"So it's all medium to small growers?"

"There are three hundred Christmas tree growers in the state of Michigan. And almost all of them are small to tiny. It's definitely a cottage industry. Still, we supply more than a third of the trees sold in the U.S."

"So what does Hank do, then?"

"He's a foreman in a furniture factory."

"Oh. What do you do?"

"I teach English at a local high school."

"And how about Marie?"

"She's an X-ray tech at Holland Hospital."

"I see."

Actually, I saw quite a bit more than I was saying. I had felt all along that there was something slightly skewed about my perception of the farm and the family. My initial view had been that they were rich, or if not very rich, at least very well off. After all, the house was large, had a lot of extra bedrooms, and the farm looked like it covered a hundred acres. But then again, studying the place more closely, there were clear signs the DeGraafs were careful with money. Possibly even strapped for cash. The siding could use paint. The house inside was comfortable, but the furniture I had seen was old, the rugs were visibly worn, the kitchen was well equipped but more functional than trendy. The barn didn't look like it had been altered since it was built, and I'd bet it was built before 1910. Of the three bicycles in the barn, one was anything but new, one was old, and one was so very old that it seemed to be used as an organ donor for the others. Come to think of it, Marie's little red car was sporty, but not pricey.

Not that the DeGraafs were being in any sense deceptive. If anything, they were extremely straightforward. There was very little around here that was for display. It was all function. The yard was laid out so that the access from house to barn was direct. The driveway was unpaved, graveled some years before, but now showing large patches of sand. It was wide, but not for looks. It had been widened over the years by the tires of workers' cars, parking along the sides. And the most impressive, most beautiful element of the farm, the land and its woods, had been there before the DeGraafs and would be there long after they were gone.

I hesitated for a few seconds in the twilight. This time of year there are fifteen hours of darkness; the sun is on loan, and night is dominant, unlike summer, when day gives way briefly to night, and then springs quickly back.

"The moon's rising," I said. It was low on the horizon and still pale in the fading twilight.

"The gibbous moon."

"What does that mean?"

"It's past the half, but not quite full. It should be full tomorrow night or the night after."

"You must be more aware of the moon here than I am in Chicago."

"Probably. The moon rides higher in the sky in the winter than the summer, you know."

"Making up for a lower sun during the day."

"Mmm. This time of year, the moon rises soon after sunset and sets close to sunrise. The moon closest to the equinox is called the harvest moon because it comes up bright at twilight and helps the farmers work into the night to get in their late crops."

"But the equinox was in September."

"The October and November moons still come up pretty close to sunset. The next one after the harvest moon, usually the October moon, is called the hunter's moon, because it comes up near sundown and lights the woods for hunters. People here hunt rabbits and deer by the hunter's moon."

I shivered a little.

"It's very beautiful here," I said.

John smiled. "You think? Not everybody sees that. We don't have any mountains, or jagged rocks or waterfalls."

"It's soft," I said, seeing the dark trees, slightly powdered with snow, the sandy paths running away between them. "The colors are all ivory and buff, or soft blue or dusty green."

"That's right. You should see the coastline along the lake. It just gets into your blood. We walk it whenever we have time free. You can take a canoe, put it in at a landing, and canoe miles and miles if you want to along the coast. Have somebody pick you up at another landing—"

Nell spoke for the first time in many minutes. "You can canoe against the wind as far as you can go before you get exhausted, and then drift back. You can just trail your paddle in the water on the way back and steer. Float with the breeze. Like you were flying."

"Her favorite method," John said, touching his daughter's hair.

They were very relaxed with each other, which isn't true of every father-daughter relationship. Where was her mother? I wondered. No one had uttered a word about Nell's mother.

I said, "You're lucky to have this place."

He looked back over the farm, then turned to the door. His face had lost its animation. "I hope we can hold onto it," he said.

"Is it—do you have high taxes? A great many farms these days are paying more in taxes than they can make from the land."

"That's part of it," he said.

· 5 ·

I was still sound asleep Friday morning when I heard motorcycle engines snarling, pickup trucks roaring, dishes tinkling and pots and pans banging, even what I thought were shotgun blasts. I opened my eyes and then wondered whether I had really opened them. It was totally dark. Then a car light played across my window and passed on. What time was it? I squinted at my watch. Seven-seventeen A.M. Not so very early; but of course the sun doesn't rise until almost eight here at this time of year. Thanking my metabolism for the fact that I had showered the night before—I tend to be an afternoon or evening showerer, something to do with a belief that no big, threatening efforts should be undertaken before I have my coffee—I got into my Levi's and sweatshirt and was in the kitchen in five minutes.

Everybody else was in the kitchen, too.

The older Mrs. DeGraaf, called Gran by the family, and another elderly woman were at the stove.

"Can I help?" I said, but they both said, almost in unison, "No. We do the cooking."

Nell giggled. "You can cut trees, write articles, or go sit on the porch, but Gran does the cooking. And Aunt Clara, of course, when she's here." Her grandmother gave her a pleased nod. Obviously, Gran liked the child.

I had met Gran last night at a sandwich supper. Turkey sandwiches. I had been expecting a plump, elderly Dutch grandmother, sturdy, with gray hair and a face like a bread loaf. Stereotypes are such a mistake. She was delicate. Pink rose-petal skin, slightly crumpled. Slender, but she moved strongly. This surprised me because she had been "resting" when I arrived, and therefore I had assumed she was sick. But then, she had probably gotten up at four A.M. to get the Thanksgiving turkey in the oven. Pure white hair fluffed up all over her head, so perfect in its little curls that it could go on top of a wedding cake. She came from the generation of women who felt utterly diminished if their hair wasn't perfectly done. My grandmother and mother both can't face any major event without a trip to the hairdresser. Not just for a cut like me, but a "perm." Mrs. DeGraaf would feel that to allow her hair to become straight and hang down would be slovenly. I'd bet that she was like my mother: When she saw women of her age without permanents, she'd say they looked "shiftless." This is the worst adjective my mother will use for anybody.

Gran was a traditionalist.

And probably with a will of iron. She was now flipping pancakes on two large, square cast-iron griddles.

"Will you have pannacakes, Catherine?" she asked. She pronounced the word with three syllables. This is Dutch, I discovered.

"Absolutely!" I said, with more enthusiasm than strict politeness required. This earned me a smile.

There were at least ten people in the kitchen. Besides Nell, Gran, and Aunt Clara (really great-aunt to Nell), there were six young men, and Luis. One looked Mexican, like Luis, and was named Raymond. Two were Hank's boys, Don and Dan, whom I'd met yesterday, one was probably Hank's eldest, Cal, the one who hadn't been here yesterday. One looked Dutch—pink skin, yellow hair, and squarely built, although if this weren't Dutch country, I would just as easily have believed he was German or Polish. His name was Ken. One was a big teenager of maybe eighteen, who looked neither Dutch nor Mexican, and whose name seemed to be "Horace, but call me Skip." Most of these large male people were drinking coffee or Dutch cocoa, made from a big box of Droste that stood on the counter. Two of them were eating pancakes standing up. Carat hung around their feet, hoping for hand-outs.

Hank came in carrying a twelve-gauge shotgun. He said, "Got a rabbit." He looked at me for approval, which I did not feel. "Early morning is best. Mom, I put it in the garage to cool. You want to cook it? Jennifer doesn't like cooking rabbit."

"I don't wonder," Gran said.

Hank walked farther into the house, and came back a minute later without the gun.

John blew in from the yard, poured coffee into a mug, saluted me, and went back out. Gran handed me a plate of pancakes and pointed to a chair at the long pinewood kitchen table. As I sat, feeling like Norman Rockwell, I saw Aunt Marie's sporty little red car pull into the drive, then reverse, and park at the very end, behind the motorcycles and pickup trucks.

A chain saw snarled in the yard, then died. Somebody said, "Damn!"

Gran looked toward the door and frowned. I was glad whoever had sworn hadn't used any worse words.

Outdoors, somebody pounded on a gong. All the male crew in the kitchen piled out the door, except Luis, who got up and went toward the big stainless steel coffee urn. When the doorway was clear of exiting men, Marie came in from outdoors at a run.

"Wipe your feet," Gran said.

Marie instantly slid to a halt and complied with her mother's order. At the same time she said "Hi!" to me, nodded to her mother, patted Nell with one hand, and grabbed a coffee mug with the other. Leaving her coat on, she tapped coffee into her cup from a second humongous urn and said to me, "If you want to see the start of this peculiar cultural ceremony, you'd better follow me."

"Take the coffee out for the men, Pieternella," her grandmother said.

"Yes, Gran."

Luis said, "I'll carry it."

"Pieternella can do it," Gran said.

"She could, ma'am, but it's pretty heavy. As long as I'm here, I might as well help."

Nell smiled at him. Gran frowned, but she said, "Thank you, Luis. I've always been told that gentlemanliness is one of the graces." I could hear the doubt in her voice.

"Come on, Cat," Marie said.

I glanced at Gran for permission while I stabbed two pieces of pancake with my fork and ate them. Gran said, "Go right ahead."

So I did.

It was still dark, but the sky in the east was deep plum red. The yard light was set on a twenty-foot pole, and underneath it hardware was massing as if for the D-Day invasion. There was a small flatbed truck with fencelike sides. There was an extremely peculiar metal object, like a huge funnel on wheels, with a motor and a cylindrical spool of orange plastic webbing and a chain at one end, the whole thing about the size of a Toyota. There were several chain saws, pruners, and hand shears. Marie carried a clipboard under her right arm, and a big first aid case, red with a white cross in her left hand. Fabulous.

It was very cold. Everybody but me was wearing gloves. Stupid! I ran back into the house—wiping my feet on the mat, of course—upstairs, got gloves, and was downstairs in under sixty seconds. Hank laughed when he saw me reappear. He was standing with Luis, looking down at a chain saw on the ground.

"Good speed in the sprint," he said to me.

"Clean living. Why are we in such a hurry?"

"This time of year you've got maybe seven hours of workable daylight. Less if it's overcast. And at both ends of that, the sun's so low you can't work very efficiently. And this is our harvest time!"

"Unlike every other kind of crop in the world," Luis said.

"That's true," Hank said. "Everything else is harvested in pretty much livable outdoor weather."

"Why don't you work with lights, at night? Couldn't you use car headlights?"

Hank said, "I'm not going to have people out in the field cutting with chain saws in the dark!" I was about to nod at his concern for his workers when he added, "Think of the liability. Shearing season is bad enough. You should see my insurance payments."

Luis caught my eye just briefly and gave me one eighth of a smile at the left side of his mouth.

Hank said to Luis, "Try to start it again."

Luis planted his foot in the handle opening of the saw and pulled the cord. This time it started with a snarl, and although it emitted a big burst of blue smoke, he pushed a lever forward and it settled down to a purr.

"Good," Hank said.

Hank went into the barn and I followed. Horace came out with a can of gasoline. Raymond came past carrying the big pruners. Inside, Cal was throwing things around. Then I realized that wasn't quite fair. He was juggling.

Don, the youngest, watched his big brother, fascinated as a hammer, a rock, a can of oil, and a pair of pliers flew around in a circle. Higher and higher they went, the circle bigger and bigger.

"Damn it to hell, Cal!" Hank shouted. "Don't you realize we got work to do? Put that shit down!"

Cal gave it all one last fling. A couple of the objects flew off around the barn. I heard one strike the wall above the loft. Another went in the opposite direction and struck one of the bicycles. Cal caught the rock and the pliers, and bowed insolently to an imaginary audience.

"What's the *matter* with you!" Hank shouted. "Cal, go pick up that hammer! Lu, find the oil. All right, everybody start moving! We've got light!"

Half the sky was now pink, and a wash of ice crystals high in the eastern stratosphere was picking up light from a winter sun that still lay below the horizon. The moon was setting. It was ten of eight. John, Horace/Skip, and Hank picked up chain saws. "Let's get out there," Hank said.

We headed for the field.

This was what I had come for. We walked through the first field of five-footers, and the next of tiny pines, and a field of spruce that looked Christmas-tree size to me, but weren't going to be cut. We arrived at a field far distant from the house, where the crew deposited the gasoline cans and other equipment. Every person knew which job to do. As the morning sun lit the trees, work began.

John, Skip, and Luis separated, each beginning at the near end of a row of blue spruce, leaving a full row between them. Safety procedure, no doubt. The chain saws snarled and they started to cut.

The rows of trees were quite close together, but at evenly spaced intervals a wider path ran through the field. Hank drove the small flatbed down this path. Behind him came Hank's son Don, with the weird funnel-truck. Marie walked next to the flatbed with her clipboard. As Luis, John, and Skip felled the trees, Hank's son Cal pushed them sideways away from the cutter with a stick and dragged them out of the field to the path. There Hank's youngest boy, Don, lopped off any branches too near the base. Raymond pushed the tree into another gadget that grabbed it and jiggled it.

"Why in the world is that thing shaking the tree?" I asked.

"Gets out dead needles and leaves and twigs and old bird's nests and stuff," Hank said.

Hank had parked the flatbed nearby, and he and young Raymond hoisted the tree onto the funnel thing. It had a small Briggs & Stratton engine, which puttered along cheerfully. Hank whipped a chain in a slip knot around the base of the tree. The tree was dragged by the chain into the funnel, which forced its branches up like a person holding his hands up over his head. As the tree was dragged farther into the funnel, it went through the doughnut-shaped cartridge of orange plastic netting. The friction of the branches pulled netting from the end of the cartridge over the outside of the tree, like pulling a nylon stocking over a leg. The netting held all the branches in place. The baler then ejected the tree at the end, compressed and baled for shipping. At this point, Ken cut the netting and knotted the end. He then picked up the tree and threw it on the flatbed. Marie had followed the tree from before it was baled, and now made a tally on her clipboard.

In the time it takes to tell it, they had done half a dozen trees.

I watched John cut for a while. He had to crouch down and lean under the bottom branches of the tree, holding the heavy chain saw far enough under to get a good bite on the trunk. The position looked uncomfortable. Compared to Hank, he looked frail for the job. Cal stood on the other side, not near the saw, leaning the tree away from John with the stick and getting ready to lift it as it came loose. The chain saw snarled and the tree fell. The kid whisked it away. John straightened up, stretched his back a few times, and moved to the next tree. He cut in a crouched position. Of the other two cutters, one knelt to cut, and one did it like John.

John cut a couple more.

"Lord, that gets to your back," he said. "Somebody invented a saw on wheels to do this once, but it didn't work."

"How much does the saw weigh?"

"Maybe eight pounds. When you start. After half an hour, it's eight hundred."

He gave the saw to Hank.

"Hey, buddy," Hank said. "You used to be able to cut a lot longer than this."

"Yeah, I used to be younger, too."

I strolled around, watching everything. When I'm on an assignment on location like this, I'm in an anomalous position in relation to the people there. Whether it's hanging around a hospital trauma unit watching, or sailing with yachtsmen to see how a boat works, or, like this assignment, actually living with the family, I'm a neither/nor. Neither quite a stranger, nor quite a friend and guest. More like an anthropologist. The DeGraafs had their own reasons for inviting me, of course. They wanted the publicity for their trees. But still, I was well aware that some members of the family, especially Nell, were beginning to treat me like a friend. This can be awkward. You see things that fall into the "I don't need to know about this" category.

For instance, I was minding my own business, asking Marie about her tallying job.

I held my pocket tape recorder where she could see it— no undercover work for me—and said, "Your job right now is to count the trees?"

"Well, it isn't only counting. I watch them before they go into the baler and I grade them and tally them. For instance, before this one went into the baler, you could see it had three good sides. The ones with four good sides are called premium grade. They're worth more."

"Naturally."

"Naturally. And the ones with two good sides are worth less. And see, this one has a three-inch handle, which is well within the allowance. We're allowed not more than one inch of handle per foot of height."

"Handle?"

"Well, the bottom of the trunk. Or the stem, as the foresters call it. A three-inch handle is a stem that's three inches in length from the cut to the lowest branches."

"Thanks."

"The U.S. Department of Agriculture gives us codes for trees just like they do for eggs or olives. USDA #1 is good three sides. We tag with the grade and our farm ID."

I clicked off. I stepped just half a dozen paces away and happened to come up behind Luis and young Cal. Cal was smoking, lounging lazily against the baler.

"Come on, Cal, let's get some work done," Luis said to him. Luis had handed his chain saw to Raymond and was now helping bale.

"Hey, I don't have to take orders from you!"

"It isn't a matter of orders. We've got a certain amount of work to get through today."

Cal said, "Get out of my face!" and walked away. Luis stood looking after him, then simply went back to baling. He didn't even bother to shrug.

Luis, according to Hank, was the crew boss. But Cal was the owner's son. Or actually the owner's grandson, I guessed, since Gran probably owned the land. That could put Luis in a bind. He seemed to deal with it all without anger. Luis struck me as an extremely mature, sane person.

It was a very chilly morning. After a few more minutes, I noticed smoke coming from the stovepipe in the roof of the old barn, so I walked back there. Time to get warmed up. The closer I got to the barn, the colder I realized I was.

Inside the barn it was wonderfully warm. My fingers ached as the cold receded from them. Nell moved back and forth, tending two huge urns of coffee, which were placed on a card table, with little cups of flammable stuff underneath to keep them hot. She said, "Hi! Come on in! This is the warming room."

Several pieces of old porch furniture, the kind with tubular aluminum legs and woven plastic seats and backs, stood around three sides of the stove. Cal was lounging in one, doing his James Dean imitation, his boots stretched out toward the fire. Carat lay near the stove. There was a smell of hot dog fur in the air.

"I'm freezing," I said.

Nell said, "Standing and watching isn't the hardest job, but it sure is the coldest."

She poured me a cup of coffee. Then she policed the coffee area. She wiped up any spills, collected discarded cups, and checked that the pots were hot. "This one's nearly empty," she said. "I'll have to go to the kitchen and get more in a minute."

Cal closed his eyes.

Stomping footsteps outside. Hank strode in, looking annoyed. He ignored both Nell and me and walked directly up to his son. Cal didn't rise from the chair.

"Hey, Cal," he said to his son. "How long've you been sitting here?"

The kid glanced at both of us. You could see him thinking that he couldn't get away with a lie, with us right there. And his father probably knew the answer anyhow.

"So the wetback tattled on me," he said.

Nell stood straight up and said quietly, "If you mean Luis, Luis is not a wetback. He's an American citizen. United States citizen," she amended. Intelligent child, realizing that Mexico is an American country, too.

"Yeah?" said young Cal. "Well, he still drops the endings of his words. 'I didn' wan' anythin' '" he mimicked.

"He speaks English better than you speak Spanish," Nell said.

"Why would I *want* to speak Spanish?"

"Never mind this!" Hank barked. "No, Luis didn't tell me. I've been watching you. You try this same trick every year! You know you don't get paid for the work you don't do. You're docked an hour. Now get out in that field. And I mean now!"

Slowly Cal rose from his chair. Slowly he walked across the floor of the barn. Slowly he slouched out the door. Slowly enough to emphasize his independence. But he went.

Hank called after him, "Straighten the hell up, will you?"

· 6 ·

After another hour, inactivity got to me—I was actually shivering from the cold—and I asked Hank to let me toss trees onto the flatbed. By then we were working on filling our third flatbed, with the other two lined up down the drive for the truckers. Hank said cheerily, "Can't pay you, but I'll sure let you work!"

It was spoken in a joking way, but underneath I could hear the clinking of coins in his head. Several dollars' work for nothing.

I soon discovered that the crew wore gloves not just to keep their hands warm but also because of the pine needles. They prick your skin, and there is something in them that is faintly poisonous. Above the cuffs of my gloves, little red dots formed where the needles had injected me with whatever it was. After a while the dots started to merge into a big, red rash.

Now Cal and Luis had passed the chain saws on to Hank and Horace, and the third saw was in the barn being sharpened. John helped at the baler and Luis stood next to me, throwing baled trees into the truck. He nodded appreciation at me. "You're not bad at this."

"You mean I'm persistent. It takes me twice as long as it does you."

"Persistent is good. Woody Allen says that ninety-five percent of success is showing up."

I smiled. This Luis was a real worker. I hadn't seen him take a break at all until Nell came out to watch, and then he stepped aside, let Don take his place, and stretched his back, bending to the left, then to the right, holding his sides. I knew exactly how he felt. It wasn't that the trees were so heavy. It was just wearing to make the same motion over and over—bend down, pick it up, step sideways to the truck, heave up and over your head. Repeat. Repeat. Repeat.

I heard Nell say, "Shouldn't you take a coffee break? Everybody else does."

"Yeah. I've got to talk to you."

They retreated a little, chatted for a moment, and then went into the barn.

I saw Marie look after them. Curious, I glanced around for John and saw him, too, staring as they left, staring at the door of the barn.

Well, all right, I thought. She was twelve or thirteen and he was nineteen, maybe twenty. A romance wasn't impossible. But let's not get totally ahead of ourselves, either. It certainly wasn't a secret tryst. People were in and out of the barn constantly and the door was open. Chat they might, but chatting would be all.

Still, fathers worry, don't they?

There were social questions here, too. Luis was an employee. He was Mexican. He was too young to have graduated from college, so probably he had not gone to college, probably he had gone to work instead. Probably also he was Catholic. Last but not least, he was much too old for Nell.

"Ah, shit!"

Somebody in the field leaped back and started jumping

around on one leg. Hank's voice said, "Oh, hell! I didn't see you. What the hell were you doing there?"

Marie calmly put her tally board on the truck, picked up the first-aid case, and walked toward the noise. I followed.

Dan—or was it Don? they looked so much alike—was sitting on the ground. His hand was wrapped around his lower leg. Blood was seeping out between his fingers.

Hank said, "Let me look." He held a chain saw up in front of his chest.

"God damn it! Just give me a minute."

I could see now that it was Don. Sure enough, Marie said, "Don, let me look. Hank, back off."

She set the first-aid box down on the ground, motioned him down, and sat next to him. She had to lift his hands away from the wound, but he let her do it without fighting her.

The cut looked huge to me. It was on the outside of the leg, about five inches above the ankle, on the lower part of Don's calf muscle. Blood had soaked all down the leg and into his ankle-high leather boot. He wasn't wearing the kind of jeans that are so tight around the ankle you'd have to cut them off to see anything. The pants leg itself was cut through in one spot, and Marie just rolled it up out of the way, up over the cut. While she did, Don said, "Shit! Shit! Shit!" I certainly hoped Gran couldn't hear.

By now the whole crew was standing around. Hank senior held the chain saw that had done the cutting. He said awkwardly, "Don, don't make such a damn fuss."

Marie said, "Well, good. It doesn't look too serious."

She took a paper-wrapped square out of the box, tore off the paper, and pulled out a gauze pad. It looked wet, probably soaked with antiseptic. She washed around the outside of the cut, then threw that pad away and got a fresh one. With this she washed across the surface of the cut, but not down into it.

The woman had done this before.

Don cursed a little more.

The cut was wide, the quarter-inch width of a chain saw blade, and about four inches long.

"It's not deep," Marie said. It was welling new blood, but not terribly fast. "I think we can just bandage you up," she said. "It's not deep enough for stitches to be any use. Okay with you?"

She wasn't asking Hank, she was asking Don, but Hank answered. "Sure. Get it covered and we'll get back to work."

"Don?" she said.

"Yeah, yeah. I don't want stitches anyhow."

It wasn't my business, but I said, "You've had your tetanus shots?"

Don simply nodded. Marie answered, "All of us. Regularly. For obvious reasons."

Hank said, "Yeah. Hey. That's nothing. Check this out." He pulled up his pants leg and showed me a long scar running from his ankle up his shin to where it disappeared under the pants fabric. It looked like a railroad track. "Had to have that one stitched. And look at this." He pulled his shirt and jacket up on the left side, and across his ribs, angled toward the spine, was another long scar. Jeez! This man is holding his shirt up in the snowy fields at the end of November just for me to see his scars. Like Lyndon Johnson. "And that's nothing," he said. "Chain-saw cuts usually don't go very deep. The blade's too wide. And not really sharp. You should see the accidents in shearing season." He held out his hands. There were cuts crisscrossed on the backs, and several on the fingers.

"Jeez!" I said. I said it really loudly, believing that this would satisfy him. It did.

Marie swiftly unwrapped two more gauze pads, dry ones. When the bleeding had slowed, she placed these gently over Don's wound, then taped them in place with four strips of adhesive.

Hank said, "Okay, let's get to work."

Marie said, "No. I want him to go to the barn for twenty minutes. Have some coffee with sugar."

"We've got work to do."

"These things shake you up. That's when worse accidents happen." She looked Hank in the eye and said, "He goes to the barn, Hank. This is not negotiable."

Hank spun around and pull-started the chain saw. Just before it caught I heard him mumble something ending with "—I was a kid there wasn't all this coddling."

Marie pulled Don to his feet. She slapped him gently on the shoulder and said, "Git."

I walked Don to the barn, figuring it couldn't hurt to make sure he was okay. "You get paid for this?" I asked him.

"Yeah."

"Enough?" Well, I wasn't really a guest. I could ask what I wanted to.

"I guess. The best thing is, it's not constant, you know? Work your ass off several days in November"—he blinked and looked at me to see how I'd respond to his language, but I didn't—"and shearing season in the spring. But most of the time the trees just sit there and grow."

In the barn, the wood stove was so hot the air around it shimmered. John was working with oily rags over two long-handled clippers and a bow saw. He had his shirt off, as Hank had last night, although unlike Hank he had a sleeveless undershirt on. He was much thinner than Hank. His chest was gaunt but his arms looked strong. There was a big chunk like a small shark bite out of the deltoid muscle at the top of his shoulder. Another sacrifice to the bite of the chain saw?

Are all these people covered head to toe with scars? I wondered.

John said, "Damn pine pitch! Might as well be rubber cement." He picked a wire brush off the floor and scrubbed hard at the teeth of the bow saw with brisk, one-way stroking motions.

Nell brought Don some coffee. She said, "I put extra sugar in it. Are you okay?"

"Oh, sure."

Nell sat back down on one of the lawn chairs. She folded her hands and looked toward the far wall, but with her eyes unfocused, that "thousand-yard stare." Thinking about something. Well, it wasn't up to me to interrupt her.

I said, "Don, what's 'shearing'? I mean, these are trees, not sheep."

He limped to one wall where tools hung in ranks. "You take one of these," he said. It was a long knife, oddly shaped. The end was squarish, not pointed. It was shaped like a very long cooking spatula or very narrow machete— possibly thirty inches long, but only two inches wide. The edge looked razor sharp.

"You make the trees grow bushier by cutting off the branch tips where they bud out in the spring. You can hand-prune with clippers, but it takes forever."

John said, "We shear spruce in April before they bud, and that makes them put out more buds the next year. We shear Scotch pine the second week of June, just the new buds, before the new growth hardens off."

"We tried a back-pack electric trimmer once, but it wasn't any faster," Don said.

"A seven-foot pine takes about a hundred cuts to shear," John said.

"Yeah," Don said. He brandished the knife. "And with one of these I can shear a whole tree in about half a minute!"

Don swept the air with the blade, swinging it fast overhand. He hooked it back, whipped it through the air again in a circle so it whistled and sang.

"Hey!" John said. "Stop that! That's not safe!"

Don said, "Okay."

He hung the shearing knife on its hook again, grinned at John, Nell, and me, and sat down to drink his coffee.

⋄ 7 ⋄

Lunch was Dutch pea soup. The family and I ate in the kitchen, but the hired crew didn't. Horace, Ken, and Raymond crowded into Raymond's dilapidated car and drove off to Wendy's or McDonald's. Luis stayed in the barn and ate some sandwiches he had brought. "Save a coupla bucks," he said to me.

Since there were eleven of us, ten DeGraafs and me, we ate in two shifts at the big pine kitchen table. Hank smoothed at it with his hand and said to me, "Look at this nice piece of white pine. See that clear grain? Twelve-inch wide stock and there isn't a knot in it."

Gran apologized that the pea soup wasn't made in the traditional way. "It's supposed to be split peas, a ham bone or metwurst, onion, carrots, potatoes, and celery. I use turkey broth instead of ham at Thanksgiving," she said. "Waste not, want not."

With it we had Dutch rye bread, a very dense, unleavened loaf, cut thin, with Gouda and some other cheeses to slice and put on it. It sounds simple; it tasted wonderful.

Aunt Clara, the only one authorized to help Gran in the kitchen, was a little butterball. Nearing eighty, five feet tall, roly-poly with a smooth cap of silky pure white hair, she was the sister of Gran's husband, Henry, who had died just this past spring. For twenty-one years, Henry had been the president of the Growers Association, the office

Hank now held. I got the impression Hank had been given the job somewhat in sympathy for the sudden death of his father.

"Such an unnecessary accident," Clara said.

"How did it happen?"

"Sheer chance. He was in the field when the crop duster came over. He should never have been out there at spraying time, with his asthma."

As we left the kitchen to get back to the fields, Gran pulled a turkey out of the second refrigerator to bone for dinner. A huge turkey. This was a bird about the size of a Shetland pony. I said, "Can I help you with that?"

"No. It's no trouble." She whisked it from the refrigerator as if it were a Barbie doll and set it on the kitchen table. Gran was little; she was beautiful; she looked like a Hummel figurine. But she was strong. I wondered again why she had been resting yesterday afternoon when I arrived. It seemed more likely she would have been doing her weight training. A hundred reps of forty pounds.

Just a few slices had been carved from the turkey. Only one drumstick was missing. "They certainly didn't finish all their Thanksgiving dinner," I said.

"Oh, I always make at least three twenty-five-pound turkeys at Thanksgiving. It's tree-cutting season. Everybody's hungry."

We started cutting on a new block after lunch. The trees are grown in blocks planted all at the same time to the same type of tree. This was a block of green spruce, their branches uplifted like the blue spruce, their needles dense and crisp. They were all six feet tall, give or take an inch. I was sad to see them fall. I tried resolutely to think of families going to Christmas tree sales yards, picking out their beautiful holiday trees, taking them home, and happily decorating them. I asked John, "What happens to this part of the field next?"

"We'll put it in white clover for a year. Build up the soil. The stumps rot pretty quickly. Then we'll turn the clover under and plant more trees."

The cycle of life.

Nell had been quiet at lunch. Thinking there was some sort of problem, I resolved to talk to her when she was alone in the barn. But finding a time when she was alone might be difficult. For one thing, although we were working closer to the house now, a rise in the ground made it hard to see the barn through the trees. For another, although we had started the day with three chain saws, at any given time we were actually working with only two. The fuel and the oil were in the fields with us, so the saws were refilled there. But chain saws are temperamental. One or another of the things would have to go to the barn to have its spark plug wiped, or its teeth sharpened, or the pine pitch cleaned from the teeth, and as soon as it got back, the next one would go to the barn for its dental work. I went to the barn twice, and both times there was somebody there working on the tools.

I didn't get a chance to talk with Nell alone.

In midafternoon, the quality of the light changed. The pearl glow in the sky altered as a roll of ropy, dark clouds flowed by. Then the light became pearly bright again for a few minutes. Then another roll of dark clouds wiped the sky.

Just behind that came another. In a few minutes the sky was dense with them and it started to snow, not flakes, but little hard pellets, something English doesn't have a word for, but Inuit would.

Work continued. The snow wasn't coming down fast. It barely salted the ground, although scarflike windrows of the pellets would blow over the sandy soil and eddy in the depressions made by feet or the farm equipment.

By four o'clock the sun was low. Don, Hank, and Horace, who were currently using the chain saws, cut a few last trees fast and then headed to the barn, while Luis and two of the kids lopped bottom branches. By quarter after four I was watching the last tree go through the baler and emerge packaged for shipping. We hadn't quite finished the block. Marie tallied her last tree of the day.

When I got to the barn, Nell offered me the dregs of the coffee. I accepted it. Why would any sane human being ever turn down coffee? And it was as good as any earlier cup, partly because I was cold, damp, and starving, but partly because the DeGraafs kept making coffee fresh all day long. My Chicago cop friend Harold McCoo, the biggest caffeine addict since Balzac, would approve of these people.

Once the work was over, the three young hired hands, Ken, Raymond, and Horace, were out of there fast. Luis got out oil and solvent and laid the chain saws on a bench to clean. Again. Chain saws to the DeGraafs were what my laptop is to me.

Nell, Dan, and Don picked up the coffee urns and cream. I said to Nell, "What can I help with?" I wasn't sure what things were usually left overnight in the barn and what wouldn't be.

"You could bring in the sugar. There's just no way to

keep mice and raccoons out of barns. Maybe bring the garbage bag, too. Do you know where the trash can is?"

"Sure." I had searched it out during the day, so I would know where to dispose of the newspaper that I used to line the bottom of LJ's cage.

The bag of trash wasn't heavy. It held mostly styrofoam cups and paper towels. I slung it over my shoulder and held the sugar box in my other hand.

The square, home-size dumpster was behind the barn, on the west side. I stepped out of the barn expecting to dump the trash and go to the house, but the sight of the land at evening made me stand still.

Far away behind the woods that lay to the west, a deep, rusty glow of sun remained. In the east, clouds obscured the sky. I walked out into the yard, where the open expanse let me see it better. Dark, invisible to me, were the acres of little pine trees, but the far woods, a mix of skeletal oaks and ash with ferny white pines, made an irregular lace against the red flush.

I could smell the spicy scent of pine, stronger now that the sun was down. There were several other scents, damp sandy soil, a hint of wood smoke, a rich, yeasty odor I thought was moss growing under the pine needle mat on the woods floor. It was easy to understand how a person could love this land.

To my right, near the corner of the barn, I heard a whisper. It's strange, but whispers can carry farther than voices.

Someone whispered, "You don't mean it."

A voice said, "I do, though."

I knew that second voice. It was Luis. He had a softer and lower voice than the DeGraaf men.

"You know, you could be wrong." Still a whisper.

I missed the next part of what Luis said. He must have turned away from me as he spoke. Then I heard, "—up to you to do the right thing."

There were several whispered words I couldn't understand. I thought about taking out my tape recorder, but it wasn't my business, and by then it was also too late. Footsteps made padding sounds on the snowy sand. One person's brisk footsteps, leading around to the far side of the barn. Probably Luis. The other person must still have been standing where they had spoken, unmoving.

When I reached the kitchen, I found Nell and two of Hank's kids, Dan and Don, being fed cookies by their Aunt Clara and Gran. In a few minutes John came in, hands covered with oil from the chain saws.

"Don't go anywhere else in the house until you've washed," Gran said.

Hank's wife, Jennifer, came in, looking for Hank. "I'd like to get home in time to start dinner," she said. "Where's Hank?"

Cal arrived right behind her, then Marie, still carrying her clipboard. She said, "When are they coming by for the loads?"

"I think first thing in the morning," John said, still scrubbing hard at the sink. This was a family that lived in the kitchen.

The door sprang open. Hank backed in, pulling, of all things, a Christmas tree, a seven-foot blue spruce. The kids jumped up. "Best one of the whole lot," he said. "Perfect all four sides."

Nell shouted, "I'll get the stand." She ran into the hall

with Don, and I heard them both clump down some stairs to the basement. Even if you raise Christmas trees, Christmas is still an event to the children.

Jennifer said again, "I'd like to get started home at a reasonable hour, Hank."

"No problem."

They finally collected Don, Cal, and Dan, and left for their home. Hank promised to tell me more about planting and growing in the morning. Aunt Clara promised to tell me about the old days on the farm. Marie promised to tell me about marketing trees. Nell seemed, ever so subtly, to be avoiding me.

Gran lay down for half an hour's rest while dinner cooked.

We had creamed turkey with mushrooms for dinner, and with it a casserole of potatoes. Gran had packed chunks of potato and some onions, tossed first in melted butter, into a huge square casserole dish. This she baked slowly for two hours. She turned the dish upside down on a platter and the whole thing came out as if molded, with the potatoes all browned and crisp on the top. The top that had previously been the bottom. I said, "Oh, gee, I want to come and live here!"

This earned a rare smile from Gran.

The family said grace before they ate. "Bless this food to our use and us in Thy service, in Jesus' name. Amen."

Because it had been fully dark at five-thirty, and because we ate at six, John and Nell and I being ravenous, by eight o'clock it seemed like midnight. They probably felt like I did, thoroughly exhausted from a long day out in the cold doing physical work, and yet deeply relaxed as a result. With the warmth and the food acting as a soporific, the whole household went to bed at nine.

Before turning in I cleaned LJ's cage, while Nell played with him on the floor. "Can we let him fly around the house?" she asked.

"Over my dead body."

"Why? He'll be safe."

"That's not the problem. Parrots pretend they can't be housebroken. Your grandmother is the most spotless housekeeper I've ever seen, and I don't intend to be thrown out."

Nell giggled and put her hand near LJ. He climbed up her wrist and from there to her shoulder. "That tickles!" she said.

I thought of trying to get her to talk to me, but it didn't seem like the right moment. Or maybe I was just too exhausted.

After she left I converted the mix of taped and hand-jotted notes I had made during the day into a file on my laptop, which I always do, no matter how tired I am. If you leave your notes too long, you lose accuracy. Let yourself get behind once, and the next day you are running to catch up. Get into a habit of putting off your note-taking, and you're one step away from finding a new line of work.

I was sleeping as inert as a sandbag, but somehow became aware that the tempo in the house had changed. Rolling onto my back, I listened. Nell's voice in the distance was saying, "Daddy! Please get up. I'm not imagining this!" It was pitch dark in my room. I turned on my light and looked at my watch. Four-thirty.

John's voice said, "All right, all right, honey. Give me half a minute." Nell must have been speaking to him from outside his bedroom door. Otherwise she wouldn't have been talking this loudly at this hour of the night. She was a courteous child, who wouldn't wake up a houseguest if she could avoid it, and besides, she had a naturally soft voice.

John and Nell had bedrooms in the same wing I did, the north wing, Gran in the south. This wouldn't wake her up.

Nell's problem, whatever it was, properly was none of my business. It was between her and her father. But when I heard her say "We've got to go out there!" it sounded like serious trouble. Besides, there's a note you can't mistake in voices when the person is really worried. Their throats close up on them.

I can get into Levi's, shirt, and shoes in thirty seconds, a relic-skill of the days when I covered fires and major automobile accidents for a big Chicago newspaper. I dressed, then peeked out my door, trying to be as guestlike as possible, and said, "Nell, is anything wrong?" The hall was dark.

That moment, John came out of his room.

Nell was too upset to notice in the spill of light from my door that a houseguest was fully dressed at four-thirty A.M. "Look!" she said.

A window in the hall faced the front yard. Nell's room was on the same side of the hall. She led John and me to the window. "I got up to go to the—you know," she said. "And I just looked out my window before going back to bed."

The yard outside lay in the glow of the safety light, which was high on a pole between the house and the barn. The light was a steely blue, and now that there was snow on the ground, the entire lighted area looked like brushed aluminum.

At first neither John nor I reacted, not quite knowing what we were looking for. Nell said, "Look in that shadow near the driveway."

"Oh," John said.

I said, "What? I don't see what you're looking at."

"That's Luis's motorcycle," Nell said, the pitch of her voice rising. "He came to work on it. He always rides it home. So where is he?"

◦ 8 ◦

"He may be hurt!" Nell said. "Suppose he cut himself cleaning a saw or something! He could be bleeding to death out there in the barn."

Darn right, I thought.

"Oh, Luis is very careful," John said. "It can't be that bad." Contradicting his words, he raced for the stairs. We hurried down, speaking softly despite the urgency as we crossed the kitchen so we wouldn't wake Gran. At the back door, John took his coat off one of the pegs in the back hall. I grabbed another coat randomly. Nell picked hers off a peg.

I said, "Um, Nell, wouldn't it be better if you waited here?"

"Why?"

John realized what I meant. "Honey, I wish you would. In case—there might be some sort of—"

"For backup," I said. "Nell, what if he's been attacked in the barn by an intruder? I hope not," I added quickly at the horrified look on her face, "but it happens. Would you stand next to the phone here, and watch us out the window? If you see us wave for help, or if you see a stranger out there *anywhere*, whether we see him or not, will you please call 911 instantly? You have 911 here?"

John looked at me gratefully. Nell said, "Yes, we have. Okay. Just hurry!" She didn't make any more fuss and didn't say any silly things about being afraid to stay in the house alone except for a sleeping grandmother, either. Admirable child.

John and I opened the back door and stepped into the blue-lit yard. There was no breeze. The snow had stopped. The land was utterly silent. No owl hooted; no dog barked. The moon showed only faintly behind a passing cloud.

Feeling John hesitate beside me, I cocked my head toward the barn but put a finger up to my lips. It was not a ploy when I told Nell to stay inside because there could be intruders. Every once in a while, a farm family is wiped out in the night. Sometimes by felons looking for a place to hide, sometimes by people who think foolishly that there's a lot of cash money on farms, and sometimes by thrill killers looking for something to do. Personally, I thought Luis had probably slipped, fallen, and hit his head, or— who knew his medical history?—maybe gone into a diabetic coma. If so, we had to find him fast, because the barn would be cold by now and he could be dying of hypothermia. But we didn't have to be reckless.

The barn had two entrances, a wide double door in the front, big enough to drive tractors and wagons through, and a smaller back door, the size of an ordinary door in a house. I thought opening the back door would make less noise, so I beckoned John to follow me around there.

It was slightly ajar. Inside a light was burning.

"This is supposed to be locked," John whispered. "Luis always locks it when he leaves."

"Yes, but we don't think he left."

I started to push my way in, but John said, "No, let me go first. It's my responsibility," and went in. We entered quietly, putting our feet down carefully on the dirt floor. Dirt floors, I found, are very silent.

A single dim bulb burned over the tool rack. The other lights had been turned off. Large areas of the barn were too dark to see. It looked like nothing was out of place, as far as I could tell, but no Luis, either. We watched for half a minute. Nothing moved.

John flicked a switch near the door and a brighter light went on, high on the near wall.

"I don't see him," John said in a more normal voice.

"Let's check for any sign of an accident."

We walked around the whole inside of the barn, studying the earth floor. But there was nothing.

"No blood," John said.

"No. Not even a scuff mark."

"There are a lot of scuff marks."

"Yes, but I'm looking for long double ones. Like heels make when you drag a body across the floor."

He stared at me as if I'd just flown in from Uranus. Then he nodded. "Right. Okay. We'd better check outdoors," he said.

"I'm afraid so. Got a flashlight?"

"Over here." He took two from the tool bench and gave me one.

We crossed into the middle of the yard, where we could see Nell in the kitchen window. We shrugged our shoulders, arms out, palms up, to show her we were still puzzled, and gestured to the field and driveway to tell her we would search there. She nodded and pointed down, telling us she would stay right where she was. Good.

"Well," John said, "we might as well be methodical. All around the outside of the house first?"

"Sure."

After that we didn't say a word. Nell watched from the window as we started around the house. We went what the English call widdershins, counterclockwise, which was natural enough because the driveway led up that way to the garage. The English say that walking around a church widdershins is bad luck, but I don't suppose anybody says that applies to houses. Still, I had a sense of bad events about to happen. We went into the garage. Sensible Nell had turned on the garage light from the house, so it was easy to see there was nothing in the garage but the old family car and a whole lot of rakes, some road salt, several cans of antifreeze, and a fertilizer spreader.

Around behind the garage it was dark. We brushed the beams of our flashlights through the dried weeds and trees beyond, as far out as they would go before they were absorbed by the night, but nobody was there and the weeds looked unbroken. In the few places where snow had drifted, it seemed to be undisturbed.

From the garage area, we patrolled the rear of the house. Nell appeared in the dining room window to watch our progress. We waved.

Then the barn side, then back to the front yard again.

"Hey!" John said.

I jumped.

He said, "Sorry. I didn't mean anything was wrong. But why didn't we check Luis's motorcycle first?"

"Oh, of course! We should have done that right away. It might have a flat tire or something!"

"Although—even if it does, where is he? He wouldn't have walked home. It's too far. He would have come in the house and phoned somebody to pick him up. And I'm sure he didn't ride with anybody else. The last time I saw him, everybody had gone except Hank."

"And Hank's truck was pretty full, with five people in it. He'd have said something, anyway, wouldn't he, if he'd given Luis a ride?"

We were walking down the drive to where Luis's motorcycle stood in a ragged lacework of shade cast by some juniper bushes. We talked, I think, to relieve our nervousness.

John said, "Yeah. Luis never said anything about a problem with the motorcycle."

Nor was there any problem. We looked at the machine, much bigger when you get near it than you realize when you pass one by in your car. Luis kept it in perfect condition. The chrome shone despite a light dusting of snow. The rear reflectors were sparkling clean. The tires looked new and certainly weren't flat. There were no tools lying around as if anybody had been trying to fix it. No spark plugs had been pulled.

I pointed at the tires. "Look. The snow has eddied up against the tires. That means it hasn't been moved in quite a few hours. For sure if he'd tried to start it, he'd have moved it. At least a little bit, backwards or forwards."

John was silent. He nodded. He turned and scanned the silent yard, the silent woods, the silent night. Far out on the highway a truck went by, humming on the pavement.

"I don't like this," he finally said.

"No."

"But we can't very well call the police. There's no evidence of, you know, foul play."

"No."

"Shall we check the fields? He could have gone back out there to get some tool that was left behind. And got sick, maybe."

I said, "Yup. Check the fields."

It was cold. It was dead silent. The beams of our flashlights went out into the darkness, picking up a few ice crystals in the air and making the beams resemble those magic sword-beams in *Star Wars*. But these beams were powerless. They swept the fields, discovering nothing, changing nothing.

Without discussion, we moved between blocks of five-foot Scotch pine toward the block of six-foot blue spruce where we had finished work at the end of the day. Getting there, we passed one block that had been totally cut yesterday. The almost-full moon was sinking in the sky and in its light the stumps of the spruces were visible against the snowy soil, all of them round and dark. Spaced in regular rank and file, all those round black circles against the white background worked oddly on my nerves. It was like a giant "go" board. It represented the deaths of a large number of trees. John may have felt the same. We hurried past.

It wasn't far. We slowed as we came to the equipment left in place for tomorrow. The flatbed stood in the lane, partially loaded with baled trees. The baler was near it, waiting for day.

Near the baler was a bundle.

Our flashlight beams found it simultaneously. It was the kind of sight that confuses the mind. For a moment I thought I was looking at a very large cocoon. Large, tapered, fibrous, the progeny of some huge, Mesozoic moth.

We ran to it.

"Oh, my God, no!" John said.

Luis lay absolutely still, encapsulated in the tough orange netting that baled the trees. His arms were up over his head, so that the bale was tapered at both ends, exactly like a moth cocoon. He had been run through the baler and left there.

"Do you have a knife?" I said to John.

"What?"

"A knife. Hurry up! Or scissors?"

"Uh, well—a Swiss army knife."

"Give it to me. Then go back to the house and call 911. Hurry!"

"Yes. Yes, okay."

He handed me his knife. "Do you think he's alive?"

"I doubt it. But hurry! Get the paramedics."

He ran. I began to cut the baling plastic. God, it was tough! I started at the center of the body, sawing at the orange fibers, not bothering to take time with the arms or legs. If Luis was alive and had any chance whatsoever of survival, I had to get his chest and head free first. And trying to revive him was also more important right now than keeping everything exactly the way it was for a later police investigation.

I sawed away at that plastic, snagging his jacket and shirt, but who cared about that? Several times I scratched or jabbed him, but he didn't respond. When I had freed the netting up past his face, I stopped and placed two fingers over his carotid artery.

No pulse.

I pushed hard three times on his chest, at the bottom of the breastbone. Nothing much happened; he felt as unyielding as a clump of grass sod. With my flashlight, finally, I studied his face. Luis's lips were blue. His eyes were wide open and the pupils, when I shined the flashlight on them, were fixed. But what was most convincing to me were the small flecks of snow on his eyeballs. The earlier snow that had fallen on him had melted, while he still had the warmth of life. But the last flakes had fallen on a surface that was cold. Luis was dead.

Neither John nor I had said aloud that Luis had been run through the tree baler. It was both too obvious and too horrible. The idea gave rise to hideous questions. Had he been put through before or after death? Was he stunned first, or could someone have been cruel enough to just lash the chain around his feet, turn the machine on, and let the mechanism pull him through? If he was alive at first, did going through the baler kill him or did he live for a while afterward, trussed up in a netting like a Thanksgiving turkey, lying on the ground as the night grew colder? God.

The baler is designed to push up the branches of the tree as it passes trunk first into a kind of funnel. As a result, a tree that has, say, a four-foot spread of branches at the base is reduced to a package about eighteen inches wide. The funnel is almost four feet wide at the entrance and narrows to eighteen inches where the tree is finally ejected. The tree is easier to ship and more protected from damage this way.

For most human bodies, passing through an eighteen-inch-wide space is relatively harmless. I could do it with no problem, but of course Luis was wider and heftier. His shoulders might be as much as eighteen inches wide. Even so, it was very possible that being sucked through the baler had not killed him.

I felt so sad for him that I put my hand on his hand. It was

cold. Both hands extended above his head and were still
held in place by the upper part of the netting, which I had
not cut. By touching him, either I wanted him to feel
someone was close to him, which was crazy, or I actually
felt a relationship to him, which was more nearly the truth.
"You know what it is, Luis?" I said softly. "I liked you. I
liked the way you handled yourself. Some people think
that even a moment's acquaintance with a person is
enough to tell you everything about his character. As if
personality were like a hologram—even a small bit con-
tains information about the whole.

"It can't really be true. I make mistakes in my first im-
pressions of people. But not all the time.

"This is foolish, talking to you. My brain must be in
shock. Talking doesn't hurt anybody, though, does it?
We're both outsiders here. You less than me, because I go
home in a few days. Or is it you more than me, because
you work here but aren't one of the family? One of the
family killed you, I think. What would you want done
about that?"

But there was no answer from Luis's spirit. Feeling increasingly foolish, and having finished with whatever last
contact I thought I was making, I backed away, and
stunned and scared, sat on the cold metal end of the open
flatbed, watching over Luis, even though nobody was going to hurt him any more than they already had. The snow
clouds had passed and stars were visible. Much clearer
than in Chicago, they were laser sharp and bright. They
look smaller when they're clear like this, but more intense.
After a while, my eyes adjusted enough so that I could see
the frosting of moonlight on the tops of the skeletal oaks
and ash in the forest.

Nell did not come, which I was glad of, and John didn't
return, either. He had probably convinced her to stay and

wait with him for the state police or sheriff, whichever they used here.

Unless they were planning to come back, attack me, and hide both bodies. No, that was silly. Nell would not have given the alarm if she'd been involved, and in any case, she was a nice child and not a killer. As to the family, though, there was no way of knowing what I might have stumbled into.

When you sit unmoving long enough, there are small sounds even in the stillest night. Maybe a piece of ice slides from a branch. Or a pinecone, its stem cracked by the passage of machines during the day, takes this moment to fall. Maybe there are small animals abroad, or larger animals, like raccoons, rustling in pine-needle litter. Whatever it is, you begin to realize that the night is alive. When you hear sounds, they seem to be creeping toward you.

I kept glancing behind me.

And then, very distant, a siren. Flashing lights, reflecting on the tops of the trees near the drive. As the trooper's car swung into the drive and slid along on its momentum toward the house, the mars lights flashed strobelike through the rows of trees and briefly shined on me. It caught just the upper surface of the dead Luis before passing on to the house. Briefly, twice, the light made Luis's cheek and mouth seem to smile, his eyebrows to lift in a question. An ambulance turned into the drive thirty seconds later.

"You cut the netting away?"

"Yes."

"You altered the crime scene. You must know better than that. Almost any functioning adult in the world knows that."

This guy meant well. He was thirty-five or so, blond, trim, and too experienced to get really angry. The sharpness in his tone was caused by nervousness—not by being new on the job, but because he didn't like this case. He glanced uneasily every so often to the spot, twenty feet away, where the crime scene team was taking samples and making photographs. And where Luis's body still lay. Sergeant VanLente didn't like the idea of people being run through balers. I had to agree with him on that score. He said crisply, "You must have realized he was dead."

"No, I didn't. Not for sure. I was working with a flashlight. I couldn't see him very well. The netting didn't help, either. Listen, I'm sorry about your crime scene, but even though he looked dead I wasn't certain. And there was no time to call a doctor. I'd try to revive him exactly the same way if it happened again."

I was having an attack of ambivalence. I wanted to stay here in the field and see how the sheriff conducted an investigation, so I could go back to Chicago and tell my buddy Harold McCoo, who is currently chief of detectives of the Chicago Police Department, how they work out here. He's always interested in police departments. For instance, you couldn't fault these people's response time.

On the other hand, I wanted to go to the house and see how Nell was. Just as the sheriff arrived, she had come running out to the field. Out of breath, gasping, she approached Luis's body.

She whispered, "Luis. Please get up. Please get up." She put her hand on his and the look of horror when she felt how cold he was made me pull her away.

"Why aren't the paramedics here?" she wailed. "Why aren't you helping him? Oh, please, Cat, *do* something for him!" I touched her shoulder and told her I had tried; it was hopeless. Really, truly hopeless—he had been dead for a couple of hours at least. She had begun crying silently, then turned and trudged slowly back to the house.

She wasn't my daughter or my responsibility. But the other sheriff's deputy had brought John out to the barn to talk and to show where the equipment was stored, which meant that Nell was now basically alone in the house. I very much doubted that she would go wake up Gran to ask for comfort. There was something austere about Gran.

In the past, in cases like this, my curiosity has always gotten the better of me, or in some cases the worst. It's gotten me into situations that could have been fatal. Usually I would not have walked away until ordered to go, and sometimes not even then.

This was new, this sense of needing to protect a child.

I'd seen enough. I said to the deputy, "That's all I can tell you. Except for my cutting the netting, this is exactly how we found him."

"And your footprints."

"I walked to the body. John came as far as Luis's feet. He handed me his Swiss army knife and went to call you. I cut the net, felt Luis's carotid, tried to get him breathing, then backed off." They certainly didn't need to know I'd held his hand and talked to him. Honesty is the best policy when taken in reasonable doses. "From then on until you got here, I sat on that flatbed. That's everything."

"Mmm-mm."

"If you want me, I'll be in the house."

I found Nell slumped on the sofa in the living room. I sat down next to her. For several minutes we didn't say a word. That would be a long time to be silent with most people, but with Nell I had a sense she needed to think. Finally she broke off her line of thought and said, "Thanks,

Cat. All of this isn't your problem. But I'm glad you're here."

"I'm glad, too."

She smiled a little.

I said, "Can I do anything for you? Or call anybody for you?"

"No. Gran's getting dressed. She saw all the lights and stuff."

"Or heard the sirens?"

"Mmm-mm. I guess. And I called Aunt Marie and Uncle Henry. They're coming. And I called Aunt Clara."

"Aunt Clara?" I said, thinking of the elderly butterball. "Doesn't she need her rest?"

"Well, no. She used to be a nurse, an R.N., and she says she learned not to sleep much. Plus, if I hadn't called her, she'd never forgive me."

"I get it. Uh—Nell—"

She interrupted. "Cat, I know what you're going to say. You're going to ask about me and Luis. Cal was always teasing, as if Luis was my boyfriend. I liked Luis. We talked a lot. He was a really honest person."

"And you don't find so many honest people?"

"No. Do you?"

"Well, actually no."

"But what I'm trying to tell you is that I didn't have any crush on him. Or any—you know—dating or romance or stuff like that."

"I see."

"I've never had a date. Dad and Gran say I have to be in ninth grade first. Anyway, Luis was too old."

"Ah. Yes." To her, he really was old. I was almost twice Luis's age, and I didn't think I was old.

"Luis was nice. He told me it was good I got good grades, and how he wished he had worked harder when he was in school. How I should work hard and go to college and all. He said someday he was going to go to college. Save money, and start evening classes."

"He does sound nice. What I saw of him, I liked."

"He was interested in doing college counseling in high schools. You know, like when they help the kids find the right college to go to?"

"Yes, I know."

"There's a lot of stuff you have to know about how to look at their tests—like aptitude and interests and all. And naturally, you have to go to college. He wanted to do counseling with other Mexican students especially. Not only, you know, but that, too."

"Yes. I see."

Nell held her head up. "I just thought I should make it clear, you know, that we were just friends. People sometimes jump to conclusions. I don't mean you, Cat. But it's always better to be clear, don't you think?"

"Yes, I do." I hesitated for a minute. Yesterday afternoon I had been trying to get a moment alone with her, because I felt she wanted to ask me about something. And there hadn't been any chance. Then last evening in my room, too tired, I blew the opportunity. This talk of honesty made me bold. "Was there something you wanted to discuss earlier toda—yesterday?"

Her hands, which had been on her knees, suddenly came together. She held them tightly in front of her chest. "I did," she said. "But I guess now I'm not so sure."

Well, she was honest, anyway.

It turned out that when you called 911 around here, your call went to an Ottawa County area dispatcher who then radioed all cars, asking what car out there was closest to the scene. It might be a Michigan State Police car or an Ottawa County Sheriff's car, as well as an ambulance if there was an injury involved. Whichever was closest responded, and then that agency was in charge of the case from then on. The idea was to get the quickest possible response in a largely rural area where the police were spread quite thin. Both agencies have detectives who take over from the patrol car if the uniforms find it's a murder case. So we had the sheriff's people, but we might just as easily have got the state police.

The detectives and uniforms that turned up from the Ottawa County Sheriff's Department reflected the local ethnic diversity. Three were Dutch—Dave Hoogendoorn, Sergeant VanLente, and Susan Kamphuis. One was Mexican—Bill Suya. Two were "other," probably the English-Irish-German-French mix common in these parts.

John had come into the house while I was talking with Nell, and it was good to see him go directly to her, without worrying about what the guest—me—would think. He put his arms around her and said, "Honey, are you all right?"

"Well, sort of, Daddy."

"I know it's terrible."

"It's just *wrong!* It's wrong! Luis had a right to live."

"Yes, he did."

"Why do things like this happen?"

"I don't know, honey. If we knew . . . You shouldn't have gone out there. You didn't need to see that—the body—him, honey."

"Daddy, seeing or not seeing doesn't make it any different. Anyway, it's not good to turn your back on, you know, facts."

Nell was a person after my own heart. I got up and left them alone.

*   *   *

Hoogendoorn and Suya were talking quietly in the hall.

In the kitchen, Gran was firing up the coffee maker. There was a smell of muffins—corn muffins, I think—coming from the oven. It contrasted oddly with the sour knowledge of death that hung in the air. Aunt Clara mixed water into frozen orange juice concentrate. How had she managed to get here before everybody else? Nell and John came in from the dining room shortly after me. John put Nell in a chair and sat near her. Clara poured Nell some juice.

Gran said, "I can scramble some eggs for you, Pieternella."

Nell's face reacted with nausea, but Gran was standing behind her and didn't notice. "No, thanks, Gran," Nell said. "I'll wait for the muffins."

I felt like a fifth wheel but there wasn't much time to think about it. The back door slammed open, the knob bouncing on the wall, and Hank blew in, his bulk dominating the room. A whirlwind of cold air followed him.

"What is this? I mean, okay, there's been an accident, but why all the bossy behavior out there?" he yelled. His big voice made the room seem even smaller. "The cops won't let me park in the driveway."

"It's an evidence scene, Hank," John said. "A murder scene."

"Well, who makes that decision? That VanLente jerk out there?"

"Henry, mind your tone," Gran snapped.

Instantly, he got quiet. In the brief lull, Marie came in the back door behind Hank. He didn't even notice her. She circled him and sat down across from Nell. She said, "Hi, darlin'. How are you?"

Nell said, "Okay."

Hank said, "The boys and Jennifer are coming over later. No point in bringing them now."

John said, "No."

"You want to tell me what exactly happened, John?"

"I'm not sure what exactly happened. But I can tell you what we found."

John told Hank, Marie, Clara, and Gran how Nell had wakened us, how we searched, and how we discovered Luis. He told it well, very calmly and matter-of-fact and without any overblown lurid details. The facts were bad enough.

While he was talking, Clara took the muffins out of the oven. They were beautiful. They were just like muffins in a picture-perfect food shot in the *Chicago Today* Sunday shopping guide. Rounded on top with a few cracks to show that they were bursting with flavor. Lightly browned. Little spirals of steam rising from them.

The kitchen was warm, walls the honey color of knotty pine, the floor yellow pine, the table clear white pine. The air was flavored with coffee and baking. And the family was picture perfect in its way. Gran was pinkly pretty. Nell was beautiful. Marie was stylish and slender, John thin but wiry, and Hank was big, hefty, and healthy. But except possibly for young Cal, who would be arriving later, one of them was the killer of Luis Montoya.

Hank caught the sergeant in the hall.

"VanLente, you guys have to be done and outta here soon. I've got a field crew arriving in three hours."

"I should have made myself clear, Mr. DeGraaf. We've barely started. We're not doing much more than preserving the scene right now. There's no light out there, except from our generators, and I don't want the generator truck's wheels rolling around on any evidence. Most of our investigation is going to take place in daylight."

"Oh, no it's not."

"We have to see what we're doing. There's a whole field out there to search."

"Hey, listen! You may not realize it, but we're tryin' to run a business here."

"I know that."

"This is cutting season. Basically, what we have here is eight days, tops, before it's too late."

"Mr. DeGraaf, what we have here is a murder."

"*You* have a murder. I have a business to run. I'm gonna call my lawyer."

John said, "Wait a minute, Hank. Think about this. You pay a lawyer, you're only gonna wipe out a lot of what we might make on the trees."

John certainly knew the way to Hank's heart. I saw the cop start to smile and then stifle it. I guess either he knew Hank's reputation or he'd paid a lawyer lately himself.

John said, "Sergeant VanLente, you want control of that particular block, right?"

"A block is a square bunch of trees?"

"Yes."

"Yeah, that block and the two-track to it and most of the driveway here. From the house down past the motorcycle about a hundred yards. Also the barn. And I don't want you in the blocks right around that one either for a while. We want to search them when the sun comes up."

Hank groaned at John. "See? You can't reason with these people."

John went on. "So you don't mind if we cut a block that's a couple of hundred feet away?"

"No. Let me walk it with you first, but offhand I don't see a problem."

"And our crew can park on the road and walk in? And they can get coffee in the kitchen during the day, if we leave the barn to you?"

Hank said, "Shit, John, where you think we're gonna work on the tools?"

"In the basement. No, the garage."

"Ah—hell!"

"And of course you realize," Sergeant VanLente said, "you can't use the baler."

Hank reared back and hit the wall a flat-handed blow. From the kitchen came Gran's voice: "Henry DeGraaf! You stop that!"

"Go sit down. I'll deal with it, Hank," John said. "I'll get a loaner from somebody."

"At cutting season?"

"Just watch me."

"Oh, sure. I'm watching. What other choice do I have?"

"And Hank, could you please turn down the vocal volume? I mean, let's not forget there's a man dead. Luis was a friend and a man who'd worked with us several years."

Hank said, "Maybe so. But it's not right, interrupting the cutting. After all, he wasn't one of *us!*"

· 10 ·

When the chain saws started to snarl again, I headed out to the field. They were cutting way over near Thornapple Street, and it was a hefty walk along the two-track, much of which was open sand. It was daylight now, and when I got to the area where the sheriff's people were working, I stopped. VanLente was dispatching a tech with samples to a white panel truck labeled OTTAWA COUNTY SHERIFF, and the ambulance was backing into the place vacated by the van. At last they were going to remove Luis's sad, rigid body from where it lay on the cold ground.

I stopped and stood with my hands tucked under my elbows. I couldn't just walk past.

The body had been zipped into a black plastic body bag. It looked longer than most bodies, because rigor mortis held the arms rigidly in place above the head. When they picked Luis up, he did not bend. I waited respectfully.

After the ambulance pulled away, VanLente came over to me.

"You're the only person from the house who came to see him leave."

"And you're going to tell me I'm not even one of the family."

"Right. Don't you think it's callous of them? Are they just ignoring this?"

"I doubt it. Most of them are hard at work."

"Still. A person they knew."

"You didn't tell them when you were going to move the body, did you?"

"They could ask."

"True. I agree they're trying to avoid thinking about it. The daughter is staying in because she's been ordered to. They don't think this is good for young girls."

"They may be right."

"And the other two women in the house are elderly."

"Yeah. Well."

"Have you come to any conclusions yet?"

"Well, Ms. Marsala, you've made it clear you're not a member of the family. Do you think somebody from outside the DeGraaf group came sneaking in here to kill Luis Montoya?"

Damn, why did he have to go to the heart of my worries? He must have an eagle eye. I was having trouble deciding what to tell the police. Should I tell VanLente that Cal had had a minor argument with Luis yesterday?

I said, "It doesn't seem terribly likely, does it?"

"No, it doesn't."

What now? Should I tell him about that cryptic but disturbing whispered conversation I had overheard behind the barn?

If it got back to Hank that I had told them about Cal, I could be out of here in less time than it takes to topple a tree. Nell might see it as a kind of betrayal of the family, too, and I had come to care about what Nell thought.

I had expected to have more time to make this decision.

But putting it in words, even just to myself in my head, had helped clarify the moral implications. Keep the information back from the police in order to stay here and get my tree story? No. Keep something back to help Nell— what kind of example would that set for her?

"I'm sorry to say it, but I agree with you," I told Van-Lente. "Unless somebody from Luis's private life decided that killing him here would be a clever idea, I think one of the family did it. And it's pretty unlikely anybody from his private life could have killed him here because—"

"Yes?"

"Because they would have had to know how to make the baler work."

"Mmm-mm. I wondered whether you'd see that."

"And just why *wouldn't* I?"

"Sorry. So you were saying?"

I took a breath. It might be right, but it wasn't easy. "There was an argument here yesterday. Probably it has nothing to do with this, but you should know about it."

"I certainly should."

"And also a rather odd conversation that I only heard a scrap of."

"Oh, really? That sounds promising."

"Probably sounds more promising than it really is. Look, Sergeant, could you keep it to yourself that I told you about all this?"

It is one thing to do what was right. It's another to make a victim of yourself.

"Afraid they'll throw you out?"

This guy had radar into other people's minds. Whee-ooo. The theme from *Twilight Zone* came to mind. This was no bumbling county sheriff. "Suppose I was?"

"Well, I was thinking. You're not a DeGraaf. But you're living in their house, right?"

"For three days altogether. I leave Monday."

"Maybe you could hold a watching brief for us."

"Let me get this straight. Are you suggesting that I spy on them for you?"

"Roughly, that sums it up."

"Well, the answer is no. Okay? I mean that I won't abuse their hospitality. I will tell you if I learn anything specific about the killer. I would have anyway. Luis deserved that much."

"Okay. Is that a distinction without a difference?"

"Not in my mind. So what do we do now?"

"Now nothing. We go back to where we were three minutes ago. What do you know?"

"No strings?"

"No strings."

"And you'll keep the source confidential?"

"Hey, you're the one who publishes stuff in newspapers."

"What's your answer?"

"Yeah. Okay. I'll keep it confidential. Unless it gets to court and you have to testify."

So I told him.

For some reason, Gran decided to serve lunch in the dining room, with full place settings and cloth napkins. She may have done this because the hired workers had to go away for lunch, since the barn was off limits, a situation that left all the rest of us with nothing to do for an hour. But personally I think she did it out of a kind of defiance. She was saying without words that although there were police officers in her house, life at the DeGraafs went on in a regular, well-bred fashion.

So the whole family and I ate together. Hank and Jennifer and their three sons, Cal, Don, and Dan, Marie, Aunt Clara, John and Nell, Gran and me. The atmosphere in general was subdued. Hank, however, was angry.

One of the effects of the police interviewing everyone

about their opportunity to do murder was that all morning one or another of the crew was called away to the house, where the questioning was taking place. The police had taken over the living room. Work was constantly being interrupted, and to Hank it was going much too slowly. He was hopping mad.

Gran, distressed though she might be about police in the house, would be all right as long as they didn't take over the kitchen.

John was worried, too, but he expressed things more mildly than Hank did. He said, "This is really a bad time to interfere with cutting. I don't mean," he said, turning to me, "that there would ever be a good time for a young man to die like this. But financially—we could be hurt some."

"This is Saturday," Marie said. "We still have time."

John said, "We'll send out the first shipments today. Adrian Oudendyk is coming for them at noon. What we cut this afternoon will go out Monday noon."

Hank was actually too furious to speak. He just snorted and seized another sandwich.

"Of course, we still won't catch up. We'll just have to cut faster Monday," John said.

Feeling sorry for him, I asked, "Why not cut Sunday, too?"

Suddenly there was a dead silence at the table. Gran turned and fixed her eyes on me. Everybody else just sat there. Outside I heard a door slam, but in the dining room there was no sound. I felt like the heroine in *Rebecca*, when she came down the stairs wearing the dress she didn't know was identical to the one worn by her husband's first wife. The dress the sly housekeeper had convinced her to wear. I didn't have anybody but myself to blame, though.

I said, "Um—I guess not, huh?"

John said, "You wouldn't know, Cat, but we don't work on the Sabbath. Don't worry about it, there's no reason you have to know our customs."

Nell said, "It's okay, Cat."

But it wasn't. I felt horrible. The fact was, I should have realized the possibility, and thought carefully before I said anything. This was a very religious family. What kind of an observer was I?

Gran spoke. "It is not a *custom*, John. The Lord said that Sunday is a day of rest and worship."

"You're right, Mother."

"Customs are insignificant matters, like placing the napkin to the left of the dinner plate. Observing the Sabbath is a moral requirement."

"You're right, Mother."

After lunch, Marie caught me in the hall. We walked into the small downstairs room that Gran's husband, Henry, had used as an office. "Cat, don't think that you've made an unusually horrible *faux pas*," she said. "Lots of people do it."

"Not family, though?"

"Oh, no. The family knows Gran. But lots of people in the community work on Sunday. The western Michigan area is in a state of transition, religiously speaking. Or maybe confusion is more the word. The early settlers were mostly members of the Christian Reformed Church or the Dutch Reformed Church, who came here because there was less religious freedom for them in the Netherlands."

"I'd always heard that the Netherlands was one of the most tolerant countries in Europe."

"Probably was. The Dutch started coming to this country, I was always told, because William I had come to the throne and had abolished Christian schools."

"When you say 'I was always told'—"

She smiled. "You *are* an experienced interviewer, aren't you? I later discovered that there were a couple of economic reasons. The first was a plague of potato disease. The second was that William raised taxes to pay for the war with Belgium and just about sucker-punched the middle class. In other words, they came here for financial reasons."

"Wouldn't be the first or the last."

"No, but Mother doesn't like to hear that explanation."

"She's very religious."

"It's not that alone, she's also very rigid. My father was the easygoing one. Of course, she grew up at a time when the whole area was very strict. When I was a child, not one single store in Holland was open on Sunday."

"What if somebody got sick and needed medicine?"

"Actually, there was one drugstore that was allowed to open from two to five P.M. or some such thing. But that was the only one."

"Strict is right."

"It wasn't just the town of Holland. In the 1880s there was a mayor of Grand Rapids who decided he was going to enforce the existing Sunday blue laws strictly. Anybody found on the streets on Sunday was arrested, unless they were either on their way to or from church. The jail overflowed the first Sunday, and among the people arrested was the pastor of the Park Congregational Church and the future U.S. assistant secretary of commerce."

I chuckled and then laughed out loud.

"When I was a child," Marie said, "we weren't even allowed to read the Sunday funnies in the newspaper on Sunday. They were put aside for Monday. We remembered the Sabbath and kept it holy. Dad would have let us, but Mom was very firm."

"Is your mother any less strict now?"

"Somewhat. By and large, though, we tiptoe around her on certain issues. There's always been a degree of discussion in the community about whether observing all the forms was the important part. Whether it was faith that counted, or whether it was good works, good behavior. It's all a very Calvinist kind of debate."

"And where do you come out in this?"

She smiled, somewhat lopsidedly. "Oh, I come down on the side of good works."

"Marie, nobody talks about Nell's mother. Was she rejected by the family? Was there a divorce, or—"

"No, she's dead."

My heart made a little jolt, for which I quickly reprimanded it. I felt suddenly so sorry for Nell, and then I thought—but wouldn't it be just as bad for her if her mother had walked off and left the family?

"May I ask what happened?"

"Sure. No problem. It's not sensitive. It was just so horribly stupid."

"Tell me."

"Her name was Susan. She was a lovely, gentle person. She was on a perfectly ordinary bike tour. You know the kind of thing—a hundred bicyclists riding up the road with those red flags on poles attached to their bicycles to warn the automobile drivers. Helmets, water bottles, all that. It was a thirty-mile round-trip run up to Grand Haven and back."

"She was hit by a car?"

"No. No." Marie put a hand to her cheek and hesitated. "I find it hard to believe even now."

"If it's too hard to talk about—"

"No, it's just so unfair. There was a storm brewing up. They can come on very fast here in the summer. Because of the difference between the lake temperature and the

land. The white clouds turned into thunderheads in minutes, and—lord. She was struck by lightning!"

"Oh, my God!"

"It traveled down the flag, they think. Flashed through
her body and over the wet tires and into the ground."

"Oh."

"And here she was out bicycling for her health. Doing
the healthful thing."

"When was this?"

"Nearly three years ago now. Two and a half, maybe."

"Were Nell and she close?"

"She was a wonderful mother. Gentle. My father very
much approved of her. She and Nell were involved in nature walks and environmental things, but besides that,
they really saw eye to eye. Similar personality types—
smart and no-nonsense. They were very, very close."

"How absolutely awful to lose her."

"It hit Nell hard. It's a bad age to lose your mother. Ten
years old. And a girl especially, I think."

"No wonder Nell is so self-possessed."

"Yes. She and John came here to live with Mother a little while after that. It works well for the three of them.
Especially for Mother now that Dad has died."

"I wonder—does Nell look like her?"

"Somewhat. Now that you mention it, more so as she
gets older."

"I assume you live alone."

"I'm divorced."

"But you don't live here, even though there are a lot of
rooms."

"Oh, heavens! I could never live with my mother. She's
much too judgmental."

Marie's story upset me. If the death of Nell's mother had been so sudden, so much like the hand of God striking her dead, there had been no time for them to prepare Nell. And no reason for her death, like fast driving, for instance, if you can ever say there's a reason for the death of one so young. It must have come as the end of childhood to Nell, and she must still be suffering. Probably she would suffer for it in some sense for the rest of her life.

The question was, Whom did Nell have to confide in, now that her mother was gone? Marie was sympathetic, more than I had thought at first when I had been somewhat blinded by her red, sporty car and stylish clothes. When I saw her yesterday and today working in the fields, I realized my mistake. But she had her own life, a full-time job at the hospital, and she didn't live here, either, so she wouldn't be available when Nell needed her.

Nell's father, John, was a perfectly nice guy. Oh, hell, that was a condescending way to put it. He was more than nice, he really cared about the child, and he was the peacemaker and problem solver in the DeGraaf family, too. But a girl child would need a woman she could talk to, wouldn't she? Aunt Jennifer, who mostly seemed to want to go home, wouldn't be any help at all. And as far as Uncle Hank was concerned—forget it.

Nell had been trying to ask me about something on Thursday afternoon. Then she backed off. She had told me she had changed her mind, but why? Was it something about me, after she had spent more time with me, that made her back off? I didn't remember saying or doing anything that would be upsetting to her. Although, of course, you never know how you appear to another person.

Or had something happened during the day to make her wary?

Had she solved her problem, whatever it was? No, I didn't think so, because she went on being troubled and in fact seemed to be uneasy that I might ask her about it.

Had Luis's murder intervened and caused her to drop it—or to become more fearful?

Maybe. No, that wasn't it, at least not causally. She had backed off asking me by yesterday afternoon, before he had died. She had avoided being alone with me for many hours before he died, in fact.

Then what?

I would find her and ask again. Any reporter knows people usually will talk if you just hang around, or failing that, keep asking them over and over.

She didn't want me to. Okay. But she was a child and there was a lot more going on here than I understood, which might mean more than she understood, and for all I knew, she was in danger. It's one thing to accept a child as a thinking person, and to grant a child every human right you grant anyone else. It's quite another to let them take a risk that because of their youth they might not recognize as dangerous.

*　　*　　*

I went looking for Nell. It didn't take long. As I entered the kitchen—everybody's base of operations in this family—Nell was going out the back door carrying a tray of eight steaming mugs. The door slammed shut behind her.

"For the workers?" I asked Gran.

"No, no. For the sheriffs."

"Aren't they in the living room?"

"No, not now. They come and go. Right now they're all out in the barn."

"This must be very hard for you, Mrs. DeGraaf."

"It's hard for Henry and John. They have work to do."

"And Marie."

"Yes, I suppose."

Was it in some way less Marie's work than John's and Hank's? Marie seemed to put in just as long hours. "What do you think happened to Luis?" I asked.

"Some—some vendetta, probably."

"Why?"

"It's hard to understand how Catholics think."

"Oh."

There wasn't any answer to that one. I said, "I think I'll go look at the work." I didn't specify whose work, the tree cutters or the sheriff's deputies. I walked toward the barn, and as I had hoped, met Nell coming back, carrying the empty tray down at her side. When she saw me, her footsteps faltered for a split second.

When in doubt, it's best to be direct.

"Nell, can we talk?"

"Uh, sure." She looked around, probably for a safe place where we wouldn't be heard. I sat on the steps. She sat, too.

There was no one around. It was chilly, but not nearly so cold as yesterday, and the sun had been flirting with the idea of appearing.

Still in the direct mode, I said, "Have I done something to upset you?"

Her face showed dismay. "Oh, no! Not at all. It's been wonderful having you here. What with—what with, you know, everything."

She was such a nice child. "Listen, Nell. When I first got here, you started to ask me about what I did, what kind of things I reported on. You remember?"

"Uh-huh. Yes." She ducked her head. The empty tray was held across her chest as a sort of shield.

"You asked specifically whether I had been involved in murder investigations."

"Yes."

"And I had the impression you were going to ask me about something that was bothering you." She ducked her head again. "Then yesterday morning, pretty suddenly, you seemed to be avoiding me."

"Well, I didn't mean to. I guess it was pretty rude—"

"No, no. That's not the point. There was a problem really troubling you. I don't believe it's gone away. I think something else has complicated it for you."

"I guess."

"Nell, do you suppose you could trust me enough to tell me what it is?"

She stared at me a moment with her mouth partly open. She didn't look foolish, just thoughtful and deeply worried. Nell was not a person who lied easily, and she would also find it hard to tell me flat out that she didn't trust me. She hugged the tray.

"Maybe I'd better," she said.

I held my breath.

She raised her head.

"I think my grandfather was murdered."

· 12 ·

"Tell me why you think that."

Nell put the tray flat on her lap and folded her hands on top of it. She was organizing her thoughts. Having made the decision to tell me, she planned to do it properly. I ached to see this unnatural maturity; that this child had had to grow up so fast, to be so adult and so cautious. All I could do for her was sit patiently and lend her my attention.

"It was last spring, during Easter vacation," she said. "We have the crop-duster airplane come over to spray for insects on the trees at certain times of year, you know."

"Okay. Sure."

"My grandfather always goes out to check the number posts that tell the airplane which field is which. You see?"

"Yes, I've noticed the posts."

"So they know that they're spraying the right field with the right stuff. Anyway, he was out in the field when the airplane came over, and it sprayed him."

"And the poison killed him?" I kept my voice even and as unemotional as possible. She'd had enough to deal with without gasps of horror from me.

"Not exactly. He had asthma. The spray isn't all that bad, they say. I mean, it probably is, and it smells awful, but it doesn't kill you, you know?"

"Yes. It triggered his asthma?"

"Mmm-mm. They must have come in right over him, and not seen him, and he ran to the creek to get away from it. But it was too late. He was already having an attack by then, and it killed him."

"Did he carry an inhaler?"

"Always. He had it in his hand, but it didn't help enough, I guess."

"But now, Nell, how could anybody know he'd be in the field right then?"

"He always checked the numbers before the spraying. They spray on schedule, you know. Not just any time they feel like it."

"But he never got sprayed in the past, did he?"

"No. But he always wore this bright orange down vest, like a deer-hunting jacket, and if the man in the crop duster sees somebody out in the field, he goes around again and gives him time to get away."

"Oh. So why didn't that happen this time?"

"Because somebody had taken his orange vest."

I began to understand why she was worried. The next question had to be asked. It wouldn't be anything new to her; she had thought about it anyway, I supposed, but if she had been avoiding suspecting the obvious people— well, I had to know, one way or the other. Things had gone much too far to pussyfoot. I could hope, at least, that talking about the event would be better in the long run for her than suffering all alone. "Who was around that day? Who could have taken it?"

"They sprayed on the Monday after Easter Sunday. Everybody was here Sunday."

"Everybody? The field hands?"

"No."

"Luis?"

"No." She made a small sighing sound in her throat, which I pretended not to hear, and said, "Just—the whole family."

"Oh."

We both sat unmoving for a minute or so. Nell was the sort of person who hurt quietly, inside, but she was hurting a lot. She curled around the tray she clutched. Not looking at me, she finally said, "And that isn't all."

"What else?"

"See, the reason it really bothered me—the reason I kept on thinking about it was—about two weeks before that he got locked in the barn."

"Your grandfather got locked in the barn?"

"Yes. He didn't go in the barn much, because of the dust. You know, he let Dad or Uncle Hank get stuff out of the barn or do the barn kinds of chores where you had to be in there a long time, like sharpening the chain saws. Because the dust made him wheeze."

"I suppose it would. What happened?"

"Well, this one day, he went in to get something. The back door—you know, the little door?—was locked from the outside. It usually is. I mean, we leave it that way. If you use it, you lock the padlock from the outside when you go out."

"I understand."

"So he was in the barn. He went in through the big door, I guess. And somebody came along and closed the big door and dropped the bar latch into place. He pounded on the door until Gran heard him and came out, but he had a really bad asthma attack and had to go to the emergency room and breathe some stuff they bubble through a tube."

"Would somebody have known he was in the barn?"

"Well—it was daytime, so there wasn't any light on. I don't know if he was making noise."

"Would it be normal to close the door if you walked by and saw it open?"

"Yes. Sort of. But Cat, you know, I didn't think about it, like it was something bad, right then. It was when the next thing happened that I thought about it. When he was sprayed in the field, I thought back. And besides that, now look what's happened!"

Right. Now they unquestionably had a murder.

Hesitating, because there was a tight edge to her voice that could mean panic, but nevertheless really needing to know, I said, "Nell, did you mention this to anybody?"

"I sort of had to talk to somebody. I really had to." She added more softly, "Somebody not in the family, you know?"

The poor child was afraid, like I was, that the killer was one of her family. She had avoided explicitly tying it up, but just barely. I said, "I can understand your feeling. Did you talk about it to several people, or just one person?"

"I only talked to Luis."

A few minutes later, after Nell had left to take the tray to her grandmother, I realized that her answer had focused my mind entirely on the death of her grandfather, old Henry DeGraaf. But he had died in April. Seven months ago. So this was not what she had learned on Friday. Something more had happened recently. Between Thursday afternoon when I arrived and some time on Friday, she had decided not to talk with me about it.

Some other event had happened after Thursday afternoon, and it happened before Luis's death late Friday night.

She was keeping something back. There was a major piece of information that she wasn't telling me.

· 13 ·

Aunt Clara appeared on the porch, her butterball body made bigger by a long quilted coat with fur around the hood. She looked like she belonged at Santa Claus's worktable, making dolls. And she carried presents. It was a plate of cookies. When she saw me she said, "Oh! It's you! Wait right there!" and ducked back into the house.

She reappeared after only half a minute, holding a sheaf of papers in one hand and the cookie plate in the other.

I was glad to see her. There was something I wanted to find out, but I didn't want to ask Nell or Gran. Although I hadn't thought of her until she popped into view, Aunt Clara would be perfect.

"I brought these from home for you," she said, breathlessly. "It's letters from Hendrik DeGraaf to a friend in the Netherlands named Katya. Hendrik settled here in 1847."

"Who was Katya? A relative back home?"

"We don't know. Most of the local historians think she was his mother's sister, who was very helpful to him as a child, when his mother had some sort of long illness and then died. But he doesn't call her 'Aunt Katya.' Some suggested she was a lady friend, a romantic involvement, but I'm not quite sure. . . . I've always wondered. You can see what you think."

"How did the letters come back here from the Netherlands?"

"They were sent to Hendrik by somebody when Katya died. And when Hendrik died, his daughter gave them to the Holland Archives at Hope College."

Studying the sheets, I said, "These look like modern handwriting."

"Well, they are, of course! They were written in 1966."

"But didn't you say 1847?"

"Well, my dear girl. These are translations."

"Translations?"

"Hendrik's are in Dutch."

"Oh. Oh, of course."

"You don't read Dutch, do you?"

I couldn't help laughing. "No, not even close."

"Actually, if you read German or Yiddish, you *are* close. We say 'You'll fall and break your tokus,' for instance, meaning the same thing as the Yiddish *tokhes*. Rump. Or we call something 'dreck,' meaning trash. Anyway, here you are. There are photocopies of the originals included in there somewhere. Take a look at them."

I did. The handwriting was beautiful, slanted sharply forward with long loops and risers, quite faded in places. Probably the actual paper would be a pale tan by now and the ink brownish. As for the Dutch words, I could make absolutely nothing of them except names and dates. I turned back to the translations gratefully. "Thank you."

"This is probably not the best time," Clara said, "but I'd laid them out for you before I went to bed last night, so I thought, why not?"

"No. This is a good time. Actually, I have something else to ask you."

"Go ahead."

"Can you tell me where to find the creek?"

She cocked her head at me. "I'll walk you there. We'll drop these cookies at the barn on the way."

"For the gendarmes?"

"Yes. My sister-in-law is very concerned with keeping up an appearance of genteel hospitality. Hopeless, of course, under the circumstances, but that's Ruth for you. She doesn't approve of showing emotion. As a matter fact, she's not too pleased about people *having* emotions. And her children take their cue from her."

"She's very strong, isn't she?"

"In her way."

"The creek rises in the marshes to the east, and runs from here into Pigeon River. Pigeon River runs into Lake Michigan at Port Sheldon. We played here, Henry, and my other two brothers Dan and Paul, and I, when we were children. Dan was the oldest. He was killed at Anzio."

Anzio. World War Two. I wondered what other wars the DeGraaf men had served in. What had happened to them. How the threads of their personal stories wove into the wide fabric of the nation's history. Sunlight bore down on us through the naked branches of oaks and ash. It was cooler here than in the yard, but even here it was much warmer than yesterday. Yesterday it had snowed. Now it was in the high forties.

Aunt Clara said, "My grandfather told us tales about the old days when they had a cool house here, in the edge of the brook. It was the only way to keep food cool, you understand? They stored butter and milk and some meats in the cool house. It was right here, exactly," she said, walking a bit farther along the bank. A trickle of water ran over deep amber sand. "Right there. You see this depression in the riverbank?"

"Yes. They had no refrigeration, of course."

"Oh, heavens, no. Now, my father said that by the time of his childhood, just before the turn of the century that would have been, they had an icebox, an *ijskast*, in the house. Some men in the village of Holland had formed a company, and all winter they cut blocks of the ice that formed on Lake Macatawa—it was called Black Lake back then, before they decided that Macatawa sounded better—and put it in this thick-walled building in Holland, insulated with straw several feet thick, and through the spring and summer they'd deliver ice in a horse-drawn wagon to people who subscribed to their service. It would go in a special little door on the side of the house, right into the icebox."

"Really."

"They even shipped ice south, and to parts of Europe."

"Europe? That was weeks by sea back then. Wouldn't it melt?"

"Yes. About half the ice melted on the trip. They packed it into the hold of a sailing ship, with bales of straw all around it—several feet of straw on all sides, just like the ice houses. In those days, ice from the Great Lakes was considered very choice in Europe. The Europeans got ice from Scandinavia, but the New World ice was considered finer. So, even though they got there with half a load, the selling price more than paid for the trip."

We sat on a fallen tree trunk. Beyond us another tree trunk spanned the little creek.

"I'll bet you used fallen trees like that to cross the creek."

"Oh, yes," she said. "Like children always do. And my brothers would push me in, like children always do. Some things never change."

"Nell told me her grandfather died somewhere near here."

"Did she? That poor child has had too much death to cope with."

I waited, hoping she would go on.

"Yes, Henry was asthmatic, you know. He must have run to the creek, because the sprayer wouldn't spray the woods, of course. But it was too late."

"How sad."

"I've wondered a little—"

Possibly she had suspicions, too, about his death?

"It's silly, I suppose," she said, "but I've wondered if he ran here partly because we had had such fun here as children. Foolish of me."

"I don't think it's foolish at all."

"Well, we'll never know. At any rate, he should never have been in the fields at spraying time. And after all those years of raising trees, he should have known that."

Aunt Clara left to go back to the house and help Gran. I sat a little longer on the log and read one of Hendrik's letters.

March 1848

Dear Katya,

> *We are all healthy, including Pieternella and little Gerritt, who are beginning, I am sorry to say, to forget their homeland. They attend a small school here, taught in a cabin two miles away, so it is often difficult for them to walk that far, as there are no roads and the weather is often inclement. Some of the children at the school are Americans, and Pieternella is learning the new language, but I fear using her old*

tongue less, even though most of the children speak
Dutch at home. I know that she must make this
transition for her own sake in the new land, but I
weep inside sometimes to hear it happen.

At the little school, the girls and boys are kept
separate, which I find appropriate. They play in two
separate yards, with a wooden fence down the middle, but Gerritt says the boys sometimes peep under
the fence to see the girls at play. If they are caught,
they are made to spend the rest of the school day in
the chicken coop for punishment.

You would be astonished at the primitiveness of
the conditions here in the New World. There are no
roads and of course no wagons plying the ways.
Most commercial traffic goes by barge on Lake
Michigan, but the lake right now is still locked under a shell of ice. There is talk of a railroad coming
through, but only between the city of Chicago,
which lies southwest, on Lake Michigan, and Grand
Rapids, a small town forty miles east. I do not think
the railroad will help us here. Twice a week a mail
carrier on foot plies between Grand Rapids and the
nearby hamlet of Holland, which now has four hundred souls. The walk takes him a day and a half. I
believe that he walks, not because they do not wish
to hire him a horse, but because all the uncut forests
and underbrush makes riding difficult.

There are many times I feel we should not have
come. I think often of returning. The old country is
so dear, and I think of the fine roads, beautiful
buildings, fine schools, and our old house, which
was small, but now we suffer here in a single room
with a floor of dirt which is actually sand, cross-
sawn logs for chairs, and blankets over our win-

dows. And we are glad to have this much. When we first arrived, we had huts made of hemlock branches set up like tents, and entered on our hands and knees.

Shall I return? I believe Pieterke would wish to, although she has not said so. She is a good, obedient wife, and does not criticize.

But when I consider it, I also think of the crowd-edness [the translator had written "congestion?" in parentheses] in our homeland and the miles and miles of open land here, almost free for the asking. The Americans want people to settle here and to farm and cities to grow up. I have many acres of timber now to cut. There are more possibilities here, dear Katya, and that makes a decision very hard.

I will write again.

Hendrik DeGraaf

· 14 ·

Still burdened with the knowledge of Nell's unhappiness, I wandered out into the field where the cutting was going on. Time for me to get back to work. After all, I had a story to write on this process. Unfortunately, events were developing into a Hal Briskman story. So much for pastoral contemplation. Or was that a stereotype, too?

They were cutting a block northeast of the house. When I got there, I saw an example of John's peacemaking. A different baler was in place next to the flatbed. It was rusty, and one side was lower than the other, as if the supports had been repaired, but not very expertly. John saw me. "Is this what you were talking about getting?" I asked.

"Sort of. I knew I could get one someplace. One that nobody was using."

"Nobody was using it because it's a piece of crap," Hank said, hurling a tree onto the flatbed.

Horace, the hired hand, unheard by Hank, muttered something about not looking a gift horse in the mouth.

"It's a different type, isn't it?" I said.

"It's a string baler." As the next tree went in, John pointed to a string, winding around the tree in a tight spiral. The string was fed out of a huge spool. "It looks less complicated than the other kind," I said.

Hank said, "Not as good, either. The string isn't as protective to the tree as a net."

Well, probably not. But wouldn't it have been nice to thank John for getting on the job and finding it? However, their sibling relationship was not my business.

Hank couldn't leave it alone. He said, "It belongs to a neighbor, Ed Sluiter. He stopped using it eight years ago. For obvious reasons."

"Well, at least it's working," John said.

I asked, "Otherwise, how's the harvest going?"

I'd asked John, but Hank answered, of course. "We're about twenty percent behind on the day."

John left to take over one of the Stihl chain saws while Horace/Skip stretched his back. I said to Hank, "What do you think happened to Luis?"

"I think some creep snuck in and got him. Some serial killer type."

"When?"

"What do you mean?"

"Well, where was he? In the barn or out in the field? When did you last see him?"

"Jeez, that cop asked that, too. But it's not so easy to remember. He was bringing in some tools when I set that tree aside. The Christmas tree I brought in the house?"

"Yes, the perfect tree."

He smiled. "It sure was. All four sides good. Dense branches. Just the way you'd like to grow 'em all, if you could. Anyhow, Luis was in the barn when I took the clipper in. I lopped the bottom two-three branches so it'd fit in the tree stand."

"So that's the last you saw him? Before you came in the house."

"Yup. He was okay then. Didn't seem worried about anything. His motorcycle was still parked twenty minutes later when we drove out the driveway. Oh—it woulda been, wouldn't it? Because it was never moved."

"Right."

"So—I don't know, then. He stayed after pretty often to clean up the tools. We let him lock up the barn. He was trustworthy, you know."

"I'm sure he was."

"And I always paid him for the extra time."

"Sure."

"Well, it beats me what happened."

Hank was big and bluff, and for all I knew, used that manner as a defense. A lot of big guys do a stupid routine when they want to duck questions, and it doesn't mean they're not smart, or not sly. I didn't buy his "I don't know what happened and I can't even imagine why you're asking me" routine. But that didn't make him guilty of murder, either.

He'd seen Luis alive just before he went to the house with the tree. Or so he said. If he was telling the truth, that pretty much let Cal out of it. Cal was in the kitchen before Hank came in with the tree, and what with leaving soon afterward, he wouldn't have had time to kill Luis. *If* Hank was telling the truth. But Hank was surely smart enough to know that as well as I did. He knew Cal had argued with Luis. He knew the police had to be looking at his son as a possible suspect. Hank's word on this just wasn't good enough.

John got tired soon and handed the chain saw to Cal. I sidled over to talk with John. He was more drawn than I had noticed before, and there were deep worry grooves in his forehead. Fortunately, he brought up the murder, so I didn't have to lead into it.

"You've talked with Nell a little bit, haven't you, Cat?"

"Yes. She's a sweet girl."

"I know." He smiled for half a second before his worried look came back. "How badly hurt by this—do you think she's very upset?"

"I don't know how to answer that, John. She's very, very sad about Luis. But I don't believe she's devastated. You have to understand I don't know her well."

"No, no. But she admires you. And I think women—girls—women sometimes say things to each other—"

"Mmmm. Well, to the best of my knowledge, she is surviving well."

"You think? I'm glad. You understand why I'm asking. Somebody must have told you that my wife died—"

"Yes."

"It's a horrible thing for a little girl to be left with no mother."

"Yes. I agree."

"And this is just so bizarre. Who would want to kill Luis?"

"What was he doing when you saw him last?"

"Hanging up some saw, as far as I remember. He was in the barn."

"When was that?"

"Oh, just before I went to the kitchen. It must have been somewhere around four-thirty."

Well, I was going to have to ask this straight out. "Was this before or after Hank left?"

"Oh, before. Hank got that tree and came in after I did."

"So nobody really knows what Luis was doing after that? I mean, assuming he wasn't killed right about then. At four-thirty."

"Not that I know of. The hired hands had gone. I saw him after they left. But you know Luis often stayed quite some time after the hands left, because he oiled a lot of the tools to prevent rust. Especially if it'd been a wet day, like yesterday, with the snow."

"Yes. Hank said so. How late would he stay?"

"Well, not hours. Maybe thirty or forty minutes."

* * *

I walked around the outside of the barn in the thin winter sunlight. Today's brighter light showed the warm pink in the sandy soil. The barn itself was weathered red, the gray old wood showing just traces of paint applied long ago. Because it had two entrances, a big double door facing the driveway and a small door facing the back, a person had a choice of entryways to avoid being seen.

VanLente would have made up a schedule of where everybody was after work yesterday and up to the time we found Luis's body. I didn't think he would tell me what he had deduced or accumulated so far. And it wasn't certain, anyway, that the answers he'd got from people were necessarily the truth. Of course, I could try him and see if he'd share. I drew closer to the barn door.

Inside the barn, VanLente's voice snapped at one of the other deputies, "Well, damn it, then look harder!"

Oh-oh. Best not to pester him right now, much less try to pry sensitive information out of him. I sat in the yard, on a five-gallon gasoline can. This seat just happened to be near enough to the barn door so I could hear anything that was said loudly. Unfortunately, at the present moment they were not yelling.

I tried to recall everything I could about where everybody was last evening right after work stopped. I had heard the voices behind the barn, ending with Luis saying "do the right thing." I had no idea who he was talking with.

By then the hired hands, Ken, Raymond, and Horace, had left, so they were out of it. Unless, I suppose, they went partway down the road and walked back. But that was pretty far-fetched.

Then after I had dumped the trash, I went from there directly to the kitchen, all of which had taken me no more than a minute or two. Nell, Dan, and Don were in the

kitchen eating cookies. Aunt Clara and Gran were there
also, feeding them. The time passed between my hearing
the voices and my arrival in the kitchen was much too
short for anybody already there in the kitchen to have
killed Luis—even too short for one of them to have
knocked him unconscious, hidden him someplace to put
through the baler later, and hurried into the kitchen.

That let out Nell, Dan, Don, Clara, and Gran.

Soon after that, John had come in. How soon? It was at
least three minutes, and I'd guess probably nearer five.
That would have been plenty long enough to knock Luis
on the head and hide him. Not long enough to get him to
the field and run him through the baler.

Hank's wife, Jennifer, had come in next. Maybe a
minute or two after John. Cal, the kid who had had the argument with Luis, followed her.

Would Cal have had time to approach Luis, lure him to
the baler, hit him on the head, and put him through?
Barely. If he moved fast. Could the whole thing have been
a two-person job?

Marie came next with the clipboard. I could not imagine any reason in the world she would kill Luis, but she
certainly had another minute more than Cal to do it in.

And finally, Hank arrived, bringing in the tree. He certainly had enough time to hit Luis on the head in the barn,
carry him out to the baler, and run him through. Or to ask
him to come see what was wrong with the baler, hit him
there, and put him in it then, which would be less time
consuming.

After Hank had left with Jennifer, Cal, Don, and Dan,
Gran had gone to lie down for half an hour while the absolutely delicious potato casserole finished baking. What
about Gran? Did I really believe that she slipped out the
back of the house, lured Luis to the baler, knocked him on

the head, and ran him through the funnel? Oh, please! That was ludicrous.

Really it came down to John, Hank, Cal, or Marie.

But Luis was a reliable, long-term employee, and a pleasant, sensible, nonviolent man as far as I could see. Why would any of them want to kill him?

• 15 •

One thing I really needed to know: Was Luis dead before he was put in the baler? It made a huge difference to the timing as far as Cal and John were concerned. John, who came into the kitchen after just a few minutes, could have killed Luis with a blow to the head, then left him concealed in the underbrush and for some bizarre reason put his dead body into the baler later that night. Okay, that was possible, given the amount of time he had. But if Luis was alive when he was put in the baler, then John was less likely. He might have hit Luis on the head, left him alive but unconscious, and gone back to get him later. But if so, he wouldn't have any way of knowing whether Luis would wake up in the meantime and go looking for help.

This applied most to John, but also to Cal, though Cal would have had less time to go back. Hank had more time than Cal.

No, wait, I thought. What about this scenario: Hank hits Luis on the head and thinks he killed him. He goes back later to check before leaving with the kids and Jennifer and finds him unconscious but alive. So, enraged at this, he drags Luis out to the field and puts him through the baler.

Well, it was not impossible, but it seemed extremely unlikely.

*   *   *

Damn. At the very least, I would have to find VanLente and ask him what the medical examiner said about the manner of death. I went to the barn, but all of the cops had left except a large blond man who stood in the doorway like Cerberus, guarding the entrance.

"Can't go in," he said.

"Okay." Since I could see through the door that VanLente wasn't there, it didn't matter. "Is Sergeant VanLente gone?"

"Nope. In the field somewheres."

Okay. I needed exercise anyhow. I headed for the field. Speaking of Cerberus, I had gone only a hundred yards when Carat bounded against my legs from behind and sent me sprawling.

"Don't do that!" I said, lying on my back on the sand. She was so proud of her eager greeting, she licked my face. "Oh, all right. How could anybody be mad at you? All you hurt was my macho-ness anyway."

And the knee of my Levi's. I took a few steps. She followed.

"How am I supposed to get rid of you? The cops won't want you here. What if you ran off with some evidence?"

Carat bounded and grinned and affirmed that naturally she would never do any such thing, not unless the evidence consisted of a nice piece of beefsteak. On that understanding we took our walk.

A deputy came past carrying a clear plastic bag in which were smaller clear plastic bags, no doubt of material they hoped would be evidence. I nodded and walked on. Sergeant VanLente was just ahead of us, standing alone with his hands on his hips, facing away toward the woods. From his body language, I assumed he was frustrated with the case.

Carat bounded forward in delight. I saw what was going

to happen, shouted "Carat!" but it was already too late. She hit VanLente right behind the knees with the full force of her body, pitching him forward. He rolled and came up crouched in a perfect semi-Weaver stance, with his Smith and Wesson Airweight service revolver in hand and the muzzle pointed at Carat and then at me.

"Don't shoot!" I said.

He saw the dog, saw me, and scrambled up out of the crouch scowling.

"What do you think you're doing?" He reholstered his weapon.

"It's not my dog," I said, taking the coward's way out. "I tried to stop her."

Carat meanwhile was eagerly licking his hand. I was cowardly, she was fawning; what a great combination.

VanLente brushed the twigs and sand and pine needles off his pants. Carat put her paws on his knees and attempted to lick his chin. "Down!" he said.

She licked harder. Licked his jacket buttons, his tie, his shirt, the holster on his hip as he tried to reholster the gun.

"Oh, hell, all *right!*" He scratched her ears, ruffled the back of her neck, and she took her paws off his knees, gratified. Still she wiggled her rump ingratiatingly. It worked. VanLente scratched her back. Rump wiggling was something I surely couldn't get away with. Carat was satisfied at last and she calmed down, contenting herself with licking VanLente's shoe leather.

I said, "See? She's not your dog either. She thinks she's everybody's dog."

"Yeah. Right. Nevertheless, it was you she followed out here. Was there something you wanted?"

"Well, actually, yes. I wondered whether you knew yet about when Luis died. Was he dead before he was put through the baler?"

"Why do you want to know that? Other than the fact that it makes good copy."

"Because—look, he was hit on the head either out here or in the barn. If it was in the barn, the person who did it would have spent less time in the attack, but had to be available sooner or later to bring him out here. Which would have been easier for some of them than others. If the blow to the head killed him, he could have been brought out here any time during the night. But if it didn't kill him—"

"Yes, I've already thought about all that. Believe it or not, I do tend to reflect on my cases now and then. Why do *you* need to know?"

"Well, for one thing I'm living with these people. I should know if I'm in danger."

"Oh, come on! The more you know, the more threat you are. Not less."

"Um. Yes, that's a point well taken. How about this as an argument—we'll find out soon enough anyway."

"Yeah, that makes more sense. You don't quit easily, do you?"

"If I did, I wouldn't be able to do the job I do."

"True. Well. The autopsy hasn't started yet." He looked at his watch. "Or maybe it's just about getting underway."

"I expected that. But you would have a preliminary inspection by the ME here to go by. Look, call it habit. Or call it nosiness." What I didn't call it was uncertainty that VanLente would figure it out without help.

He said, "All right. All right. He was still alive when the killer put him into the baler."

My heart sank. This made it all more horrible. "How do you know that?"

"Abrasions from the netting on his elbows. And finger-tips where he tried to pull apart the plastic netting. He struggled."

"Oh, my lord." I couldn't help biting my lip. Luis didn't deserve this.

"The killer stunned him, Ms. Marsala. I don't know whether he was knocked out for long, and I'm not real sure whether the autopsy can tell that. While he was unconscious, he was put into the baler."

"How do you know that?"

"No signs of a struggle on the palms of his hands, and he would have fought going in, if he had known. He would have tried to grab the edge of the funnel part. You don't go gently into a machine like that."

"Oh. Of course."

"And there are marks of his thrashing on the sand."

"Oh."

"The killer wrapped the chain around his ankles the way they do around the handle, as they call it, of a tree. We had Horace demonstrate for us. The chain pulled Luis unconscious through the funnel into the netting, and it compressed his arms upwards, just like it does a tree, but not enough to kill him. Then it ejected him, just like it does a tree."

"God!"

"Then the killer simply walked away and left him. He woke up and found himself alone, wrapped tight in the netting. Then he died slowly of hypothermia. He'd shiver and pick and pull and tear at the net with his fingers and shiver, until finally his core temperature got so low that he stopped shivering and became torporous. All alone. Unable to move. Unable to put his arms down to warm himself. Lying on the ground with the snow falling. And then he died."

He paused a few seconds and said, "So what do you think of your friends now?"

*   *   *

That was a low blow, of course. Even if one of the DeGraafs was responsible for this hideous thing, nobody in their right mind would think they had all done it. This was not a murder on the Orient Express.

VanLente stomped back to the road to talk with some minions, leaving me with instructions not to enter the crime scene. "And please get that damned dog out of here, too."

Okay, I would.

I walked with Carat to the edge of the grove of trees. If I had gone farther in, I would eventually have reached Pigeon Creek, but I didn't want to fight my way through the underbrush; Carat wanted very badly to fight *her* way through the underbrush, thinking there might be rabbits or partridge or wild turkeys, but sometimes you have to be firm about these things. Also, from here I could see the back of the barn and the side of the house, so if anything major happened, chances were I'd know about it.

I sat on a stump. There was an open area between the edge of the woods and the first block of Christmas trees to the west of the tree field. Most likely Henry senior had felled some of the native oak, maples, and ash in order to let afternoon sunlight reach the pines. Enough sun would mean round, well-developed trees, "good on four sides" or at least three sides.

Carat gamboled about. She barked at an imaginary flying dragon, then dug for an imaginary burrowing dragon.

I scratched her ears when she came to sit near me. But mostly I worried. The death of Luis, by itself, didn't make sense. Look at the possible killers.

The chance of somebody from outside killing Luis was next to nil. In the first place, the killer had to know how to use the baler. Second, the killer had to have met Luis in the barn, unless he or she made an appointment to meet

him in the field where they had been working. And since
they cut several fields over this week in no particular order, how could an outsider know where to find the baler in
the dark? It had to be somebody who was here that day.

One of the hired hands? Two went away right after work
in an old car, and one on a motorcycle. It did not seem
likely that the two would kill him as a pair—after all they
weren't related—or that one would have asked to be let
out at the end of the road, walked back, and killed him.
Asking to be let out was a way to get remembered, for
sure. And even the one on the motorcycle probably didn't
do it. If you really wanted to kill a fellow worker, why not
do it off site someplace, so you wouldn't be connected to
the crime? In this case, why not wait for Luis out on the
road a couple of miles from here and run his motorcycle
off the road, then stop and bash him on the head?

Because angry or desperate people do stupid things?
Indeed they do, but counting on stupidity to explain a sequence of events that doesn't make sense is sloppy thinking. You come down to the irrational explanation only if all
else fails.

Far more likely was that one of the family killed Luis.
Unfortunately. And if so, somebody had to have had a very
serious reason. Even a family member would have been
smart to kill Luis someplace else, if possible. Unless it was
somebody who couldn't get away easily. Or unless killing
Luis was an emergency.

Would young Cal have killed Luis just because Luis
kept riding him to do his share of work? Not much of a
motive. Especially not since his father also wanted him to
pull his own weight. Cal seemed more slothful than vicious anyway.

Hank? Why would he kill Luis?

Would John have suspected a sexual relationship be-

tween Luis and Nell and killed Luis to prevent it going
any farther? John didn't seem to be the type for violent
rage. If anything, he was a thinker. Thinkers are often wor-
riers, but surely he would talk with Nell first, and ask her
to break it off, if in fact he thought there was any dangerous physical relationship going on. What about the whispered conversation I'd overheard? It certainly wasn't John
telling Luis to "do the right thing" and leave Nell alone,
because it was Luis telling somebody to do the right thing.
It didn't fit.

To be fair, consider Gran as a killer. She was certainly
very religious. She certainly disapproved of Catholicism.
She would certainly disapprove of Nell becoming involved with a Catholic. No doubt about it. She would believe that whatever she said was right *was* right. But
would Gran kill Luis, even if she were physically able to?
Gran would probably believe she could just issue an edict
that Nell stay away from Luis and assume that she would
be obeyed.

Religious mania? Who could tell?

Marie? I knew of no reason Marie had to kill him.

Of course the "I knew of" part was the problem. There
had to be something else going on here. Some family situation that was not apparent. Nell believed that her grandfather had been intentionally killed, indirectly and by
sabotage rather than direct violence, but intentionally
nonetheless. If she was right, there was a very dark secret
here. A DeGraaf family secret.

• 16 •

The family. I felt so sorry for the family. They were good, loving, hardworking people. Whatever had gone so terribly wrong here, one of them might be evil, but the rest would suffer.

From where I sat, the house lay beyond the barn, both backed by the far woods. From the house, the driveway ran as a long, slow curve, the row of eleven huge oaks following the curve to the end of my view, then out to the distant, invisible road. I let my gaze drift over those oaks, noticing that ten of them were huge, with the immense span of branches that red oaks achieve in this climate. The lowest branches reached straight out far from the trunks, parallel to the earth. What enormous strength they must have to support the weight of heavy wet snow in the winter, with the leverage of that length of branch. No wonder oak wood was used in furniture and in ships and in buildings where great strength was required. The one tree of the eleven that was smaller than the others was still a good-size tree. I would have to ask one of the family members about it. And four of the remainder were largest of all, a hundred feet tall. Each branch was as thick as most tree trunks.

The house and the land in some sense symbolized the family's unity and its persistence through the years. Luis's death might change all that. If it turned out to be as woven into the family secret as I suspected, it could be the end of the family. Unraveling it could pull the family apart.

Thinking about this reminded me of the photocopies of letters that Aunt Clara had given me, which I carried folded into my note pad. After the first letter I read, written in March of 1848, I had found a long, sad letter that Hendrik had written just before Christmas 1847, shortly after the Dutch colonists had landed in Michigan. Now I picked one that turned out to have been written four months later, in the spring.

April 15, 1848

My dear Katya,

> *Today I am thinking that we must return to Europe.*
> *Life is very hard here. I cut wood a great deal of the time. Our trees are oak, maple, ash, and conifers, but there is much brush grown up between them, and it can be very difficult to cut a tree as one has to cut the brush from around it first. The trees they call beech [beuk] here are very beautiful, but like ours quite brittle. They have wonderful silver bark that is almost blue, and wrinkled like the skin of an elephant. As they grow in pure groves, you might think you were standing among the legs of a hundred elephants.*
> *I cut logs for lumber, but then have to hire a sled to transport the logs to Holland or Port Sheldon to be collected. They are shipped by barge, on Lake Michigan, to the city of Chicago, but of course I receive only a fraction of the dollars the logs fetch by the time they get to Chicago.*

The good thing is that we are warm. I have endless branches and small wood and have bought used a stove in Zeeland, the American Zeeland, of course. I break all small branches in pieces and store them under a tarpaulin [dekzeil] and it is always dry for fires.

Pieterke is not feeling well. I must tell you that perhaps we will be five, not four, come spring. I hunt and sometimes get squirrel. Once a church member gave us two pounds of salt horse, and Pieterke made stew for two Sundays. Occasionally Potawatomie Indians pass through with dried trout to trade. They are very fond of wheat bread, which they don't make and which Pieterke bakes on occasion if we have wheat, and we trade that. But rarely. It is mostly corn, corn, corn. I cannot say whether I am justified in placing Pieterke and little Gerritt and Pieternella in such a condition.

I will pray about this. I do not know what to do. Jan Steketee has offered me a job at his dry goods store, but it would mean living in the little town of Holland, as I could not possibly walk the whole eleven miles into town and back each day. Then there would not be the chance ever to have a fine farm, which is the reason, as you know, that I came here in the first place. It has never been my goal to be a shop clerk, or if it were, I might have been able to do so at home. I cannot ask Pieterke, as I ought not share doubts with a wife.

Hendrik DeGraaf

"You're sharing the hardships," I mumbled. "Why not share the doubts? Better yet, why not share the decision?"

*   *   *

I saw a bustle of activity around the house, but I couldn't
figure out what it meant. Cal was carrying something
around the corner of the porch, and then the hired hands
came trooping in from the field. It was two o'clock.
Nothing special had happened yesterday at two o'clock. I
walked toward the house and found Nell coming out the
back door with a large pot of coffee. By the time I reached
her, Cal was setting up a card table in the garage. Nell put
the coffeepot on it, and as if they had choreographed the
whole thing, Aunt Clara appeared at that instant with a gigantic plate of almond pastry she called "banket" and a
stack of Styrofoam cups.

"Can I help?" I asked Clara.

"You could bring out the cocoa."

I got the cocoa from the kitchen, wiping my feet, of
course, on the way in. Gran gave me the cream and sugar,
to take to the garage along with the cocoa.

Then the family trooped inside, leaving the three hired
hands, Raymond, Ken, and Horace/Skip, to eat in the
garage. It seemed kind of like separating two classes of
people, but at the same time I could understand that the
family, under stress, might like to be alone. And since I
was also an outsider, where did that leave me?

But Gran said, "Take these in, Catherine," as she handed
me cookies for the dining room table, so I guessed I was
one of the elect.

"We thought we'd better let the kids have one refresh-
ment break all at the same time," John said as he sat down.
"Ordinarily we let one or two of the hands go to the barn at
a time, like you saw yesterday, but under the circumstances—"

"Yes. And today they don't need to warm up—"

"Nearly fifty in the sun," Hank said. He wiped a spill of tea from the table with his hand. "Water is the enemy of wood," he said. "And this is a nice piece of ash."

"You work in a furniture factory?"

"Yes, but I hate to call it a factory. Some of the best furniture in the world is made around here. Baker, Widdicomb, Herman Miller. My place, Vanderlyn's, makes custom pieces. I'm the foreman."

There was silence for a couple of minutes as people added sugar to their coffee, chose between peanut butter cookies and something Gran called "krakelingen." I reflected on how calmly the family was taking the death of a long-time employee. I might have said they were even too unemotional. Nobody showed any apprehension about being arrested, and there wasn't any nervous tension or backbiting, either.

Which shows how wrong I can be. Someday maybe I'll learn.

Cal reached for the last peanut butter cookie. He and Dan and Don had eaten more than a dozen in two minutes. I have brothers and I know how teenage boys eat.

Don, the youngest, had been reaching for the last cookie, too. He said, "Hey! You had the one before this!"

"I got it first!" Cal said. And he had.

Hank said, "Oh, let him have it, Don."

"Why do I always have to give everything up?"

Hank said, "Be quiet, both of you!"

Jennifer, Hank's silent wife, put one hand over her mouth, which was hardly necessary, since she never spoke anyway. Don said, "Why do I always have to be quiet?"

Cal said, "Hell!" and jumped up and left the room.

Gran said, "Calvin! Language!" though he wasn't here to hear her. Gran folded her hands and started to pray.

Hank leaped to his feet also, pointed at Don and Cal, and said, "Now see what you've done! Go out in the yard and get to work!"

Nell burst into tears. Marie turned to Hank. "Oh, get a grip, all of you! You're all—" and then she started to hiccup and couldn't stop.

Aunt Clara took her arm and helped her out of the room, saying, "—brown bag and just breathe into it until you stop—"

Nell was still crying.

John said to me, "Cat, you have a car." His face was stern, and I saw an intensity there that he did not usually show.

"Yes. What—"

"Could you take Nell out for a drive? We've got to get back to work and I just think she—"

"I understand. I'd love to go for a drive with Nell. At any time."

Nell smiled damply. She knew she was being got rid of, but probably it was a relief.

· 17 ·

"There are tissues on the floor in front of you."

My car isn't new, and usually it isn't clean outside or neat inside, either. Because I go into a lot of different communities for stories, I keep a variety of clothes in the back of my car. I can change clothes and blend into quite a lot of different sorts of places fast—a leather jacket, a long wool coat with fur trim that I got in a thrift shop, a baseball cap, a purple knit hat with silver discs, a Russian sort of fur hat, a gray fabric rain hat that totally hides my face, and several different colors of scarves. Also a baseball bat, car phone, pepper spray and Mace, and half a gross of pencils. As I say, it may not be tidy, but I have all kinds of equipment for emergencies, and tissues are the least unusual of these. I have plenty of tissues.

We were on U.S. 31, heading south. My heart ached for Nell, but I knew if I hugged her right now, she'd just break down again and then feel more embarrassed. Right now it was best for her to have something to do. While she mopped her eyes, I said, "I know a cure for sadness. Always works. Foolproof."

"I didn't think anything was foolproof."

"Only this one specific thing."

"What is it?" She looked at me with big, wet eyes, the lashes damp with tears.

"Chocolate."

She almost smiled. I said, "Where's the nearest source?"

She came slightly closer to smiling, and pointed. Up ahead was a mall, and in the mall were ice cream places. We were only a couple of miles from the farmhouse. I was surprised that a shopping area was so close, because the farm had felt extremely rural. I had passed this spot on my way to the farm on Thursday, but didn't remember it. At that time I hadn't known how much farther I was going, and I'd been totally focused on not getting lost.

Nell pointed me to a Dairy Queen. I went to the window, bought her a double hot fudge, and then thought, well, hell, it was a crisis for me, too, and got one for myself. We took them to the car to eat. By the time we were several bites into the things, she looked less damp. "Here we have at least three of the four basic food groups," I said. "Sugar, fat, and chocolate."

"What's the fourth?"

"I don't know. Salt?"

"Food coloring?"

"Preservatives?"

"Cholesterol?"

We ate in silence for a while. The sun on the roof made the car warm enough. Nell relaxed. There were a lot of questions that I wanted to ask. It wouldn't be fair to push her right now when she was vulnerable, but if she wanted to tell me anything or ask me anything, here I was.

Finally she said, "I'm just so scared."

"About what, Nell?"

"Everything."

"Well, sure, but there must be some specific thing. Or things."

"It's not easy to say."

"You're in a horrible situation right now. I know that much."

"I'm afraid of—" She backed off again. "Of a lot of things."

"Nell, you should be. It's all right."

"I'm afraid that—that—that one of *us* killed Luis. And that would be just so totally horrible." She went on in a fast rush of words, "I mean, I know it's horrible that he's dead, no matter who killed him, and I don't want you to think that I'm worried about our reputation or some stupid thing like that, because that wouldn't be right—"

"Don't explain. You would be perfectly justified if you worried about your family's reputation. People are allowed to have their own concerns."

"Because, see, when you think about who was there, there's only Gran and me and Uncle Hank and my dad and Aunt Marie and I suppose my cousin Cal and Aunt Clara, but Aunt Clara couldn't have done it, you know, that would be just totally ridiculous—"

"I know."

"And neither would Gran. She's so, you know, so totally concerned about what's morally right. And Dad wouldn't, because he's just not like that, and Cal, my cousin, is kind of a jerk, but that isn't the same thing as being a killer, and Aunt Marie wouldn't kill anybody. And Uncle Hank really is a lot nicer than he seems when you first meet him. Aunt Jennifer is too dweebish to kill anybody. But it just doesn't make sense that somebody came in off the road and just saw Luis there and killed him, because who would even know how late he'd stay at work, and besides the person who came in went to the block they were cutting, you know, and we'd be the only people who would know that, or went to the barn, which is so close to the house somebody might see them, or somebody might be in the barn. They'd know we'd remember seeing a stranger. So it just doesn't make sense."

"And they wouldn't know where the baler was."

"You've thought about all that, too?"

"Oh, yes."

"Do you think my dad knows this, too?"

"I'm pretty sure he must."

"I guess so. He must be *really* worried."

"I'm afraid so."

"Which is why I've been trying not to worry him more by asking about it, but I'm just so scared."

"You've been taking the whole burden on yourself. You really don't have to."

"I guess not. But I can't just put it out of my mind."

"Let the adults deal with it. Let VanLente do his thing. Have you talked with your dad at all?"

"He's been looking tired and worried and, no, I haven't. I'm glad *you're* here, Cat. Because you're not one of us. I don't mean that, you know, like it sounds, like you're an outsider, which I guess you are, but I mean that's a good thing. It helps to talk with somebody who isn't really, you know, involved."

"I don't think I've relieved your mind much. Frankly, I agree with you. It isn't likely any outsider killed Luis."

"But it's nice, you know, to know you'll be honest with me. I mean, not that you wouldn't be honest, but you know what I mean. It helps to get treated like a grown-up. Gran either says 'Stop fussing' if she sees me looking worried, or she tells me to read my Bible, and I don't mean there's anything wrong with that, or say my prayers, but sometimes you just have to *know stuff.*"

"I understand."

"And Cat, it's all okay to say let VanLente deal with it, but what if one of us really *did* kill Luis? I mean, I just can't believe it; it's not possible, but I keep saying it's real.

It's really real. And what if Sergeant VanLente arrests one of my family? What will we *do?*"

Nell began crying quietly, tears just flooding out of her eyes. As she wiped them, I took away the ice cream dish and put my arm around her, and she broke into loud sobs, deep gasping, desperate, moaning sobs. She was so little and thin, the despair shook her whole body. "And what I want most of all," she said, gulping, "is to bring Luis *back.*"

I let her cry. "Don't cry" is one of the stupidest things you can tell anybody. And selfish, too. People say it so that they won't have to deal with tears.

Nell cried for at least five minutes. It was amazing that there were any tears left in her. Toward the end she began hiccupping, and finally that trailed away, too. She whimpered a little bit and got quiet.

With her head down and her hands over her face, I couldn't tell whether she was embarrassed or just exhausted. When it seemed enough time had passed, I said, "I think that was the right thing to do."

She looked sideways at me.

I went on. "You know how teachers are always talking about 'appropriate behavior'? If your friend is murdered and your family is suspected, then crying about it is appropriate behavior."

"I must be *very* appropriate then," she said. A small joke. A big sign of improvement.

"How about if we drive around a while?" I asked her.

We drove west, toward Lake Michigan. She said, "Go right at the next corner, if you'd like to see the lake."

"Okay."

We drove along Lake Shore Drive. "Looks to me like there are some pricey houses here," I said.

"Yes. And you know what? Aunt Clara says that in the

old days, when the early settlers lived here, it was so poor
it was nicknamed Hungry Street."

We came to a park, directly on the lake. There was a
large stand of oak and beech between us and the water.
The trees grew on a dune of pure pale sand, with hardly
any plants of any sort underneath them except a thin scat-
tering of ferns and Solomon's seal. I said, "Want to walk for
a few minutes?"

Lake Michigan has many personalities. In Chicago it
curves into the city, which forms a crescent cradling it.
Because of the curve and the beauty of the architecture, in
Chicago Lake Michigan has a flavor of Rio. People who
don't know Chicago are amazed at the magnificence of the
lake front. Three hundred miles north of Chicago, where
the Wisconsin beaches are rock and the water is cold,
Lake Michigan resembles Hudson Bay.

But it is the Michigan coast of the lake that is most
changeable. Because the prevailing winds are westerly,
the surface water, warmed by the sun, is blown here in the
summer and you can swim in water that is sometimes as
warm as eighty degrees. In the winter, as ice forms in the
lake, northwest winds push it along the wave crests and
pile it up on the Michigan shore. Icebergs form. The bot-
toms of the bergs ground on the sandbars and form a long
barrier reef. Waves in the open water break against this
solid line, and the spray freezes on top, making a mountain
range of ice. The icebergs stretch north and south as far as
the eye can see. In about one winter out of twenty, the lake
freezes all the way across, and icebreakers ply the middle
to keep a lane open for shipping.

In northwest storms that occur in the fall, the waves are

highest as they reach the Michigan coast. A north by northwest wind eats sand away from the beaches, cutting into the land. Houses, trees, piers, and dams fall into a torrent of ice water rushing south.

But today the lake was calm, though the air was cold. Nell and I stepped out onto a beach of clean, pink-tan sand, decorated at intervals with silver driftwood. Six-inch waves broke with the sound of kisses on the shore.

For a couple of minutes we walked north on the wet sand just above the little waves. Every so often a larger wave would sweep up and make us jump back. Finally, laughing, we walked farther from the water, up in the dry sand, which squeaked at our footsteps.

"My mom said that during the last ice age the ice cap right over this spot was two miles thick."

"Nell, is there anything else you're worried about? I mean, you seemed troubled even before Luis died."

"Oh, yeah, yes," she said. She avoided my eye, looking out at the horizon. "I think we're going to lose our home."

We paced on. I didn't respond right away, wondering if she could possibly know what she was talking about. But she was a serious child, and very accurate. She had had terrible losses in her life, particularly the death of her mother, and I certainly hoped she was wrong about losing her home.

We sat finally on a mound of sand, where beach-grass seed heads rocked in the slight breeze. The sand was cold, but not bitterly cold, and the sun warmed the tops of our heads and our shoulders. The damp sand nearer the water had a smell similar to the concrete sidewalks in my neighborhood in wet weather, and I was well aware how perverse the comparison was. The cement smell at home was good, but it was always overlaid with gasoline smells, motor oil, wet discarded paper, and waste of all sorts, unlike this place. Here the breeze came in from the northwest, over a hundred miles of open water. Seagulls glided on the air without moving their wings, lifting at the turn of a feather, crying like cats mewing.

"Nell, how could you lose your home? Do you mean the farm?"

"Yes."

"But it's been in your family practically forever."

"I know."

"I remember Thursday night your father said something about taxes. Or actually I asked him something about taxes, and he said, 'That's part of it.' Is that what you mean?"

"Sort of. I don't understand it very well."

"Are the taxes higher than what you earn from the trees?"

"Well, maybe. They keep saying the taxes have gone up. But not exactly. It's got something to do with the value of the land and inheritance taxes."

"Oh."

"It's real confusing. The land is supposed to be valuable for development, so if Gran dies, it gets evalu—valued—whatever—at whatever you could sell it for even if you're not going to sell it. So there are these big taxes coming if Gran dies, but they could sell the land for a lot of money, but if they don't sell the land they still have to pay taxes that are, you know, as high as if they sold it. So it's because we have something that's gotten valuable that we may wind up losing it all."

"Oh. I don't like the sound of that."

"It doesn't seem reasonable. But it must be true. It's what my dad said, that it's gotten too valuable for our own good. My grandfather was real worried about it."

"I see. Did he have any ideas what to do?"

"I don't know."

"But your grandmother seems well and healthy. I know she's elderly—"

"Seventy-eight."

"But she might live for a long time still."

"Y-yes. She's got some kind of heart thing. Not like a heart-attack kind of thing. She takes pills for it."

Nell stirred the pink-white sand. I said, "You only came to live at the farm a couple of years ago, I think?"

"That's right. After my mom died." She said the last words quickly and without intonation. The implication was clear. She didn't want to talk about that part of her life.

"So are you so very attached to the farm?"

"Oh, yes! It's home."

"But before you moved here, you must have—"

"We had a house in town. In fact, it was walking distance from the high school where Dad teaches. But it wasn't anything special. I mean, it was okay, you know, but it just had a plain little yard with grass and all that. The farm is so wonderful, you know, with the creek, and the woods, and there are all these wildflowers. And we always went to the farm anyway, for Christmas and Thanksgiving and all the holidays. Summer vacations. Then on top of that, a couple of times Mom and Dad took trips and I stayed with Gran and Grandfather. My grandfather always took walks with me a lot, and he told me about the wildflowers and what they were used for in the old days. Like, bouncing bet was used like soap. He always had time to talk to me. He taught me the names of birds and trees, too, you know. So it was always like I lived there."

For a moment I had that sense you get with an occasional person—she's just like me! I had been that kind of child, not very excited about clothes, more interested in how things worked and what things were called, including a period in high school when I wanted to be a biologist and spent a zillion hours in day camp at the prairie state parks, learning the names of insects. Life didn't turn out quite that way, but I'd reflected sometimes on the similarities between investigative reporting and studying and cataloging insect life forms.

At school Nell was probably liked by most of her classmates but seen as a little too studious. A little too serious. She probably didn't giggle enough about clothes or make-up or spend much time hanging around the mall.

And she certainly did not have any sense of how beautiful she was. She would probably say that her face was undistinguished and her hair limp. But she looked like the women in Vermeer's paintings of Dutch wives going about their home tasks, pouring milk, drawing water, opening the top of a Dutch door to look out at the farm fields beyond the edge of the picture frame. Her hair was the color of Lake Michigan sand, pale beige with a hint of red, and her skin was milk white.

She was a lovable, valuable child. I hoped there was some way I could keep her from being hurt again.

· 18 ·

Taxes, property that was soaring in value but was a liability if held and valuable only if it was sold . . .

I knew it. I knew it. There was a financial motive lurking somewhere behind Luis's murder. Never in this world will you find any two, much less half a dozen, family members who feel the same way about money and property. And—call me a cynic, but there's no impetus to kill quite so strong as money. Gain usually. Avoidance of loss sometimes.

When I stopped the car in the driveway, Nell thanked me for the ride with a lot of extra thank-yous. Getting away really had helped her. She was visibly more relaxed than she had been when we left.

She took off for the kitchen. I lingered at the Bronco, casting my glance around the yard, but not much had changed. Two sheriff's squad cars were still there, along with Marie's little red car. Raymond's car and Horace's motorcycle were farther down the drive, out of the way of the investigation. There was a strange car in the driveway, a Lincoln, not a likely squad car. As I watched, a man came out of the house. He wore no overcoat, just chinos, a turtleneck, and navy blazer. He got into the Lincoln and drove off.

The hired hands had left the garage and were back in the field.

I had done my good deed for the family. Time to go to the house and see what could be discovered.

I stopped abruptly on the walk, one foot skidding on the gravel. Had it really been true that John thought Nell needed time away?

Or was it me they wanted to get rid of for a while?

How much money could people make growing trees? How much do these people have to struggle to make a buck? And somehow the murder was connected. Who owned the farm? Gran, I was pretty sure. Who got it in her will? What was it worth? Would somebody kill for it? What had Grandfather DeGraaf been planning to do about the possibility of losing the farm?

Hank, Marie, and John came out of the house. Marie held a clipboard. John looked tired and ill. "Mom's lawyer," John said, gesturing down the drive where the Lincoln had recently passed.

Marie said, "We realize the police might think—well, the point is, we needed to know our rights."

I said, "Of course."

The sun was now behind the far woods, and blue, cold shadows inched toward us. Raymond, Horace/Skip, and Ken appeared, carrying tools back from the field. Work was over for the day.

"How much more to do before the end of the season?" I asked.

Marie said, "Eight blocks."

"We're still behind," Hank said.

"How many trees do you have?"

Hank said, "Oh, I don't know. This is a small block. It's twenty rows long and fifteen wide. That's um—two—"

"Three hundred trees," Marie said.

"Oh, right. Three hundred."

"But I mean how about on the whole farm?"

"A whole lot," Hank said.

Marie said, "We have eighty acres in trees. About fifteen hundred per acre, give or take."

"So you cut how many blocks for this Christmas?"

Hank said, "Well, we've done six blocks of blue spruce so far."

Marie said, "One thousand, eight hundred spruce trees so far. We cut three thousand Scotch pine in October."

"I had no idea it was so many! Listen," I said, "I don't mean to be rude, but at some point for this article I need to get an idea of the profitability. I mean, I know a house guest shouldn't ask things like how much money do you make, but I'm kind of half guest and half reporter—"

"Don't apologize," John said. "We understand that."

"Thanks. So your profit—"

"Profitability isn't what it oughta be." Hank smiled with one side of his mouth. "In 1985 Michigan was planting seven times more trees than they were harvesting. It's always a question how the market's gonna be any given year. If the sales aren't going well, you might as well stop cutting and wait for next year."

"So all the next year the trees would still be growing taller. So they'd be more valuable, wouldn't they?"

Marie said, "Yes and no. The other growers would probably have stopped cutting, too, so the next year you'd have a lot of larger trees flooding the market."

"Oh, right. I hadn't thought of that."

"Plus, Scotch pine gets straggly if it gets too large, no matter how much you shear. Spruce doesn't. You can cut it larger."

"So you can hold them over."

"Yes, but that goes to the question of the number of trees per acre. They used to say you could check-row them. That means you don't plant them like pieces on a checkerboard, but staggered, like cells in a honeycomb. Then you could get twenty-seven hundred an acre. But then you're really locked into harvest. You have to cut them, or as they get bigger they shade each other, and run out of light, and drop branches, and become unmarketable, and you've wasted your whole crop. The maximum spruce you can get out of an acre is seventeen hundred, and if you want to leave yourself some marketing leeway, twelve hundred is better. Even a thousand. So you're trading off between cost of land and allowing for market fluctuations."

"Just like other businesses," I said. "I was sort of hoping Christmas tree growing was more—ah, pure."

Marie said, "I wish."

"It's always something," Hank said.

Marie shifted her clipboard to the other arm. "Fifteen, twenty years ago," she said, "you would have presold your whole crop by August. Now it's November."

I asked, "How long does it take you to grow a crop of trees?"

Hank said, "Averages out about seven, eight years to grow a Scotch pine to the six- to seven-foot size. Longer for spruce."

"That means you cut one eighth of your trees each year."

"Market conditions being normal, yeah. Scotch pine grow faster than spruce. Spruce sells for more."

"How does it work? You plant seed?"

Hank laughed out loud at my question. John, again the courteous one of the siblings, said, "Come on, Hank! A person doesn't know until they ask."

"All right, all right. See, Cat, if I just took a bunch of seed and plowed a row and planted it, I'd get spotty germination. Long areas with no trees at all, and then places where a whole bunch came up. They wouldn't be evenly spaced. It doesn't pay to farm a row that's all straggly like that. The ones that were close together wouldn't have more than one good side. And you'd have gaps where you could have raised trees but didn't. You couldn't cultivate properly. We get our trees as seedlings mostly, from a nursery. Seedlings are grown close together in beds." He pointed at a field of miniature spruce and we walked toward it. "I got these this spring as 2-0s. Basically, that means they grow two years in a nursery, then the nursery digs them and ships. Or they dig the seedlings and plant them out in rows in their nursery and grow them another year or two, which makes them 2-1s or 2-2s, then sell them as transplants. Two-year-old seedlings are four to eight inches tall."

"So what do they cost?"

Marie said, "A hundred dollars per thousand for seedlings, three hundred dollars per thousand for transplants."

"Depending on type," Hank said. "And size. A 2-2 is more than a 2-1."

"Uh-huh." I made notes. Hank and John crossed the tractor lane to another block of trees, which Hank began petting. "These little guys are the new big deal in trees. Frazer fir, a variety of balsam," he said, stroking the tops of some three-footers. "Been here four years. Doin' beautifully, aren't they?"

"They look great. How much do they grow a year?"

"About six inches."

"So what do you sell them for? You sell through a wholesaler?"

"A marketing co-op," Hank said.

"I knew that, now that you remind me. You're the current president."

"Right."

"So you sell the grown tree—"

"A six- to eight-foot tree," Hank said. "Under six is considered tabletop. Bigger than eight feet is hard to market, but we do sometimes sell a larger one for companies or municipalities."

"Mmm-mm. You sell the tree for—"

"Scotch pine is down this year," Marie said. "A Scotch pine, depending on quality, will go for four to seven dollars. A blue spruce this year will go for about thirteen."

"So then the consumer pays how much?"

"Maybe eighteen to twenty for a blue spruce. We sell at a lot of prices to a lot of people, though. We're wholesaling some near our cost to the local Boy Scouts so they can sell them and raise money. In New York, people are paying ten dollars a foot for Frazer fir. But they're real slow growing."

"I suppose you fertilize the trees to push them along."

"Not really. We all used to think so, but agriculture schools like Michigan State have been running these comparative studies, and it turns out the only things that really make a tree grow fast are enough sun, enough water, and keeping all the competing weeds down. Turns out fertilizer is a waste of money."

"No kidding? In a way that makes sense. Conifers are supposed to have evolved before deciduous trees, isn't that right? Maybe they go back to a time when the earth didn't have as much fertility."

Hank looked at me blankly. "Maybe so," he said, without enthusiasm. I felt put down. Maybe his religion did not believe in evolution and I had offended him. Maybe he didn't like women to know things, however sketchily. He'd certainly been happy enough when he was lecturing me.

John, though, was nodding his head. "You think? That's interesting."

I said, "So can I get down to the nitty-gritty and ask you how much profit you make per tree?"

"This year?" Hank said. "Because last year the market was glutted and the price went down and a lot of trees didn't even sell. We stopped cutting and we lost money."

"Yes, this year," I said. "Just so I have a picture of it."

Marie said, "Say we sell a tree for fifteen dollars. At that point we have maybe eight dollars in it in cost of water, labor for pruning and weeding, insecticide including overhead spraying by plane, and other odds and ends."

"So you make seven dollars per tree."

"No. You might have a little more than eight in costs into a blue spruce and a little less than eight in a Scotch pine. This year the Scotch pine will sell for seven dollars and we lose a dollar. The spruce will sell for maybe fifteen and we make five."

"And how many will you sell?"

"We're cutting five acres of spruce."

"So that's—"

"About four thousand trees. You don't have trees over the whole acre. You also have to leave room for the farm equipment. Trails between the blocks, you know."

"So if you cut five acres of spruce at eight hundred trees an acre and make five dollars per tree—"

"We would make twenty thousand dollars. This year. If the market in trees doesn't fall. If that was the whole story."

"It isn't?"

"We have the cost of land."

"Land cost, like taxes?"

"Yeah. Ten dollars per acre ten years ago. Thirty per acre today. Even though earnings on the trees aren't going up. The piece with the house on it is more. We pay over three thousand a year in land taxes."

"So why are taxes going up?"

"Because the land value is going up."

"And why is that? Although I have a pretty good idea."

"I'm sure you have. Because we could probably sell it for a mall or housing development. Or a theme park."

"And it keeps climbing?"

"Every year."

One thing was clear. This was a marginal business already, and the squeeze was on. If the land continued to go up in value and taxes kept pace, Christmas trees were going to have to be raised someplace else. Where would that leave the DeGraafs? Sell the land and make money? Lose their home?

And did that make a motive for murder?

· 19 ·

May 20, 1848

*It is so strange, dear Katya, to see the ways that
Gerritt and Pieternella develop. Have I told you that
the school here is one room only, with all ages in the
one room? So that, of course, the teacher must attempt to give to each child the lessons that are appropriate to that child's age. You would think that was
difficult, would you not? But the teacher is a very patient young woman. Pieternella has been in school
only six months, no seven, starting in November. The
teacher sent a note home with her yesterday, telling
us that she is advancing at a great rate in mathemat-
ics. She has gone from the eight-year-old lessons to
the eleven-year-old lessons in that time. The teacher
seems to be praising us for it, but I have done nothing. It is just Pieternella. I see her sometimes teaching
Gerritt his numbers, sitting on the floor with rows of
pinecones. She is trying to teach him subtraction
now, but he is much too young. She has taught him
the numbers, however, and will keep at it, I think, until he understands the rest. Gerritt, for his part, is
more talkative than Pieternella, who is rather a quiet
child, and when any passerby stops here at the cabin,
he wants to ask questions.*

*I have worried somewhat about Gerritt and
Pieternella attending school with the Americans.
They do not observe the Sabbath so strictly as we
do, and are loose thinking in other ways. Still, I am
conscious of the importance of education for
Gerritt. Even Pieternella, while she does not truly
need an education in itself, may well have to keep
accounts for her husband's farm or business some
day.*

*It seems at times that the difficulties here only
multiply. . . .*

I looked away from the letter. John, Marie, and Hank were
putting the borrowed baler to bed for the night. I walked
back toward the barn in the dusk. The police cars had left,
and two of the hired hands, Ken and Raymond, were inside the barn. That meant the police had released it for
farm use. Hank would be crabby but pleased. Possibly the
DeGraafs would be able to use their own baler tomorrow—no, no, not on Sunday. On Monday.

I was supposed to leave Monday morning.

Sergeant VanLente was never going to solve this case.
There was no way for any specific piece of evidence to be
tied to any individual. Suppose the detectives found a fin-
gerprint on the baler? Everybody's fingerprints could be
on the baler. Even Gran's, since she might occasionally go
to the barn, where it lived during the year. Even Clara
went out to the barn fairly often. Other evidence?
Footprints from anybody could legitimately be anywhere.
Hair? Fibers? Get real—these people lived here. Of
course there would be hair and fiber.

If VanLente did not solve the murder, how would Nell
get along in the future? How would she get along if, in

the end, nobody found out who had killed Luis? She would live all her life with public suspicions about her family.

The family. The family was important to these people.

I peered into the barn, which had a dirt floor just like the old DeGraaf cabin. I pictured Pieternella playing on the dirt floor, teaching her brother numbers in English, which would have been a foreign tongue to Hendrik, only partly mastered. . . .

"One, two, three. . . ." The child would use pinecones to illustrate counting, Hendrik had said. I imagined her using little stones when it was summer and she couldn't find pinecones. Or possibly acorns from the oak trees, I thought, seeing dozens of them lying in the wind drifts of leaves.

"Four acorns take away two is two acorns."

"Two acornth," little Gerritt might have said.

"Now what is four acorns take away one?"

"One, two—three!"

"Good boy!"

Ignoring the young men in the barn, I sat on the gasoline can near the barn door to finish reading the letter in better light. At the end of the letter, the tone changed:

> *This is too difficult. I have worked all winter and cleared only nine acres. Now it is spring and the insects have arrived. The flies and the mosquitoes as one works the land are unbearable. There is a type of black fly that carries a material to keep the blood of the victim from clotting, and when they bite you bleed. Lately they are saying there is malaria in the town of Holland. And most of the vegetables I sowed in the spring had to be replanted twice. . . .*

I finished the letter, then gazed at the woods and imagined Hendrik.

He stood near the creek and rejoiced at the evidence that summer was coming. From here he could see across the land he had cleared in February and March. He had planted on April first, having turned the sandy soil with the aid of a plow and a borrowed horse, and then everything he planted had been frozen by a snowstorm on April 15. Except the peas; they liked cold weather. By the end of April the peas were up and growing and he set out cabbage. He replanted the squash. Both the cabbage and the peas were almost flattened by wet snow on April 25, and the squash died of the cold.

He asked himself, how was he to know winter never ended in this new land?

The carrots, peas, and cabbage didn't mind the cold, thank the Lord, he thought. But the squash he had replanted twice more, once on May first when it was immediately killed by frost, once on May 15, not yet up and growing. He had no idea when the first fall frost would hit, but people said mid-September was possible.

Ninety or a hundred frost-free days! Back in Borculo, in the Netherlands, they could have a hundred and twenty growing days.

He thought of the cost of seed, the cost of nails for the house, the cost of the assistant who had helped him drill the well—thank the Lord the water table here was high— and he wondered how they could survive. His small stake of money was almost gone. His wife, Pieterke, was pregnant and therefore not able to do much heavy work. Pieternella and Gerritt were too young to be much help in the fields. They would pull weeds later, but they couldn't use a hoe.

Hendrik picked up his heavy field hoe. The blade was fourteen inches wide, and it took a lot of force to cut through the earth with it. It was pierced by two holes in the top part of the blade so that clods of earth would fall off more freely, but it was still very heavy to work with, and in five minutes he was sweating again. Despite the coolness of the day, early mosquitoes began to bite his neck, and then a cloud of midges formed a whirling cluster in front of his face, making him feel dizzy from the dancing spots before his eyes.

Who knew what insect plagues the summer would bring? He was already hot and tired, but he had to break down the clods of earth he had turned earlier into finer planting soil. He absolutely must open a patch for onions before it became too late in the season. At least they'd have cress. Cress would grow in three weeks, if it got enough water. But the soil was so sandy it would dry out fast. He and Pieterke would have to carry water from the creek in a pail.

Then squirrels and woodchucks would try to eat his crops.

Hendrik made grunting noises as he hacked at the clumps of turf with the hoe. Coming to the United States had been a mistake. He certainly never uttered a word of doubt to Pieterke. It was important for women and children to feel secure, and to that end men must stand by their decisions and present a confident appearance.

It was unending effort, though, with no reward for it. Possibly he should not have settled so far outside the new village of Holland. But he was a farmer, not a townsman. He thought longingly of the village they had left in the Netherlands, where everything was so settled, so civilized. The church there was three hundred years old.

The market—you knew what price your vegetables would bring. . . .

He must stop thinking this way. In Borculo, he had farmed twenty acres and owned a cow. Here he had a hundred acres and a chance someday to farm even more. Here there was opportunity.

Or was it only the opportunity to starve and freeze? The house, hastily built while they stayed with a family in the village, was a single room. The outhouse was far away from the door, as it should be, but the nights were so cold.

It was wrong to have these doubting thoughts. The Lord sent the weather and the Lord sent challenges. And man did as circumstances required.

His neck and back itched from the running sweat. His ears itched from mosquito bites. The work shirt, rough and growing much too hot, scratched his body. The heavy boots on his feet were made of wooden shoes topped with deer-leather ankle pieces. The soles were picking up a thick coating of mud, making them even heavier. They chafed his feet. He wore no stockings; stockings were a luxury few people had. Henry closed his eyes, bent his back, and chopped at the earth.

I put Hendrik's letter at the bottom of my sheaf of papers, under the other letters and my notes on tree farming. I stared across the fields and wondered who among the present-day DeGraafs most resembled tough, stubborn, persistent, stolid old Hendrik.

*   *   *

John, Nell, Gran, Aunt Clara, Marie, and I sat around the big ash-wood dinner table. Hank, Jennifer, and their large, loud male brood had gone home, and the hired hands all had left. The cops were gone, too—for how long nobody seemed to know. In fact, nobody alluded to the police at all or in any direct way to Luis's death.

His murder hung over us, though, as intense as if oil-soaked rags were burning in the dining room and everybody was trying to ignore the smell. Gran said grace, as usual, and added a very brief sentence. "Let us pray for those departed."

In the living room, the Christmas tree that Hank had brought in on Thursday night stood in the tree stand, undecorated. Gran had declared it inappropriate to do anything so festive as decorate a tree the day after Luis died, and for once I agreed with her.

One thing about Gran—she might be affronted by police in the house, she might be careful to observe the proprieties at the death of an employee, but none of this affected her cooking.

We had an immense casserole of turkey, mushrooms, and onions. The salad was what the family called Dutch lettuce, actually a warm slaw of lettuce with bits of ham in a sweet and sour dressing. And as always, potatoes. These were quarters slowly roasted in butter, with home-grown parsley and chives. What's not to like?

Nell did not say a word from the moment we sat down to eat. I wondered whether she was sick.

There I go, I thought, worrying about her again as if I were her mother, even though I saw her father give her a brief hug after he pulled out her chair for her, his arm across her shoulders and his eyes looking into her face for signs of unhappiness.

The mood was somber. The family had probably talked among themselves while Nell and I walked on the beach. They certainly realized that the police thought one of them had killed Luis. Whether they themselves believed one of them had done murder was harder to say, but judging by the air of constraint, maybe they did. Carat lay under the table, with that guilty air of a dog whose people are unhappy.

Thinking to lighten the mood, I said, "Living on the same land your ancestors lived on must give you a sense of having the land in trust."

Marie said, "It does. If you plan to go on living on the same plot of land, you care for it differently."

"I wonder if Hendrik DeGraaf felt that way."

Clara said, "He certainly believed he was making a life here that he would pass on to his children and grandchildren."

Marie said, "Oh, come on! You make it sound as if he was an early environmentalist."

I said, "Well, I know they didn't understand land conservation back then. But he would try to keep the soil productive, I would think."

"They started by cutting down the forests," Marie said. "They thought of themselves as taming the land. This is sandy soil. Underneath, it's just beach sand. It's what's left after the glaciers moved through and then receded. When they cut the trees, the sand was exposed to the winds. And it started to blow."

Clara said, "When I was a child, there were living dunes here."

"Living dunes?"

"Dunes that moved across the land. They'd advance a few feet every year, from west to east, because the prevailing winds are westerly. They'd move right across roads. Sometimes they'd even smother towns."

"Really?"

"Yes. The town of Singapore near Saugatuck was swallowed up by living dunes."

"Singapore," Marie said, "was about fifteen miles south of here."

Clara said, "The living dunes would leave hollows behind in the sand where sand had blown away. We called them sand blows."

"The worst of the erosion," Marie said, "came in the twenties and thirties. The wind would simply blow the farms away, like the Dust Bowl, but here it happened even though there was rain. People were losing farms. And then the Depression hit."

John said, "The early settlers didn't have the time to respect nature. They fought nature. They were extremely pragmatic. They did what they had to do to survive."

"Well, naturally they had to cut trees and—"

"Do you know where Pigeon Lake and Pigeon River got their name?"

"Not exactly. From pigeons, I suppose."

"Not just any pigeons. Passenger pigeons."

"I remember reading about passenger pigeons in school."

"Yes. They are a symbol of environmental catastrophe. Man's rapacity. And it happened right here. In the 1850s this was one of the largest breeding grounds in the entire United States for passenger pigeons. They say when the flocks arrived in the spring the sky turned black with them. One man wrote that he watched a flock of them that took two and a half hours to pass overhead. He guessed it was twenty miles long. The pigeons were hunted right here. Passenger pigeons were almost as large as chickens and they were so gregarious that they flew together and nested together and you could catch them by tying a living pigeon by his feet to a thong stretched from a post. You'd take your end of the thong and hide in the bushes and hold it tight, so the bird would be standing on it as if it were a wire or a branch. Then when a flock came by overhead, you'd let the thong go loose a little bit. You know, when a bird feels himself sink down he stretches out his wings and flaps. The flock would see him flapping and come down to visit him. The farmers and hunters could club them with sticks or hit them with rocks. They shot them too, but you hardly needed to, they were so unafraid."

"Oh."

"There were professional bird hunters who killed the pigeons by biting their throats. A good hunter could kill fifty a minute."

"Good Lord!"

"Yes. You could say that. They'd cut the wings off the dead birds and pack the bodies in barrels. The barrels went to cities like Chicago and New York. For a while they were getting a dollar fifty a barrel, but finally there were so many birds being killed that the bottom dropped out of the market. Pigeon meat was practically worthless."

"But they went on killing them?"

"Sure. And it was as easy as ever," John said. "The birds were so gregarious that as they got fewer and fewer they still congregated in dense flocks, and because they were all in one place they were still easy to kill. By 1878, Michigan was the last of the great passenger pigeon breeding grounds. They were pursued to their nesting ground—here. And finally they were all gone. The last passenger pigeon, called Martha, died in the Cincinnati

Zoological Gardens in 1914. I think of that sometimes. This gregarious bird, all alone, and even though she wouldn't know it, all alone in the entire world. The last of its kind. Absolute extinction."

"I don't know what to say."

"And it happened right here."

It seemed to me insensitive of him to say all this in front of Nell. Wouldn't the child be upset? Or maybe he believed it wasn't good for people to pretend reality didn't exist.

John said, "Do you know what they called the bird they put on the thong to lure other birds to land there?"

"A decoy?"

"A stool pigeon. That's where the term came from."

Gran said, "John, I want you to stop this talk right now." I thought, good, a champion for Nell's sensibilities. But I was wrong. She said, "You shouldn't talk about your ancestors that way. They were God-fearing people, and I'm sure they did what was right at the time, even though we might not see it that way now."

"Mother, they killed those birds unnecessarily."

"Well, even so, they were only birds."

"But Gran," Nell said, "birds suffer. And they can feel pain."

"We don't know that they do, Pieternella. And we certainly know that they don't have souls. Killing a bird is not the same thing."

In a sharp voice, Marie said, "The same thing as killing a person?"

Dead silence.

The quiet was so horribly uncomfortable that I wanted to say something, anything, into the gap. But what? "What do you think of the Detroit Lions?" was too obviously a diversion. "How long will you go on harvesting blue spruce?" was just plain stupid. I had decided on, "Gee, this is a beautiful table. Was it passed down from one of your ancestors?" when Aunt Clara, feeling similarly awkward, made a somewhat similar decision.

"When Hendrik came to the United States," she said, "he was thirty-two years old. It was 1847. He had two children, Pieternella and Gerritt. Our Nell was named for the first Pieternella."

Nell said, "That's nice. But it's too long a name to use."

"Nonsense," Gran said.

"Old Hendrik's third son was also Hendrik, and he was born here, in this country, in this house. Well, not this house, but on this piece of land."

"The hearth from the old house is still here; it's part of the barn," Marie said to me. "It's that piece of beautiful Zeeland brick that the wood stove stands on. The pink brick, Cat, you know?"

"Yes, I saw it."

"It's made in Zeeland, Michigan, not Zeeland in the Netherlands."

Aunt Clara said, "Hendrik had eight children. Three died in childhood. Two moved away as adults, both of them farther west. Iowa and California. Pieternella married a dry goods merchant and moved to Grand Rapids. Gerritt went to fight in the Civil War in 1863. He was twenty-one. He was wounded in Tennessee and died of malaria in camp there."

Little Gerritt, who liked to talk with passersby and whose sister taught him to count. "Is he—did they send his body home?"

"Yes. He lies in a cemetery on New Holland Street. His brother Hendrik lived on here after his father died, and had seven children, one of them named after his dead brother, Gerritt. One died of scarlet fever. Another

died young of what they called 'a decline.' In those days
that sometimes meant tuberculosis, but in his case it was
cancer."

Gran frowned. Like many of the older generation, she
felt the word "cancer" was indelicate. Aunt Clara went on.
"Hendrik's son Henry—the first one they called Henry instead of Hendrik—was born in 1894. He went into the
army in 1917. So did his brother Calvin, and they were
both sent to Belgium. Calvin was gassed and never really
recovered. He lived here all his life, in the room you're
staying in, Cat, lived in his brother's house and with his
brother's family, but he was never strong, never married,
never could work the land. He did their bookkeeping.
Another brother, Harold, went to Grand Rapids and into
the furniture business. There were also three girls, who
married, of course, and moved away."

"And lost their home here?" I said. She looked at me
sharply. The same thing had happened to her, except that
she had not married. She had gone into nursing.

"Yes, they did. Henry had a son, Henry junior, born in
1919—he died this spring—and Daniel, born in 1923,
and the later children, Paul, myself, and Helen. Helen
married and moved to Battle Creek. She died a few years
ago of cancer at the age of seventy-one. Daniel was in
World War Two and was killed at Anzio. Paul became a
physicist and is teaching at UCLA—well, technically he's
emeritus now. He'll be coming home to visit at Christmas." And find what situation here? I wondered. One of
the family arrested for murder? She went on. "And Henry,
of course, married Ruth Bos—" she gestured at Gran "—
in 1948 and was the father of John, Marie, and Henry III,
whom we call Hank."

They were a picture, all grouped around the dinner
table, in the yellow glow of the brass chandelier with

milky-yellow chimneys. The color of the light was similar
to that of firelight, and under that glow the family took on
an air of timelessness. All these DeGraaf faces. Vaguely, I
heard Aunt Clara saying, "There's always been an academic
strain in the family. My brother Paul. And John, now. He
teaches English, you know, at the high school, but he went
back to the University of Michigan this summer to take
two courses and finish his second master's."

John said, "Well, you know, you get a raise if you have a
second degree—"

But Gran cut in. "And worked himself to the bone and
came home twenty pounds thinner. Too much thinking."

Nell smiled and said, "Gran has spent months trying to
fatten him up."

Yes, John was lean. So was Marie. Clara, Hank, and
Hank's three sons were chunkier. Still, they all looked very
similar. The blond hair—pale blond with reddish highlights in Nell, washed-out blond for John, white with a few
yellow highlights in Clara, tan with an almost orange cast
in Hank and his sons, ash blond for Marie. They all had
square hands, workman's hands, or craftsman's hands. A
basically lanky, bony frame, whatever muscle or fat they
put over it. All had green or hazel eyes. Gran, who was
shorter and had blue eyes, seemed to have contributed
very few dominant genes.

The individual person was a new human being in a new
generation, but the characteristics flowed unchanged
down through the ages. I saw the original Pieternella's
mathematical ability appear in Marie. And Paul the physicist. Marie, who kept the books and calculated trees per
acre and profits per tree while Hank was still standing
there, working up to figuring 20 times 15 is 300. Marie,
who could calculate 6½ percent of something in her head.

Marie, who knew just exactly how the tax numbers worked out.

And Hank—he had inherited the family tendency to make things with his hands, and like little Gerritt would talk to anybody who came through. Would little Gerritt have become a craftsman if he'd survived the Civil War?

I said, "Clara, what use did the second-generation Hendrik make of the land?"

"He grew apples and had a cider mill here and trucked cider and apples in to Grand Rapids. Made a very good thing out of it, too. But *his* son discovered there was more money in Christmas trees."

In her debunking voice, Marie said, "There weren't any Christmas trees in this area until 1871. The Henry Post family had the first one. They aren't a Dutch tradition."

"Christmas stockings are Dutch, though," Clara said. "The story is that eighteen hundred years ago there was a poor family with several daughters. They had no money, and therefore no dowry, and therefore they could never marry. One night they had washed their stockings and hung them near the fireplace to dry. Sinterklaas passed overhead and dropped gold coins down their chimney. In the morning they found the coins, which had fallen into their stockings."

There was a narrative strain in Clara. Was this a link to John, who taught English? And perhaps back to Hendrik?

Each generation had had its stay-at-homes, like Nell's grandfather, Henry. Like the first Hendrik's son, Hendrik. And like John, I thought. And each generation had had its rebels. The first Hendrik had been rebel enough to leave his homeland and sail across the ocean to a new, comparatively primitive, comparatively inclement, uncivilized land, simply on the basis of the rumor that it was bigger, and more open to expansion. Clara was a rebel of sorts herself, living alone, earning her own way. Marie, I thought, was the rebel in her generation. She was an iconoclastic thinker. She probably would have moved farther from the nest if she had not been a woman.

They all shared an ability to work, and a kind of enjoyment of working with their hands. They all shared the pale hair, pale skin, and a bony frame. Mental and physical traits, woven together, repeated over and over.

The generations were a kind of tapestry, with recurrent themes and colors. Threads would be buried for a time under others and then resurface. And each generation, with its donation of strengths and weaknesses from the last generation, marched into the future and confronted new problems with the age-old characters and bodies.

Now they were confronted with losing their home.

I stood on the back porch after dinner, breathing in the air. It would be wonderful to live here, where the air smelled like spiced cider. John, who had come out with me, said, "The scent of the pines is stronger in the winter."

"Why is that?"

"When I was a child, I used to think it was because the trees were getting themselves ready for Christmas. Christmas smelled like pine, so it made sense to a child. But I suppose it's really that the competing vegetation has died back. The evergreens are the only ones keeping their leaves alive and working. This is their triumphal time of year."

"You must have enjoyed growing up here."

"When you have fields and a creek and woods right outside your door, there's always something to do. I was one of the world's all-time tree climbers, even though you might not think it now."

"Why wouldn't I?"

"Oh, I know I look like a cautious type—we get more sedate as we get older, I guess. I used to go across the creek to the woods to climb so my mother wouldn't see me and have a fit."

We walked around the corner to the side porch. "You see that oak sticking up above the others?"

"I see a hundred oaks sticking up."

"The one that comes out of the bunch of lower pines."

"Yes."

"That's one I used to climb. I could see the house from there. Unfortunately, I didn't realize that if I could see the house, people in the house could see me. My dad came running out to get me one day."

"What did he say?"

"He said"—John smiled—"next time don't do that where your mother might see you."

"He sounds like a nice guy."

"Well, he was, he was a lovely, understanding, kindly man, and also it was a tree he had climbed himself as a kid, so he didn't really think I was taking my life in my hands."

"No. I fell out of a tree once, but I grabbed a lot of branches on the way down."

"Yes. If there weren't any branches, you probably wouldn't have been able to climb up. Uh, Cat?"

"Yes?"

"I appreciate you befriending Nell."

"It's not an effort. She's a delight."

"Yes, she is. But I mean, it's very nice for her right now to have somebody to talk with. From outside the family. It's—everything is very intense for her, because of—you can imagine."

I was about to answer, but as we came around the side of the porch, we noticed that the sheriff's car was back.

"Damn it! What do they want now?" John said.

"The light's on in the barn. We could go ask."

"No, I'm sick and tired of talking with those guys. You go ahead if you want. I'll be in the house if they need me."

*   *   *

"Hi."

VanLente said, "Have you come to see what we're doing?"

"Sure. What *are* you doing?"

"I'm sorry to say, nothing very exciting. We'd intended to take a few more soil samples from the barn floor than we did."

"Oh. For comparison to what? Is there any reason to think Luis was killed in the barn? Is there blood in the barn?"

"No. I don't think there's any blood in the barn. But it'll take a while to be sure. There's a lot of oil, and spots where gasoline soaked into the sand, and spilled paint. Over the years all kinds of stuff has spilled in the barn."

"So?"

"So we took samples of all the different stained sand and none of the *un*stained sand. It's just a matter of having a base line."

"Have you found any indication that anybody came in from outside to kill Luis?" Grasping at straws? Why not?

"No. Nobody walked in by coming from the road into the fields. We checked all along the property line when the sun came up, and there were no new footprints anywhere. That doesn't mean somebody couldn't have come walking in the driveway, you know."

"All right. Try this. The only one who could have found Luis and persuaded him to go to the field, started the baler, and so on is somebody familiar with the place—"

"Obviously."

"—and therefore either one of the people we know or possibly a former associate of the DeGraafs. Was there anybody they've fired recently? A tree farm employee?"

"Two. One has since moved to Tucson and the other was

working on Friday at a tree farm near White Cloud. They cut Norway spruce until dark and then went out for beer and spent the rest of the night in a bar."

"Oh."

"The young kids they have this year, one has worked for them for two years, that's Raymond. Skip worked for them last year for the first time, and Ken is new this year. There's a lot of turnover because the hired hands only work a few weeks a year here. All these people have regular jobs the rest of the year."

"Oh. Well. So—do you have any idea who killed Luis?"

"I have a couple of notions."

"Such as?"

VanLente said, "Well, you're probably aware there's a certain amount of tension in the community between the Dutch and the Mexicans."

"I haven't really talked with anybody about that."

"Then take it from me. It's not just the difference in appearance. It's also the religion. In the Netherlands, about half the population is Catholic and half Protestant. But this particular area was settled by Protestant Dutch, and they think Catholics are going to hell."

"Uh-huh. People never change, the world over, do they?"

"Not but very little. Anyhow, the DeGraafs must've been highly uneasy that Luis was romancing the girl."

"Luis was not romancing Nell. They were friends."

"Oh, sure. He was twenty—she's what? Thirteen? She's an attractive girl."

"There was *no* romance."

"He was an exciting older man. Plus, a little bit more exciting because of the ethnic difference. The forbidden is always more interesting. She may have fallen for him hard—first love, you know."

"That's simply not *true.*"

"Hank's kid Cal tells me they were always whispering and playing kissy-face behind the barn."

I could feel myself getting hot. "He's wrong. Cal's a little snot. I know Luis and Nell were talking. Quietly, not whispering. They talked about life and stuff. Nell's had worries and she needed somebody to talk to. But they weren't kissing!"

"Yeah? How about this theory: Nell's father John killed Luis in a rage, trying to protect his daughter. The idea of her being seduced by a Mexican was too much for him."

"She was not being seduced—"

"The killing has all the earmarks of that kind of thing. Fury. Cold fury. It was vicious, real, *real* nasty, leaving him out there to freeze to death. Wonder if she realizes she got her boyfriend killed."

"He was *not* her boyfriend, damn it! *You're dead wrong!*"

"Oh. And just what makes you so goddamn sure?"

"She told me so!"

"Ha! And you believed her?"

"Absolutely. Nell is totally straightforward." I could hear my voice rising in pitch, but I couldn't stop. "I'd be lucky if *I* had such a nice child as a daughter. Anybody would. She might try to protect her family, but basically she doesn't even know *how* to lie! She is the sweetest, *nicest child you'll ever—*"

He was staring at me.

I quit in midsentence.

There was an awkward pause, and finally VanLente said, seriously and quietly, "Ms. Marsala, do you have any feeling that maybe you're getting overinvolved?"

*   *   *

How impenetrably blind we can be to our own motivations! I had absolutely no idea that I was more than reasonably fond of Nell. It seemed to me she was a child in trouble, a child in a house full of adults who were all well intentioned, interested in her welfare—all except for one particularly nasty murderer.

I thought natural humanity made me care about her, not some irrational desire for a child of my own.

I lay in bed that night, wide awake. The garage light, which they did not usually leave on, shone on my bedroom ceiling. All the outdoor lights had been left on tonight—the front and back porch lights, the exterior barn light, the garage light—not just the yard light on its pole.

It wasn't the light that kept me awake.

The pillow that had been comfortable last night was full of stones tonight. The room temperature was still in the low seventies and now felt much too hot. Except when it was too cold. The sounds of the old house creaking, which had been as comfortable last night as the creaking of an antique rocking chair, now had the impact of rifle shots that went off at exactly the moment I began to doze. The blanket had developed thorns.

Nell *was* a good person. Thoroughly good. I could not be so mistaken. Or, face it, so biased.

What worried me was that up to this moment I had been utterly unaware that I saw Nell as a daughter. Not just as someone who was the sort of person I would wish a daughter to be, but as someone whom I actually wished was my daughter.

I was old enough to be her mother, if she had been born when I was twenty. At twenty I had decided not to marry or have children any time soon. My decision to go on building my reputation as a features writer had been thoroughly thought out. I knew precisely what I was giving up by not marrying, not having a child yet. Never had I felt any serious pain as a result.

Or so I thought. Apparently I didn't know what was going on beneath the surface—my own surface.

And what worried me even more was Nell. Had I misunderstood, because of my own unperceived needs, what was going on beneath Nell's surface?

Could Nell have been having a love affair with Luis? She was very young, but no younger than Juliet when she met Romeo. If there was a romance, could John have known? And last night, when he thanked me for befriending Nell, was he really giving me an opening to tell him whether she had confided in me about a love affair with Luis? Did he want to find out whether I knew? Because if I knew and intended to tell the police, it might show that he had murdered Luis.

Or worse, could Nell have killed Luis? As long as I was facing the impossibility of truly knowing people, could there have been a lovers' quarrel? Was Luis going to break off their romance? Or on the other hand, was Luis going to tell her family about their relationship against her wishes?

Or didn't they have a romantic relationship at all?

I had thought Nell could not have killed Luis because she had been in the house continuously from the time before Luis left until after dinner. Also, could she have lifted him into the baler? Was she physically able to do it? Well, I had thought Gran was, partly because the baler was not high off the ground. Its entrance was arm height, to make it easier to feed it trees.

Uneasily, I realized that Nell was the one person in the family Luis might have been willing to wait around to talk with later, after work. Any of the others might have said, "Let's go out in the field to discuss this where we can't be overheard," and taken a stroll with him out to the block where the baler was. And certainly one of them could have killed him right then. But they would have had to do it soon after quitting work. If he was killed later in the night, and he could have been, Nell was the main possibility. Luis would not have sat in the barn for hours to wait for John or Hank or Cal to show up. Particularly not Cal. He'd have told Cal to take a hike.

For Nell, I think he would wait. He liked her. They talked frequently, and I suspected that he felt sorry for her loss of her mother and grandfather. Possibly he admired the way Nell handled her loss, just as I did. Whether he was attracted to her, I didn't know and couldn't guess.

But if she had said, "Can you work awhile in the barn, and then meet me in the field after we have dinner?" I think he would have agreed. He might have agreed to stay even later than that.

I pictured them walking toward the block of trees, sitting down on the flatbed or possibly on the edge of the baler itself. Nell, maybe, feeling that he is the only person in the world who understands her and cares about her. Have they had a relationship, and he is tired of her? Or does she want his love and he rejects her? "No, Nell, I have a woman I love, and you're only a child." Is that possible?

And then she has had simply too much of people leaving her, through death, and she snaps. Hits him on the head with a piece of wood or pushes him over so suddenly that he strikes his head on the side of the baler. Then while he's unconscious, she lashes his feet with the chain and turns on the baler motor.

Would she know how? Of course. She hasn't been in the fields much while I was here, but there must have been many times when she helped load trees or lop branches. That part is not heavy work. Of course she'd know.

And then late that night, did she wake us because she had misgivings? Did she hope to save him? Had she been lying awake all those hours and finally, unable to stand it any longer, did she wake her father and ask him to check? Or so that she wouldn't be suspected?

Did she?

No, I didn't believe it.

But at the same time, I still didn't think Nell had told me everything.

· 21 ·

Maybe I slept some. I heard the Dutch clock in the dining room strike six A.M. This was a clock I had admired earlier— an ornate green-enamel-and-brass wall clock with weights and a pendulum that hung down unboxed. Gran had said the Dutch called the pendulum a wigwag. Who would have thought that the damned thing increased tenfold in volume during the night?

It would not be daylight for two more hours. But I was finished with lying there feeling stupid. I turned on the light and made some notes on my laptop. I got LJ out and let him fly around for a few minutes, whispering to him that airborne exercise was probably aerobic. He got tired of that and hopped around the floor, cocking his head for dust balls—he's found plenty of them at my place, and he rolls them by fanning them with his wings, but he wouldn't find any in Gran DeGraaf's meticulous house. I sat for a while reading one of old Hendrik's letters. Finally I put LJ in his cage and turned off the light, thinking I might go to sleep now, but no. The bed was still full of rocks. Putting on a white angora sweater, my best white wool pants, and white boots—no Levi's because it was Sunday and they had invited me to church with them—I tiptoed down to the kitchen. For once, I was the first one up.

Except for the glow from the garage light, the kitchen was dark, but it still smelled wonderful. The ghosts of generations of apple pies and coffee and roast turkey flitted through the air.

The DeGraafs, being thrifty people, did not throw out coffee, but left what had not been drunk on the side of the stove for people to heat up in the microwave as needed. I did the same thing at home. Freelance writing is no way to get rich. My friend Chicago Police Chief of Detectives Harold McCoo, the wizard of the coffee pot, arbiter of coffee beans from around the world, would be horrified at anybody drinking old coffee. But he wasn't here.

I nuked a mug of coffee and then sat at the kitchen table in semidarkness for a couple of minutes, waiting for the coffee to cool. But I got bored. There was nothing to see from here, as the kitchen window was high over the sink. The DeGraafs didn't eat in the living room, but surely, if I carried my cup into the living room and curled up into a chair, I could manage not to spill it on Gran's spotless carpet.

I staggered sleepily toward the living room, planning to sit and watch the day wake up and the house come to life. And worry about what was going on here.

The living room was dark, too, but turning on the lights might bother somebody. Suppose John or Gran saw lights shining from the windows into the yard outdoors and got up to find out what was wrong. This was Sunday morning, and they might want to sleep late. No, not very late; there was church, but at least there was no work in the fields, so they might sleep a bit later than usual.

I paused in the doorway to the living room. In the faint spill of bluish light from the yard lamp, I could scarcely make out the furniture. A high-backed chair looked like a tombstone. The oval coffee table was polished to such a high shine that in the bluish light that glanced off it, it looked like a lake. A wall mirror was a square hole into yesterday. The clock ticked loudly.

Placing each footfall with care, I approached the coffee table. On one side was a sofa, on the other side were two chairs. I rounded the end of the sofa, intending to sit facing the window and watch the dawn come up.

I leaned over to the table. And jumped almost out of my boots. There was a body on the sofa! The mug jittered in my hand.

"Oh, careful, Cat!" Nell said.

"Yikes!" Coffee sloshed over the rim. I made a grab for it with the mug, as if I thought I could catch it in midair. More overflowed.

I put it down on the table fast, pulled some Kleenex from my pocket, and mopped the spill.

"Gee, I'm sorry," Nell said. "I heard you in the kitchen, but I didn't hear you come out here—"

Thank God no coffee had splashed on the rug. I wiped the bottom of the mug to make sure I wouldn't leave a ring on the tabletop. As Hank might say, that was a nice old piece of burled walnut.

When my heart had settled down and my body was in the chair, I said, "What are you doing here?" She had heard movement in the kitchen. That meant she had intentionally not called out or come to see who it was. She had remained here alone in the dark.

There must have been some irritation in my voice, because she said, "Nothing. Just sitting."

The combination of all the thoughts I had been having about her—not quite doubts, just thoughts—plus the annoyance at having spilled the coffee made me feel crabby. But now I looked closely at her. My eyes were adjusting to the light somewhat, even though it was still very shadowy in this room. The outdoor light reflected on her eyes, making them glitter as if they were filled with unshed tears, and turned her hair to silver monofilaments. She looked as insubstantial as an old silverpoint drawing. I could read sadness and loneliness in every line of her face. Immediately, I felt guilty.

"Nell, you should be asleep. What's the matter?"

She exhaled. "Well, almost everything, I guess."

"I'm sorry. That was stupid of me."

"I tried to stay in bed, but it made me twitchy."

"Me, too. Can I get you something? Cocoa? Or juice?"

"No. As a matter of fact, I don't feel so well."

"Are you sick?"

"Not really. I just don't feel so well."

We sat there for a while in silence. I sipped coffee that I found I didn't want. Now that Nell had mentioned it, I realized I didn't exactly feel so well, either.

"Cat, are you mad at me?"

"Oh, honey, no!"

"Okay."

"But I'm worried."

She smiled. "That makes two of us."

"Well, yes. But Nell—" I paused. She just looked at me, a little fearfully.

"Nell, there's something you're not telling me."

No answer.

"It's not that you need to tell *me* specifically. I mean, I'm just a stranger, really. But if there's something you know and you're keeping it back, it could be dangerous for you."

"I don't know what to do."

"It could also be dangerous for someone else. If you know something that might help the police solve the murder, it's important to tell them. Because—see, it might seem like you could just wait and hope the whole horrible mess will go away, but it won't. If nobody is ever arrested for Luis's murder, everybody who was here that day will go on being suspected. Possibly for years and years. People will look at them differently. They'll think, Well, he or she couldn't possibly have done such a thing—but just maybe . . ."

"I hadn't thought about that."

"It shouldn't be that way, but it is. Suspicion can be very, very nasty."

She turned it over in her mind. I knew her well enough now to know she was habitually honest with herself. And possibly stubborn, in the way that self-directed people can be. It wouldn't do any good to nag her. Let her think about it. She'd face the facts.

I drank more unwanted coffee. The night was still dark. Didn't the sun ever come up in this place?

She said, "Okay. I guess maybe I have to tell somebody."

The moon had sunk behind the woods. We moved silently across the yard, lit by the fake bluish moon of the yard light. The back door of the barn was locked tonight, unlike last night, when John and I had come out here looking for Luis.

Although there were more lights on in the yard tonight than last night, the effect was to make the sky seem darker beyond the lights and the shadows deeper. As Nell inserted the key in the lock, we didn't speak. The lock whispered as she turned it. The door, as well oiled as the lock, opened with a soft draft of air.

Nell walked straight on in, but I shut the door after us. I didn't like the idea that someone might creep up behind us when she showed me whatever she planned to show me.

But with the door so silent, we wouldn't know if it opened behind us, would we?

She was already crossing the floor, past the stove. The solid cast iron still gave off a hint of warmth. Chain saws lay on the bench. The heavy anvil clipper, oiled and ready to go, lay near them. The place was filled with sharp steel, a thought I tried to put out of my mind.

Nell walked carefully but steadily past the tools. I didn't know where she was headed. She passed the borrowed baler; the other one was still out in the field where Luis had died. She passed the card table where coffee usually was served, passed the porch furniture. She crossed to the far end of the barn where the two old bicycles, the bicycle parts, the hoes, the rakes, the lawnmower, the rototiller, a trombone sprayer, and rolls and rolls of garden hose were piled against the wall under the raised gallery.

Nell moved a bicycle, then started to move the rototiller. It was too heavy for her to do alone. We both shoved hard and it shrieked. We jumped, startled. Looking back over our shoulders, we shoved harder. It moved a couple of feet out toward the center of the barn.

I realized that Nell had not turned on any additional interior barn lights. This must have been intentional on her part. Even though the single dim bulb near the door had been left on, it was gloomy enough in here so that anyone would immediately turn lights on. Therefore she didn't want anybody to know we were out here or see what we were doing.

Now she stepped over a couple of tool handles to a ladder nailed vertically to the wall, and started climbing. I followed. We went up through a veil of spiderwebs. Some of the webs were recently broken, indicating that the police might have checked up here, too.

The gallery was about six feet wide and twenty feet long, running the whole width of that end of the barn. It was skimpily floored with one-by-six pine boards that gave a little as you stepped on them. Old furniture, some of it ornately carved, some of it cobbled together out of rough boards, was tumbled up here. There was also a condenser from an old refrigerator—the kind with the coils on top— and several dusty mirrors with their silvering flaked off in places. They reflected me as a pale ghost with holes.

In the dim light, Nell looked carefully at the furniture and the spaces between, searching for something but not knowing exactly where to find it. She worked her way slowly down the gallery. I stuck close to her. For her safety or for mine, or just because it was so eerie here that a person needed companionship?

Suddenly she stopped. She pointed. I could see her hand shake.

"There."

I heard her voice shake, too.

I said, "What?"

"This. This is it." She reached forward but not far enough to actually touch the thing. At first I couldn't make out what it was. It was just a lump, lying on top of an old table that was behind a lopsided chest of drawers. A lump that even in the dark was bright enough to show its color.

It was a bright orange down vest.

· 22 ·

I held out my fingers, poked the vest, and found it wouldn't move. It was partly stuck to the tabletop. I poked it again, and it came unstuck, leaving a whitish, discolored blotch underneath. There was a lot of dust on the upper side of the vest, and it had the somewhat wrinkled look of cloth that had been wet and allowed to dry while lying unsmoothed.

We left it there.

"Nell, sit down." I pulled two of the aluminum porch chairs close together, sat in one, and pointed at the other. It was still dark in the barn, but the sky in the east must have been giving hints of the coming day, because the crack between the double barn doors let in a rosy light.

Nell said, "Are you mad at me?"

"Good God, no. Why do you always ask me that? Do I seem like an angry person?"

"No. Sometimes it feels like people go away from me. No, I'm sorry. That's stupid. And it isn't your fault anyway. I mean, even, you know, if it's true."

She sat. I said, "Nell, it isn't true. You've had real tragedies. People haven't gone away from you, they've died, and it's not your fault. We have to save what you have now, and to do that we have to figure out what's behind all

this. I don't understand what's been happening around
here. But it's not only horribly serious, it's long-standing.
It didn't just happen last night. The night before last, I
mean."

"I know that. That's what makes it scarier."

"Are you willing to help me?"

"Mmm-mm." She nodded. She was tense, and her
hands wove together tightly, but she seemed resolute
when she added, "I want to get this over with."

"Then let me ask you some questions—let me interview
you as if you were an informant for a story I was writing.
Impersonally."

"Okay. If you say so."

"Only if you want to. It's got to be your decision."

"Yes. I'm sure now."

I had more than a moment's qualm. It was hard to imagine any outcome of Luis's murder that wouldn't hurt her,
one way or another. Still, she had hit the heart of it when
she said she wanted to get it over with. Although Nell herself probably meant that she couldn't stand the tension any
more, it was still true that, one way or another, this child
had to get past the murder and get on with her life.

"Can you really do this, Nell?" I asked.

"I think so."

"All right. How did you know about this down vest being there?"

"Luis told me."

"Luis? Really? When?"

"Friday morning."

Yes! That figured. It was Friday morning when she became withdrawn and I thought she was avoiding me.

"And you didn't want to tell me or anybody about it?"

"It really scared me. I was already worried before that. I
never believed my grandfather would just make a mistake

about the spray. It had been around his whole life. I mean, they started crop dusting from planes way, way back, they always told me. Like after World War Two. He always wore his orange vest at spray times."

"Okay."

"But worrying about what happened isn't the same as seeing. Seeing the vest was real."

"I understand. You had talked with Luis about your suspicions before all this?"

"Well, yes, but it wasn't like I was telling him something new. When he heard about Grandfather's accident the first time, last spring, he wondered, too. He knew my grandfather was careful, because of his asthma. And also Grandfather was just a careful sort of person, you know? But Luis didn't say anything to me that he had doubts until I said something to him. You see?"

"Yes. So he came to you Friday and told you what?"

"He'd been up in the barn loft—"

"Why?"

"Oh, Friday morning Cal was clowning around like he does, juggling some stuff, pliers and some stuff, and he threw the 3-in-One oil and it bounced off the barn ceiling and landed in the loft, and Uncle Hank said to Luis to go get it. I mean, half the time, Cal would do something dumb and Uncle Hank would have Luis straighten it out."

"Right. So Luis went up in the loft?"

"Yes, well, he heard it bounce high up and he didn't see it on the ground, so he went up, and the can of oil was pretty small, so he had to look everywhere before he found it. He was crawling under the furniture up there and everything—"

As she talked, I thought she was going into detail in order to distract herself from the unpleasant fact she was approaching.

"—and he was rummaging around, looking on top of things and underneath things, and, you know, that's when he saw the down vest."

"And he left it there?"

"Yes."

"Why?"

"He said he had to think about it."

"And later he talked to you about it?"

"Yes."

"Did he tell anybody else about it?"

"I don't think so."

But he had. I knew that now. I had heard him.

"Did he say what he had to think about?"

"No. He probably wouldn't know for sure what it meant," she said. "I mean, the vest could have been up there for some other reason, he said. Although—"

"Although?"

"Well, when he told me that, I kind of felt he was trying to make me feel better."

"So he was wondering whether he should tell somebody in the family?"

"I guess. He didn't exactly say that."

"Or the police? The sheriff?"

"Yes. But he was wondering—I mean, if you told some-body like the police, he thought, wouldn't they say, Oh, what does a jacket mean?"

"They might. But of course, a jacket doesn't get up into a loft by accident."

"I know." Nell briefly put her hands over her eyes. When she took them away, her eyes were sober, but there were no tears.

"Nell, could your grandfather have thrown the jacket into the loft himself?"

"Why would he?"

"I don't know. Maybe it ripped and he was disgusted with it, so he threw it away from himself angrily. Do you think he might?"

"No. He wasn't the kind of person to get angry and throw things. He was nice. And I'm not sure he could, even. He had bursitis in his shoulder, from hunting ducks as a young man he always said, and the shotgun recoil was real strong and it hurt his shoulder"—she was talking again to avoid thinking, but that was okay—"so he never threw baseballs or stuff that you had to throw hard, or sticks for Carat to chase, and I think you'd have to throw a down vest fairly hard, don't you, to get it all the way up there?"

"Yes. I guess I do."

We huddled close together.

"Nell, why do you think the vest is stuck to the table? It looks to me like maybe because it was wet when it was thrown up there."

"Mmm-mm."

"What are you thinking?"

"Well, the day before Grandfather died, the crop duster didn't come in because it was raining. And grandfather was out looking at the trees, because he always does—did—and besides with scale insects you have to spray right away, so he probably came in that evening with a wet jacket."

"And you think somebody took it then?"

"Yes."

"The evening before? And took it to the barn and threw into the loft?"

"Yes."

That meant premeditation, of course, whether it was thrown up there just before the crop duster came over or the night before. But the thought of the killer planning to do it the night before, getting rid of the jacket, then going to bed and waiting all night for the death to occur the next day—the idea was sickening. I hoped Nell had not realized all this, but she was very bright, and I was afraid she knew as well as I did what it meant.

"I think I just heard the kitchen door opening," I said, gratefully.

"I did, too. I bet Gran's putting out trash."

"Let's go help."

"All right."

We found the lights on all over the downstairs and the kitchen in an uproar. It wasn't disheveled—not Gran's kitchen, ever. It wasn't dirty—not Gran's kitchen. But Gran was sitting in a chair—I realized I had never seen her sit in the kitchen in all the time I'd been here—and John was talking loudly, which he never did, on the phone. He was wearing pants but no shirt. His shirt was hung over his left arm, where he seemed to have forgotten it. He had the phone book open on the kitchen table, and was shouting, "Well, then, come by here for just a minute on your way to church!"

Nell immediately went to the table and took her grandmother's hand.

"Gran," she said, "are you all right?"

"I certainly am. Your father just gets easily upset."

John said, "Okay. We'll be here," into the phone and hung up. After hanging up, he said, "Good-bye," which the person on the other end could not have heard. John didn't notice that, either. And he didn't notice me.

"He'll come by in half an hour, Mom."

"That wasn't necessary," Gran said. "I was just a little faint."

"You were *not* just a little faint. It was that rhythm thing again." He backed up and stepped on my foot.

I said, "Yipe!"

"Oh! Sorry! I didn't see you."

"No problem." I was wearing my better boots, in honor of Sunday, but at least they were solid leather.

"My mother has a heart rhythm problem," he explained. "It acts up sometimes."

"It's nothing to worry about," Gran said. "I get a little faint when it happens, but it always goes away if I rest awhile. I feel perfectly well now."

John caught my eye as if to say the heart problem was not so negligible as Gran pretended. Then he realized he was half dressed and hastily pulled on his shirt. I noticed again the slice-cuts on his arms and the chunk out of his shoulder.

"Well, there!" he said, as if everything were all decided.

Nell said, "Is Dr. Brink coming out?"

"Yes, on his way to church. Honey, what are you doing up and dressed?"

"Oh, nothing much."

"You aren't sick, are you?"

"No, Daddy. I feel fine."

"Can you stay with Gran while I get shaved?"

"Sure."

Gran said, "This is a lot of fuss about nothing!"

By the time Dr. Brink pulled up outside, Aunt Clara and Marie were both here, too. Alerted by John, they'd sped over instead of meeting the family at church and coming later for Sunday dinner.

John sat with his mother in the living room, despite her constant assertions that she was just fine. I made coffee, being extremely careful not to spill anything in the spotless kitchen, and Nell made toast. Aunt Clara made scrambled eggs and fried potatoes.

"Is Hank coming?" I asked Clara.

"Not until later. Ruth gets over these things pretty quickly, but while she's having one I think it's just as well not to have three teenage boys clattering and banging around the house."

"You're probably right. How long does it take her to get over it?"

"Oh, she's better already. But we make her sit for a while to be sure."

"Clara, how serious is it really?"

"It *can* be serious. She faints when it comes on. According to Dr. Brink, it's a form of tachycardia. The heart beats too fast for a while." Clara watched Nell leave the kitchen with coffee for Gran, John, and Dr. Brink before she added, "The heart beats inefficiently, which is why she faints. If the fast beat went on too long, she could die. But she takes some medication that's supposed to limit the attacks."

"I see." Another person in Nell's family who might die. I wasn't especially fond of Gran; she wasn't a warm person. But my heart sank at the thought of Nell losing her, too.

Dr. Brink chatted with Gran, listened to her heart, and told her she was in good enough shape but shouldn't go to church this morning.

"Now wait, Morgan—" she said to him.

But he immediately added, "And *no* strong coffee. Put that cup down right now."

I was watching from the doorway and saw the look of horror come over Gran's face. No coffee? I really sympathized with this. Giving up coffee would plunge me into an utter blue funk.

"A little coffee never hurt anybody," she said.

"Ruth, I told you at the office. One cup in the morning, okay, but no more. No drinking it all day. You can drink decaf."

"Decaf! You know what Henry used to say about decaf? 'You might as well open your mouth and let the moon shine in!' "

Dr. Brink laughed. "Well, I see you haven't lost your spark, anyway." He looked around at the family. "I deduce Ruth didn't report to all of you what I told her in the office. Well, you've heard it now. Keep her away from the coffee."

John said, "Oh, sure."

Marie said, "Easier said than done."

"Well, I leave it to you. Be good, Ruth. I've got to get to church."

"So do we. Or some of us anyhow," John said. "I'll stay here with her."

Clara said, "No, I'll stay. It's no trouble."

Nell said, "Why don't I—"

Breaking into this welter of selfless offers, I said, "Look, why don't I stay here with her? It's your church, not my church, and it's important to you to go."

So there I was. Gran sat on the sofa, irritable at the inactivity. "I am perfectly able to get up and start dinner," she said.

"I know that. But later."

"Hmmp." She shifted, getting ready to rise.

"Come on. Don't make them think I didn't do my job taking care of you. The doctor said you could cook dinner later. He just wanted you to sit still for a while first."

Smiling slyly, she said, "Of course, you couldn't stop me."

I smiled, too. "You are certainly more than I could handle. I wouldn't want to try to stop you from doing anything you wanted to. Why didn't you just insist on going to church anyway, then?"

"I wouldn't want to faint at church."

"Aren't there people there who could help? Your doctor goes to the same church, doesn't he? Or they could call an ambulance?"

"That isn't the point. Fainting right in front of everybody would be so embarrassing."

That made sense. That was Gran as I perceived her. Worried about maintaining appearances. This thought made me realize more strongly how very difficult Luis's death must be for her. To have a man murdered on your own farm and your own family suspected would be an utter horror for her.

I know this was not the same as feeling sorrow for Luis himself. That would have been a more admirable reaction. But events that are catastrophic for one person have consequences for other people as well, and it wouldn't really be sympathetic on my part to belittle her feelings.

Now that I studied her more closely, she did not look well. She was a tiny little pink and white doll, but she was less pink than she had been on Thursday, and her cheeks were pinched. I thought she had lost a bit of weight. And yet, through all this crisis she had been keeping up her end of the work, cooking, providing coffee for the farmhands, even coffee and cookies for the sheriff and his crew of people. She had put breakfast, lunch, and dinner on the table, maintained her end of all the conversations, and kept up a brave front as well, all the time.

It had cost her more than I realized.

*   *   *

With a start, I realized something else: Gran's sudden illness had made me forget that Nell and I had found the orange down vest. We had planned to notify the sheriff. Nell had forgotten, too, and now the whole family had gone to church. What should I do?

I could tell Gran about the vest, and then call the sheriff. Oh, sure—then she could have a heart attack and then how would I feel? After all, that vest related to the death of her husband, and not just his death, the *murder* of her husband. Maybe the vest would be the first hint she had that it was murder. I couldn't just blurt it out to her.

Maybe I could go to the phone in the kitchen, call the sheriff secretly, and tell him.

No, that was just too sneaky. Besides, what if he came right over? The family ought to be here to take care of Gran when the sheriff arrived.

There was nothing to do but wait until the family came back from church. Then either I or Marie, John, or Hank could call the sheriff.

"You must be proud of your family," I said. "All with jobs, all responsible people."

"You do the best you can. Marie should learn to control her sarcasm, but I suppose she could do worse. Her husband drank, you know."

"No. She didn't tell me anything about him."

"Hank earns a good salary. Jennifer, of course, is a flibbertigibbet. But harmless, I suppose. But Hank's job is rather blue collar. John has done well."

"Marie is a technician—"

"Mmm. If she'd watched her mouth, she could be mar-

ried and at home with children. Oh, well. Henry wasn't
strict enough with them."

"Oh."

"I remonstrated, of course. But a wife has to do what
her husband says."

I put a hassock under Gran's feet—over her objections
and under her feet, so to speak. Finally she stopped ob-
jecting and closed her eyes. Good. Because I needed to
think. I was filled with dread.

Finding that down vest was the end of hope, really. If
there was ever any faint chance that an evil stranger had
come onto the farm and killed Luis, that was now gone.

Only a family member could have gone into the house
on Easter, taken the orange vest, walked out to the barn
with it, and slung it up into the loft. No one else—except
possibly Luis himself—would have known exactly where
it was on its peg, plus what it meant to old Henry
DeGraaf's safety, plus what time the crop duster was likely
to come over, plus old Henry's habit of walking the field
before the duster came.

And if Henry had been murdered by a family member,
there was little point in looking around for a dangerous
stranger to have come in half a year later and killed Luis.

Which meant a family member had done it.

A family member had murdered an elderly, kindly man,
and then killed a hardworking employee in a hideous way.

There was a monster here, and it was one of these:
Gran, Hank, Hank's wife, Jennifer, their boys Cal, Don, or
Dan, John, Marie, or Clara. Or Nell.

For twenty-four hours now I'd known this horror was
approaching, and it sickened me. I felt like I had felt three
weeks ago when I visited a maximum security prison in
Indiana. It wasn't so bad at first. We went in the entry gate,

which had the fall-browned remains of chrysanthemums bedded out around the walk. Then inside, we handed over our driver's licenses, which the admitting guards held, and they took away from us any "dangerous" materials— our coats, our pens, our pencils, keys, whatever. Then they searched us and let us in through a second airlock-style double gate.

The bars closed behind us. We entered a long hallway next, with double glass-and-bar doors closing behind us. The farther we went, the more doors closed behind us, the farther we were into the center of the prison, the harder it would be to get out. There were fewer and fewer options.

I felt just like that now. Maybe I should have left the first day, as soon as the murder occurred. But doors had closed off behind me now; there were few options left. The choice was to find the killer or leave the family with a murderer in its midst—a killer who had no restraint and no pity.

There was one last door that had not closed. I could still escape. I could leave this noon, when they all got back from church. I could just say, "Thanks, I've got enough on Christmas trees now. Appreciate your hospitality. Hope your problems work out."

Hope you have a nice life, Nell. You're too honest and too smart to pretend the killer wasn't one of your nearest and dearest. So if he's never caught—well, gee, I hope that doesn't bother you too much. 'Bye.

Good God, I really couldn't leave, could I?

· 24 ·

While Gran napped, I tiptoed to the phone. Once inside old Henry DeGraaf's office, I closed the door. Using my calling number so as not to leave a charge for the DeGraafs to pay, I called Jeb Wine at his home in Winnetka. He would not be in the office on Sunday, hot-shot attorney or no.

Jeb was a partner at Katz, Wheeler and Wine. His friends, including me, referred to the firm as Cadge, Wheedle and Whine.

Jeb isn't the guy I'd call if I'd just been accused of murder and needed a tame tiger to defend me. But if I ever make zillions writing freelance—about as likely as my playing for the Chicago Bulls—he is the person who can tell me what to do about taxes.

"Jeb, I need some advice."

"Do you know it's Sunday morning?"

"What a coincidence. It's Sunday morning here, too."

"I charge quintuple for Sunday morning."

"And the next time your daughter needs a female journalist to take to school for role-model show and tell—"

"Go ahead with the question."

"Actually, there are several questions. I'm on a Christmas tree farm in Michigan—"

"Hey! I'm about to go out and buy a tree. What do you recommend?"

"Ask for a Frazer fir. But Jeb, a Christmas tree? You're Jewish."

"I have blue and silver ornaments. Frazer fir, huh?"

"Jeb—why would a family with a lot of farmland be in danger of losing it, when the farm ordinarily makes enough to pay taxes?"

"Oh-oh. Now let *me* ask the questions. Who are the family members?"

"An elderly mother whose husband recently died, her three children, four grandchildren, some others."

Again he said, "Oh-oh. They on an urban fringe?"

"Suburban. There's a mall three miles away."

"Oh-oh. Sentimental value?"

"Been in the family for a hundred and fifty years."

"The adult children know they could sell for serious money?"

"Yes."

"They don't all agree that they should?"

"I assume not."

"Do they have other large assets?"

"I don't think so."

"Big incomes?"

"No. Regular incomes, but small."

"The father make any estate plans before he died?"

"He was going to put some kind of restriction on the land, but he died too soon. Actually, one family member thinks he was murdered."

"Oh, *shit!* Here we go again!"

"What?"

"Cat, you need to know that they are in the middle of the same thing as a huge number of people in this country. This generation is the first in this nation's history that can't just leave the farm to their children."

"Why?"

"Taxes. It's a disaster. Not just a disaster to the family. Once a working farm is gone, its contribution to scenic beauty, open vistas, and produce are gone forever. For any community that wants to preserve the quality of life, this is a disaster."

"Why? Why? Jeb, I don't get it."

"Let's assume your people have land worth a million dollars, if it was sold to a 'developer.' "

"Okay, let's assume that."

"But they want to keep it. Suppose the present owner—"

"Gran."

"Gran dies. The estate is valued at a million dollars for tax purposes. Six hundred thousand dollars' worth is allowed to pass to her children untaxed."

"That's a lot of money, Jeb. Two hundred thousand for each of them."

"Remember it's land, not cash."

"Oh, right."

"Now, the tax on the remaining $400,000 is $200,000. I'm rounding off, here."

"Sure. Be my guest."

"In other words, they have to pay the government $200,000, and they have to do it within nine months according to the regs. So where does that money come from?"

"Not from their incomes. They're not rich."

"So where?"

"Jeez. Yeah, each one of them would have to come up with $66,666, which is a lot more than they have. They have to sell land."

"Right. Plus, they have to sell it fast, which means not waiting for the best price. Get me?"

"Yes. Isn't there anything they can do?"

"Yeah. They can get a large chunk of the value out of the

estate ahead of time, by giving away a conservation easement. All that means is they deed a right to some conservation group to enforce certain restrictions on the land,
like no new building. That reduces the value of the land. If
the restrictions are severe enough, the value of the land
may be so low that the estate taxes are insignificant."

"That sounds great."

"Well, there are subtleties."

"Aren't there always."

"Like finding a conservation group willing to accept,
and so on. But if they do it right, they could go on farming,
but no one, in perpetuity, could develop."

"That's what Henry wanted to do. I'm sure of it."

"You see the disadvantage for the children?"

"Yes. They can't sell the land, because after they give
the easement to the conservation group, it's not worth
much. So—since Gran isn't rich, anyway—they don't inherit any money or anything they can sell for money."

"Exactly. On the other hand, if they have no easement
and sell the whole thing when Gran dies, let's say they
could get a million. Take out the $200,000 they pay the
feds—there will be some state and local blood money
owed here, but forget that for the time being—and suddenly they have $800,000."

"Which is $266,666 for each of them. More than a quar-
ter of a million dollars."

"Right."

"And all they have to do is give up their home and let
the family farm be destroyed."

"You got it."

*   *   *

I met Marie's car in the driveway when she got back from church. "I've got to talk with you. And Hank and John."

Marie slammed her car door. "Has something else happened? Is it Mom?"

"No, no. She's fine. I just want to talk about a problem where she can't overhear."

Together we walked to John's car, which he had pulled into the garage. Marie said, "Mother's all right, but Cat wants to tell us something."

John's face fell into worry lines. He said, "Okay. Nell, can you go inside with Gran?"

I said, "Nell knows about it."

By now Hank's wagon with Jennifer and the three boys was turning the corner off the main road.

"And Hank, too," I said.

The five of us walked to the barn, Hank, John, Marie, Nell, and I. Jennifer showed no desire to come along. We pulled the aluminum chairs into a semicircle. Then everybody stared at me except Nell, who already knew what was coming. She had her arms wrapped around her chest and was staring at the floor.

"All right," Hank said. "What the hell is this?"

So I told them about the vest.

When I finished, John said, "Wait, wait, let me ask—"

Hank interrupted. "I don't get it."

And Marie said, "Let's get this straight. You think somebody intentionally hid the down vest so that Dad would be caught in the insecticide? In other words, you think somebody murdered my father?"

"Yes. It's not so much what I think as what the evidence points to."

"Now wait," John said. "Anybody could have thrown that vest up there, just for fun."

"Why would they? Did you?"

"Well, no—"

"Did any of you?"

John said "No," Marie said "Of course not," and Hank shook his head.

"But what a minute," John said. "Hank's kids are always clowning around. Maybe one of them threw the vest up there just to be funny."

"Hey!" Hank said. "Cal clowns around some, but I don't like you blaming it on him. I was there all day and he didn't—"

I said, "And anyway, why? When? I've been told it was on its peg on Easter Sunday. You all went to church, and then came back here. Right?"

They nodded.

"Then you ate Easter dinner, and sometime along in there it started to rain?"

Marie said yes. John thought so. So did Hank.

"So did anybody even go out to the barn, after it started to rain?"

John said, "I don't know."

Marie said, "Only Dad. He always went out into the fields in the morning and the evening. He loved the farm."

Her eyes filled with tears, but she shook her head and stopped herself from crying. "He came back in a while, after the rain started."

"So the jacket would have been wet?"

"Sure, I guess so."

"So if it was wet, *why* would one of the boys put it on and then go to the barn and throw it into the loft?"

Hank rumbled, then spoke. "They didn't. They were wearing suits for Easter. Dad changed into more casual clothes because he was home, but the boys didn't. They wouldn't put a vest on over their suits. And as far as I remember, they didn't go to the barn."

John groaned. "Oh, God."

"So," I said, "between then and the next morning, some unknown person took that vest and threw it into the loft. And probably soon after your dad went out in it, because it was still wet when it was thrown up there."

"How do you know?" Hank got to his feet. "I'm gonna go look!"

"I don't think you should do that. You should let the police look at it first."

"What difference does it make? You've been up there."

"The more people who go up, the more likely they'll confuse the evidence."

"You know what I think? I think I'm getting pretty tired of you interfering in our business."

Softly, Nell said, "That's not fair."

I said, "I sure don't want to interfere. This just happened."

"Well, maybe you'd better leave us alone to figure it out, then!"

"Make our own decision," John said.

"Look, I can't simply forget I saw it."

"I think she's right," Marie said.

"Well, I don't see that we *have* to tell the police about this. They could have found it themselves. They've tied up our barn for a whole day! Why look for trouble?"

"That's a good question," John said. "They can investigate Luis's death without this to confuse them. Think what this would do to Mother!"

Marie said, "She'd have to face the idea that somebody murdered Dad."

"Yeah, plus," Hank said, "it's gonna make us all look really bad."

Well, now he was beginning to realize the implications, at least.

"But we're talking about your *father!*" I said.

"Moving a vest isn't really a method of murder," John said. "What if Dad had waited ten minutes longer to go out in the fields? We don't know for sure that it was intended as murder at all."

Nell spoke again. "Remember when somebody locked him in the barn?"

John started to say, "That was an accident . . ." but his voice trailed away. Then we all sat silent. I was proud of Nell. She could look straight at facts, even if she didn't like them. At least two minutes passed. John rubbed his eyes. Hank groaned and put his head in his hands.

Marie finally said, "I'll go call the sheriff."

"Why didn't you tell me, Nell?"

"I did, Daddy. Right after Grandfather died. I said he wouldn't make a mistake like that. And you said it was just an accident."

"I guess I did, at that. But why didn't you tell me about this now?"

"I was—it was just too—I didn't want to worry you, and I know that was stupid now, but it seemed like I should find out whether I was just being silly and there really was no problem, you know, so I asked Cat."

"Okay, honey." He thought a moment. "This should never have become your burden. You did fine."

"Daddy, we'd better go explain to Gran."

John said, "Maybe we can keep it from her. The sheriff can certainly look at the vest without involving her."

I said, "No way. You might hold off until you see what the sheriff thinks, but you'll only get a short delay. I can't imagine him disregarding evidence in your dad's death, especially with Luis so obviously murdered. And soon after he gets into it, he's going to want to know what your mother remembers about that Easter weekend."

Within half an hour, VanLente was back at the barn with an evidence tech. The police car parked square in the driveway, and the white panel truck that the evidence tech came in took up a position directly in front of the barn. Between them, they emphasized the return of the heavy hand of the law. I felt more and more burdened by what I had done.

VanLente interviewed each of the family singly again, this time about the death of their father, or husband, or grandfather, Henry DeGraaf.

Too saddened to stay in the house, I walked out into the fields, which lay green and gold under the late afternoon sun.

I walked through the first field of Scotch pines closest to the barn, the ones that were up to about my forehead, five-footers, in other words. They were a yellow-green, a beautiful brassy color in the gold light. Hank had told me growers touched them up with green dye for sale. Beyond that was a field of little ones. My favorites were in the next field, the blue spruce.

This particular field was six-foot blue spruce. They could be harvested the next year, but would be even more valuable the year after. By then they would be big, grand Christmas trees, almost seven feet. They were so regular, all conical, upright, with evenly spaced branches and evenly colored blue-green needles, that I had to admit someone could say they looked artificial.

Not to me, however. They looked brave. There is something so feisty, so courageous, about a plant that stands right up and looks back at the sky through sun and rain and snow and wind, that you just have to smile at it. All these soldierly blue trees with their arms out straight and their heads tall and rising. By now they'd gone through years of sleet storms, high winds, and baking heat.

They smelled wonderful. I stopped to distract myself, sampling all the other odors of the field—moist sandy soil, distant scents of the lake shore. Chickadees sat on the pine branches and chattered at me. The old settlers said that chickadees could be tamed.

Can you actually love land? I thought so. This was a living world. It was not a parking lot, or a street. Not yet. A hawk drew a half circle in the sky. Quite suddenly, he folded his wings and went into free fall. Somewhere a mouse had been incautious, had ventured out into the open, and the hawk had seen it.

A breeze sprang up, and the pines waved at me. I walked as far as the driveway and sat down on the cool sand, with my back against the trunk of one of the eleven oak trees, a trunk that was nine feet around.

"I have decided to stay in the United States, dear Katya," Hendrik wrote in the letter I had read last night, when I was trying to get to sleep.

We have a new baby now, named Hendrik. Gerritt was named after Pieterke's father, and the new boy is named for mine and, I suppose, for me. Pieterke is well enough, but much weakened, and I can only hope she will recover quickly, as I intend to have a large family.

Intend indeed! I thought. Much weakened indeed! Having a baby in the middle of the wilderness, after months of being fed only on cornmeal mush!

> *The beets are up and growing, and the carrots. I am told this sandy soil is good for potatoes, as it fails to harbor many of the potato diseases, and the church has given me a half bushel of sprouted potato eyes, which I have planted this day.*
>
> *I have great hope. It seems to me now that I cannot subject my sons to the constrictions of life in the Netherlands, where their future would be no more than mine. This is a broad, big country, and by working very hard on the land here, we shall establish a grand farm. Gerritt, I should think, will inherit the farm from me, and Hendrik will most likely either buy an adjoining farm or go into business. There is talk now of a railroad from Chicago through the town of Holland to a small port north of here, called Grand Haven. If this comes to pass, we will easily be able to market crops to Chicago, and as Chicago is the rail hub of the United States, from there to all of this huge country.*
>
> *It is the children I must think about, dear Katya, not how long all this will take, or the work, but the children.*

"Hi!" said Aunt Clara.

"Yikes! You scared me. I didn't hear you coming." I clambered to my feet.

"I couldn't stand the atmosphere in the house anymore," she said.

"Neither could I."

"Have you read the letters?"

"Yes. I was thinking how Hendrik would have hated this scandal."

"He wouldn't have understood," Clara said. "He would have thought the family would always follow the straight and narrow."

"And I think he followed the straight and narrow himself."

"I suppose."

I said, "Yes. Given the attitudes of the time."

"So you don't think Katya was a lady friend?"

"Not in the sense of a romantic involvement," I said. "The tone isn't right. He would not be talking to a lady friend about what doubts about the future to share with Pieterke and what not. He would either say 'Pieterke wouldn't understand what I'm writing to you' meaning that the other woman was superior to Pieterke, or 'Pieterke is too gentle, too wonderful to bother with such thoughts,' meaning that he was wise to leave the other woman and come here with Pieterke to find their fortune."

"Isn't that an awfully modern way of looking at it?"

"Do you think human nature has changed?"

"Well, no. All right. I suppose I agree with you."

"Who else would he be writing to? Who else would be named Katya?"

"Well, like I said, there was a Katherine, who was an aunt."

"Mmm. Maybe."

"And a Katinka, who was a teacher. Twenty years older than he, and some sort of second cousin. Certainly not a romantic interest."

"Teacher? That's promising. Teacher of what?"

"Of writing."

"That's her!"

"Why do you say so?"

"Because of his descriptions. He describes the trunks of beech trees as being like elephant's legs. Don't you see? He's showing her how well he can write."

"Oh, my, yes. Yes. It could be. There's a family story that Hendrik had wanted to be a professor of literature."

"Why didn't he?"

"My dear child. In those days in the Netherlands you didn't just decide to be a professor when you had been born a farmer. That just didn't happen. He would have had Katya as a teacher in what we over here would call grade school. I doubt he ever went beyond a fifth- or sixth-grade level, if that."

"But he had aspirations. He wished for more. Poor Hendrik."

"Well, he came here because he chose to," she said.

"Yes," I said. "And he found the future he was looking for. He found it for his children, didn't he?"

· 25 ·

Sunday dinner was a large farm-style meal at four o'clock. We gathered around the big dining room table, with a white cloth and blue-and-white cloth napkins, as the dusk thickened outdoors, the yellow light deepening from pale tea to the color of maple syrup. Sheriff's deputies continued to measure and sample the barn.

There was a huge beef roast, easily ten pounds. Gran eyed me, thinking, I'm sure, that her Chicago guest had expected another Phoenix-like reincarnation of the turkey. There was a gravy boat the size of a small canoe, full of rich brown sauce, about fifteen pounds of mashed potatoes, hot slaw, peas, and rolls.

In other words, everything that could be done to make the meal seem normal had been done. Gran had cooked most of it, her fainting spell earlier in the day notwithstanding, and Aunt Clara had done the rest.

It looked normal, but it was *not* normal. It was horribly tense and awkward. Marie kept glancing at an empty chair. Quite suddenly, I realized that the one chair they always left open was the one at the head—the place where Henry must have sat through all the years of his adult life. He would have sat there last Thanksgiving. He was gone now, and now nobody could evade the knowledge that he was murdered.

Nobody said so. Nobody said anything about it.

For a long time nobody said anything at all.

"We grew apples here up to twenty years ago, Cat," Aunt Clara remarked conversationally as John carved the roast, putting a thick, juicy slice on each plate. "It was quite a struggle, though. Apples have every kind of insect and disease you can imagine. Getting a perfect-looking apple was terribly difficult. When we picked, naturally we kept the ones with apple scab and insect bites and so on for ourselves and marketed the other ones."

"We still have three or four apple trees next to the back of the barn," Gran said. "Good apples. Winesaps and Green Transparents."

"I remember when I was young," Clara went on, "DDT was considered a miracle. It would do away with insects. It was going to replace all the awkward substances we'd been using—nicotine, sulphur sprays. It was going to bring in a new era of plenty for all Americans. Plentiful food, inexpensively produced."

"Yes. I remember, too," Gran said. She passed the potato bowl, and after it the gravy boat.

Marie said, "And then of course, after they'd been using it for twenty years, they started to hear about the bad effects of DDT. Dad decided to raise more pines."

Equally conversationally, John said to me, "Cat, for the purposes of your article, I want you to know we're into integrated pest management these days. We don't use grass killers here on our land, even though a lot of growers do. Or pre- and post-emergent herbicides. We just till through twice a year to keep weeds down. Chemical insecticides are used surgically, only when they're needed. When you know the crawlers are emerging, for instance, you have two or three days to get them, and you don't spray willy-nilly after that, the way they used to."

He stopped abruptly when he saw most of the rest of the family averting their eyes or staring at their plates. The "surgical" use of pesticides was exactly the reason why someone could sabotage Henry DeGraaf. They knew the spray schedule within a couple of days. We all ate a few bites of beef. It was delicious. The potatoes were wonderful, the gravy was rich with beef juices and a large dollop of butter. But in my mind there was dread.

John stumbled on. "Uh—and we use biological controls now wherever we can. Dormant oil. Some botanicals. You know, certain insects won't eat a plant that's sprayed with lemon extract, for instance. Insects decide what to eat largely on the basis of scent."

I said, "Integrated pest management."

"Oh, absolutely. We always opt for conservative management. This is where we *live,* after all. I don't want to use something that causes, uh, cancer in twenty years. My *daughter* lives here!"

"It's different when you intend to go on living on the land," Marie said. "You treat the earth differently. It's a member of the family."

They were maintaining an appearance of normalcy, but the horror was in their voices, half a tone higher than usual. They were awkward; they didn't converse, they lectured. And Hank's boys, Cal, Don, and Dan, said nothing at all. I was surprised when Nell spoke.

"That's what Mom used to say."

"What, honey?" John said.

"Well, we had a social studies section in fifth grade on the early settlers in the United States. I mean, as they moved from the east coast where they settled first toward the west. They used to say 'cut down, wear out, walk off' about the land."

"They thought it was inexhaustible," Marie said.

"Yes, but it isn't. Let me read you something."

Nell jumped out and ran away from the table and up the stairs. We all just waited. Nell, I supposed, was trying to distract everybody, too. She came back with a brochure.

"Mom used to like this," she said. "This is the tea party scene from *Alice in Wonderland*. It's printed in a brochure from the West Michigan Environmental Action Council. The one Mom worked for."

John blinked and passed his hand over his face. Nell read:

"'Then you keep moving around, I suppose?' said Alice.

'Exactly so,' said the Hatter, 'As the things get used up.'

'But when you come to the beginning again?' Alice ventured to ask.

'Suppose we change the subject,' the March Hare interrupted, yawning. 'I'm getting tired of this.'

"See?" Nell said.

Marie said, "I do see. I like it. You have to give to the land if you stay on it. You can't wear it out and walk off if you're planning never to walk off."

"And," Nell said, "Mom said if we treat the land well, it will treat us well. And we can live here always."

I saw a look of pain cross John's face. He said, "That's true, honey, as far as it goes, but first you have to be able to live." He leaned toward her, as if just nearness would help her to understand his view.

"In Europe, in the old days," he continued, "a family could just own a huge tract of land forever and ever. A baron would be like a small king on his estate, and then his son after him, and his son after him, and his son after him. And no peasants, no matter how hard they worked, would ever have a chance to own even a piece of it. They worked the land their whole lives, but never owned the ground they labored on."

"We've gotten far away from that," Marie said.

"But that was the reason for fairly stiff land taxes in this country. So that nobody would become a land baron and hold onto land like a dog in the manger, without contributing anything back for other people. If you have land, you pay taxes on it and the taxes go to benefit the county or the township. They go to schools and roads. If you hold the land, you have to pay and benefit the other people, and if you can't pay, you sell it and give somebody else a chance."

"That isn't the point, John!" Marie said. "The point is the world's different now from when those laws were made. What we need now is to preserve the remaining land as raw land. It benefits everybody when we keep the woods as it's been for thousands of years. It maintains the pool of animals and plant life. It maintains diversity, it generates oxygen. The forest detoxifies all kinds of poisons for everybody, but *we have to pay for it, not the public!*"

"Well, maybe the government ought to realize that and give people specific benefits—or tax rebates or something—for holding land in pristine condition."

"Good Lord, John, don't you understand? Of course they should! But they *don't*. And we're living right now, not twenty years from now, when every acre that's green may be precious! We're going to be forced to sell! And we are going to lose our home, and the woods is going to be leveled, and the oak trees cut, and the earth paved, and the creek will be 'landscaped' and tamed and killed!"

"That's all very well," John said, his voice throbbing with intensity, "but my child needs money for her survival." He meant it with all his heart. I had been less aware than I should have been of John's fierce love for Nell because of my own partisanship of the child. I had been taking the attitude that nothing was good enough for her, even her father, but in fact she was the world to him.

"Oh, horsepukky!" Hank said. "She's got you to provide for her, while she's young. You've got a good job. And besides, like I tell the boys, they have to learn to make their own way in life. Learn a trade. Get out and work. Like our ancestors did."

"My daughter will start her life with more than Hendrik DeGraaf!"

"But I want to live *here*," Nell wailed, sounding for the first time since I'd met her like a ten-year-old child, not a thirteen-year-old. "Grandfather was going to keep it for us forever!"

"He'd have kept the land, honey," her father said. "But without any inheritance."

"The land and the house and our home!" Marie said.

Gran said, "It was a very foolish notion of your father's, Marie. He was going to give it all away."

"No, Mother, he was going to keep it!" Marie said.

"He was going to give away the value of it. He'd keep it locked up as a farm forever, even if we needed the money terribly badly. He was wrong."

"This is my *home*," Marie said sadly, sounding very much like Nell. "You couldn't sell it. You just couldn't possibly, Mother."

"If he put those restrictions on, we couldn't ever have changed our minds later. This way, we can decide for ourselves."

"Mother, you never understood. The decision *has* to be made ahead or not at all. If you were to die suddenly— heaven forbid, but we have to think about this—but if you were to die suddenly, now, we'd *have* to sell, just to pay taxes."

"But you'd have the money," Gran said.

"But I'd have lost my home! Mother, I have tried hard not to say anything about this, but you're *wrong*. You're stubborn and unreasonable. You didn't grow up here, and you don't understand!"

"Marie! Don't speak to me that way—"

Hank yelled, "Shit, Marie, you don't even live here!"

Gran gasped and said "Hank!" about his language, but Marie was sobbing now. "I love it here. I always thought I'd move back when I got older. I want to retire here. I want to spend my last years here!" Tears were running down her cheeks, and Nell was crying, too. "I love the farm. I'm only—I'm only *camping out* where I live now. *Someday I'm coming back!*"

Aunt Clara, who had not uttered a word since bringing up the subject of DDT, said quietly, "I am, too." She had grown up on this land, of course.

Hank's wife, Jennifer, pointed her finger at her sons, Cal, Don, and Dan, beckoned sharply, rose, and left the room. They got up and followed her out. This was a woman who truly hated confrontation. Or did she, perhaps, hear the prison doors clanging shut, like I did?

For reasons of strict politeness I should have left the room, too. I was an outsider; they had forgotten I was even here. It was rude and callous to stay. But I was paralyzed.

I knew now who had killed Henry and Luis.

I ached. My eyes prickled, and I didn't know whether it was tears or anger. My chest felt like I'd taken in a breath but couldn't exhale. I tried to swallow the bite of beef in my mouth but could hardly taste it, and my throat didn't work.

Hank's fair skin was turning a bright pink. He said, "Land is just an *asset!*"

Marie said, "Land is a living thing!"

Tears were running down Nell's face.

John whispered to Nell, "Would you like to leave the table?" but she shook her head, still crying.

"We could keep the house," John said. "By selling some of the farm, we'd have enough money to pay estate taxes and land taxes."

Marie said, "Don't be stupid! I've already explained this to you. You'd have to sell a little more of the farm every year. Ten acres now, ten acres next year. 'Development' would creep closer and closer to the house. In five years we'd have neighbors where the barn used to be and pavement up to the door, and that's if it doesn't turn into a shopping mall! You want to look out at night and see McDonald's fifty feet away?"

"That won't happen."

"That's what's happened four miles from here!"

Nell put her head down and sobbed.

"Now you see what you've done!" John shouted. "You've put these ideas in Nell's head, and she'll—"

"I've *never* spoken about this to Nell."

"No, Daddy. She hasn't."

"Your mother then."

"Partly. But Daddy—it's really just me."

Oh, my God.

John. So fond of his child. Willing to do almost anything for her. Just like Hendrik, who gave up his native land, and his relatives back home, and all the hours of his life, tilling the sandy soil to make a future for his children.

I looked into his face—his scholarly, well-meaning face—and knew he had killed two people. It was John who had killed his father and a hardworking, innocent young man.

• 26 •

Nell took her father's hand, and he smiled at her. He put his other hand over hers and held on.

Oh, my God, what should I do?

I swallowed, feeling like I was swallowing a huge clot of blood. I must have looked like I felt, because John said, "Oh, Cat, I'm sorry. We shouldn't have dumped our family troubles on you."

"No, no. Don't even think about it." My voice sounded reedy to me. "Listen—" I turned to Gran. "The roast beef was delicious. But let me go out for a little walk, so that you can talk without an outsider at your table."

Gran looked at my plate. I'd eaten most of the beef and all of my potato, so she was satisfied. "We'll call when dessert is ready," she said, gracious in the face of every-thing.

I fled.

When dessert was ready? Lord! How could I possibly eat?

Get in the car and leave! That was the thing to do. Go upstairs, pick up LJ in his cage. He'd love to get back to the apartment, where he could fly free. Get in the Bronco and head home to Chicago.

The DeGraafs' problem wasn't my problem. I didn't cre-ate these people. I didn't create the disaster they were re-acting to. I could always write an article on the crisis of the

family farms and the loss of open lands and woods. Sure.
That was the real way to help. That would get the message
out to a lot of people. This particular family was just a
bunch of ten people. What did they matter in the larger
scheme of things?

Plus, even if the DeGraafs never knew who had killed
Henry and Luis, that was their problem, wasn't it, not
mine? It certainly wasn't *my* fault if they went through the
rest of their lives wondering, and suspecting each other. I
didn't cause this to happen.

And anyhow, wasn't it better for them all to suspect each
other than for Nell to know—to know for sure—that her
own father was a killer? A particularly nasty murderer?

Of course it was.

She'd be better off if she never knew.

Uh-huh. Sure. Lying and covering up the truth was my
mission in life, was it? That's why I went into journalism in
the first place?

Wait. Hold it. I can't stand this.

I won't do it. It's not fair for me to have to make this decision. Why can't I just let Sergeant VanLente do his job?
Either he figures out who killed Henry and Luis or he
doesn't. That's his job. What do we pay taxes for?

And Nell would hate me if I got her father convicted.

Is that a reason?

That's really totally chickenshit, isn't it?

One way or another, I was getting out of here soon.
Even if I didn't run out tonight, I was scheduled to leave
in the morning, to follow the Monday shipment of
Christmas trees going to Chicago, to watch how they were
shipped and then marketed. I couldn't stay longer and—
oh, lord!—I couldn't leave John loose in the family any
longer, either. Suppose he decided to kill another person?
Suppose one of Hank's boys had noticed something suspi-

cious—or just got to thinking about it? Dan, maybe, who struck me as an observer, not a talker. They knew John much better than I did, and they knew the other family members. They could come to the same understanding I had. And if they let on, he might kill them.

I discovered I was leaning against one of the old oak trees. And it was starting to snow.

What should I do?

I had to decide. Now.

The falling snow both hid and revealed the soft landscape. The woods in the distance had changed again, this time to a chalk and charcoal sketch, quickly done, on rough paper, with lots of white showing through.

If I convinced VanLente that John was the killer, the consequences to Nell would be hideous. Her father would be taken away from her, the third loved figure in her life that she would lose in the space of three years. That was the kind of horror a person never really recovered from.

But truth had to be served, didn't it? It was right to accuse a guilty person, not wrong. Hurtful, but not wrong. It was Right with a capital R. The hurt was the result of someone else's wrongdoing, not mine.

Suddenly I imagined I actually saw old Hendrik, out in the field in the snow. He was digging, and I imagined all the years he would have spent doing exactly that on this land, these very grains of sand turned over and over, on the surface one year, under the roots of the cabbage the next year, digging, digging, turning the leaves under in the fall to enrich the earth, to make it less sandy and more fertile. I had tried digging half a dozen shovelfuls, and it was hard work. I could not even imagine the effort involved in hand-digging a whole acre. And after he had first broken the sod with a borrowed horse and plow, he had kept ten or fifteen acres in food crops.

Out of all that labor, that investment of all the hours of his life, wasn't there something he could say to me?

Talk to me.

I had little in common with the man, I hoped. A different century, different values. I didn't even like him much, if you can like or dislike a person dead a hundred years before you were born. He was rigid, bigoted, authoritarian, paternalistic, self-righteous—and lord knows I tried not to be any of those things, although I suppose one never is aware of the ways in which one is self-righteous.

Was I being self-righteous to say that truth was more important than comfort for Nell?

But I kept seeing him, Hendrik, standing upright, rigid as a red oak, wearing blue bib overalls, leather boots so stiff the ankles wouldn't bend, a long beard, and a frown. You would know all about sinful ways, Hendrik. Wasn't that what you heard about every Sunday, the deadly sins? Lust, greed, envy. Sloth, pride, gluttony, anger. Both Marie and Hank contained quite a bit of anger.

Sloth surely was not one of the DeGraafs' sins. But some of them went in for greed. What was this murder for? Greed? Greed on John's part? Sell the land, make a profit, move on? Greed for a house and land? No, not greed, but it was pride in a way—pride in one's own family, his daughter, who would carry on the next generation. A type of pride that valued her above the lives of other people.

What should I do?

What about it, Hendrik?

And then Hendrik came striding toward me. Not an evocation from a collection of letters and swirls of snow, but a real man, coming from the edge of the field.

He had appeared as an image on photographic paper

might, because of the intervening snowflakes. First he was a pale image, white-flecked brown on a white-flecked tan background of sand. As he drew closer, and less snow danced in the air between him and me, I could see that he wore leather boots of a darker brown, and a tan coat that swirled in the light breeze. He carried a hoe, I thought, but now there came an eddy of thick snow and there were snowflakes on my eyelashes, and even though he drew closer, my vision was increasingly poorer.

"Do you always stand out in the snow with no coat, Ms. Marsala?"

"Sergeant VanLente!"

"Did I frighten you?"

"Not exactly. It's more like—more like seeing Nemesis."

"If you say so."

I took a shuddering breath. Before I could let cowardice get the better of me again, I said, "I think we should talk."

"Come into my office." He strode to the barn. Inside it was warm. He had built a small fire in the wood stove, as the DeGraafs had urged him to do when he worked there. He gestured at the porch chairs and sat in one, putting the yardstick he had been carrying against the chair.

"So what's the problem?"

I was too upset to sit. I paced to the stove and back. The evidence tech was nowhere to be seen. Was I about to be a Judas? Or a righteous person?

"I know who killed Luis. And Henry, too."

"Who?"

"John DeGraaf."

VanLente crossed his legs. "And just how do you know this?"

"Look, are we agreed that the killer was one of the DeGraafs?"

" 'Are we agreed'? I don't think you and I have agreed to much of anything. You're not really part of the investigation team, Ms. Marsala."

I stepped on my anger, with difficulty. This was hard enough without VanLente acting like an ass. But there was nothing to be gained by trying to improve this jerk right now.

He said, "What do you care if I agree? I thought you said you *knew* who killed them."

"I do. I do. I just wish I didn't." Suddenly I started to cry. I knew I was going to, and I couldn't stop it. I was absolutely humiliated. I was a professional, and what was more important, there were people with real trouble to be considered.

"Hey!" VanLente said. "Here, sit down. Don't take it so hard."

He shoved me into a chair and got a Kleenex out of his pocket. I wiped my eyes. Sagging into a chair, I decided to go ahead.

I got my breath. "All right. Let me tell you the sequence of events. Nell's grandfather, Henry DeGraaf, loved his farm. He loved the land, not just the productive part of the farm, but also the woods and the creek. The actual trees and earth. Because the land has gone up and up in value, he knew that when the day came that he and his wife both died, the family wouldn't be able to pay their inheritance taxes without selling it, either piecemeal or all at once for 'development.' Saving just the house, which they might be able to do, wouldn't be the same. In ten years they'd be in the middle of a suburb. He could save it all by putting certain irrevocable restrictions on the land, which would avoid most of the inheritance taxes, but that would also make the land effectively unsalable for the children."

"Yeah, okay. I like money as a motive, but why kill Henry right then?"

"He was about to make this irrevocable change."

"Okay. I'll buy that."

"And to make it more urgent, Mrs. DeGraaf isn't well. She has some kind of heart rhythm problem. Ruth DeGraaf disagreed with Henry, but she would have gone along with her husband. She was raised that way, and she's a traditionalist. Or if she died first, that would still leave Henry free to make the property change. It was only if Henry died first, before making the change, that John was in good shape, because Mrs. DeGraaf always wanted to consider the land an asset. It wasn't *her* ancestors who settled here, after all."

"Even if you're right so far, it applies to all the children equally."

"It doesn't apply to Marie at all. She wants to keep the farm forever. I didn't realize that at first. I had her pegged wrong. But I know now that she does."

"Hank, then?"

"Hank would like to inherit the farm and sell it for the money, but he's not rabid about it. Hank has a good job, and he also has the notion that his boys should go out and work for their money like he did. And deep down, he's just not as fond of his children as John is. He's a cold man in some ways. John loves his daughter beyond anything."

"I'm supposed to believe he's the most likely killer because he loves his daughter so much?"

"There's another indication. I know it's weak—"

"Go on."

"Hank loves wood. Furniture. He's basically an Old World craftsman. I've known people like that. They love what they can do with their hands, and well-made things, and good materials, much more than they love people."

"So?"

"I don't think he'd have thrown a soaking wet down vest onto an antique table up in the loft."

"Oh, come on! He was thinking murder! He's gonna be upset about the finish on a table?"

"We're talking a lifetime habit here, VanLente. All he had to do was hurl it a little farther to the left and it'd have landed on the old refrigerator. Nobody was hurrying him. Nobody else was hanging around the barn that evening. Lifetime habits can be stronger than anything. Like, I always throw my keys in the kitchen drawer when I come home. Usually I'm not even aware of it."

"I'm not convinced."

"Let me go on to the conversation I overheard."

"Now you think the whisperer was John?"

"Yes. And not because I've suddenly decided it sounded like him or anything lame like that. It really leads to what I think is the strongest proof that John killed Henry. In fact, it's so compelling that I don't know why I ever considered anybody else."

"Try me."

"We know from Nell that Luis found the vest by accident when he went up into the loft to get the oil Friday morning. He told Nell about it, because he knew she was already fearful that her grandfather had been murdered. I doubt if he'd have told her otherwise. He seems to have been protective of her."

"Maybe."

"And that's the point. He then went to the person he believed responsible, confronted him, and asked him to give himself up, to 'do the right thing.'"

"All right. Suppose he did? It could have been anybody."

"No, it couldn't. If it had been Marie or Gran, or especially Cal or Hank, he would never have taken that chance. He'd just have turned the person in. Called the cops. There was a reason he went to this effort and risk—to protect Nell. John was Nell's father, and Luis liked Nell. He wanted to give her father the chance to confess in his own way, maybe even work a deal, plea bargain."

"But John killed him."

"John killed him. Asked Luis to wait after work, meet him at the barn so he could explain what he was going to do. But he didn't want to confess, he wanted to survive. He went out to the barn after Hank and his family left, while Gran was napping right before dinner, and knocked him unconscious. He carried him out to the baler. John was lucky they'd been working a field not far from the house. He's not strong, and although Luis wasn't a big man, he wouldn't have been able to carry him far. Then he put him through the baler."

"What did he knock him out with?"

"I assume you didn't find any of the tools had blood or hair on them."

"No."

"Probably with a piece of wood, which he then put in the wood stove. It would either have been burning or still roasting hot."

"So he started the motor on the baler. A Briggs and Stratton gas engine and nobody heard it?"

"Sure they heard it. With all the motorbikes and motorcycles around, who'd notice?"

VanLente stretched, then leaned back in his chair, and the rickety aluminum frame nearly collapsed. He sat forward.

"It's not enough, Ms. Marsala. There's no evidence."

"You can't get a conviction on it, I know—"

"Conviction? I couldn't even get an indictment. The state's attorney would laugh at me. There isn't a particle of physical evidence. I'm not sure it even convinces me, although I have to admit some of it rings true. For instance, everything we turn up on Luis suggests he was a pretty okay guy. But it's just not enough."

"Exactly."

"Exactly what?"

"I have a suggestion."

"A suggestion? Forget it."

"You've made my point for me. You haven't any evidence. I want to suggest a way to trap him."

"Ms. Marsala, I don't even know that he did it at all!"

"Suppose he did, though? Somebody killed two innocent people."

"That's for sure."

"And that somebody became particularly vicious when he thought Luis was going to expose him."

"Yeah. Matter of fact, I agree with your interpretation of that conversation behind the barn. I just don't think it points to any specific person."

"Then let's find out."

"Mmm-mm?" VanLente folded his arms and stared flatly at me. He wasn't going to go for this, unless I sold him just right.

"John—or let's say the killer—could kill again. Next month, the month after that? Suppose young Don suddenly figures out who did it? What does John do then?"

"He kills the kid."

"Yeah."

"Get to the point."

"All right. You and another cop stay in the barn. It's almost dark. Turn the light off in the barn but leave the yard light on as usual. Go away in your car and then come back quietly through the field and let yourself into the barn by the back door, the one that can't be seen from the house. Or have somebody else drive your car away, leaving you here."

"Already I don't like this."

"I'll wait half an hour. Then I'll tell John I need to talk with him alone. I'll intimate that I know he killed Luis and Henry. I'll tell him to meet me outside at the barn. When he gets there, I'll tell him what I know and ask him to give himself up, for Nell's sake. You tape his response, and we've got him."

"No. Nope. No, no, no."

"It's the only way we can stop him."

He unfolded his arms and gripped the arms of the chair. "Look, Ms. Marsala. I don't appreciate being used this way."

"What?"

"I said I don't appreciate being used this way. I know you're a reporter and you have your income to earn and all that, but I don't think it's ethical to exploit a situation like this."

"*Exploit a situation like this?* What the hell are you talking about?"

"You're going to write one of those trashy 'How I Helped the Cops Catch a Killer' pieces. And I won't be a party to it."

"Damn you, VanLente! I hate this whole thing! I would do anything on earth to put the clock back to last spring, and change things, so Nell didn't have to go through this. My only reason—damn it!—the only reason I'm not in my car right now headed south is that I think truth is important."

"Oh, sure."

"I don't do exposé reporting! The stories I do have substance. They're *journalism!*"

"Uh-huh. Sure."

I was absolutely seething, and doing my very best to suppress my anger. On top of the pity I felt for Nell, this was just too much.

"Suppose I could prove it?"

"Yeah, right."

"You have a car phone?"

"Of course."

"Suppose you were to call the Chicago Police Department. Suppose you were to talk with the chief of detectives about me. Would that satisfy you?"

I saw that thin-blue-line look go over his face. They almost all do it—that dividing of the world into two groups, cops and noncops.

I pushed it. "Suppose a fellow police officer told you I was trustworthy? Suppose he said that I don't write that kind of article, and my word is good. What then?"

VanLente took a minute thinking. I've noticed with cops in general that the best bosses don't feel they have to make rushed decisions. They think awhile, and they let you wait while they do it. I respect that.

VanLente said, "I'm willing to talk with him."

Obviously, VanLente wanted to make an arrest.

"You'd better call information in Chicago," I said. "I know the number, but if I give it to you, you'll think it's some sort of setup."

"Even you wouldn't have left somebody in Chicago who

would pretend to be a chief of detectives on the off chance you needed it."

"I could have called somebody from here half an hour ago, though."

"Yeah. That's true. Anyhow, I don't have to call information." He flipped open a small black book. "I keep these in case I get a fleeing felon situation and need a number right away."

"How nice."

What if McCoo wasn't in the office? It was Sunday, after all. I knew his home number, but how was VanLente to know it was really McCoo, if it was just a phone at a house? I needn't have worried. VanLente reached him immediately. McCoo was almost always there, days, and he was there now. VanLente introduced himself, told McCoo I was here, and then laughed at McCoo's response.

"All right, what's so funny?" I said.

"He said, 'Better there than here.' "

"I hope he means that he's glad I'm having a nice change of scene." I took the phone. Okay now, I said to myself. It was important to sound cheerful and competent no matter how I really felt. McCoo knew me too well, and if he caught onto the fact that I was emotionally involved in this, he'd shoot the plan down, just to save me. He always thinks I take unnecessary risks.

"Hi, McCoo."

"What kind of mess have you gotten yourself into now?"

"None at all. In fact, you must realize I am not messing around on my own. I have the Ottawa County Sheriff's Department here."

"Uh-huh."

"So how are you? How's Susanne?"

"Oh, better. She's finished the chemo and her appetite's back. In fact, it's come back more than she'd like, and she's gained fourteen pounds."

"Well, that's good, isn't it? What are you doing?"

"Making coffee." McCoo was the best coffee maker in the world. He had all the equipment in his office—the only luxury items in the office were the Krups grinder and a new Danish pot—and he even had a tiny refrigerator to keep real cream.

"What kind of coffee?"

"Ethiopian Harrar, which is an excitingly light-bodied coffee, a bit gamy, with a lively acidity."

"Sounds like an old boyfriend of mine."

"Listen, Cat, it's lovely to chat on this guy's battery, but you're up to something. What do you want?"

"We have this suspect. I know he's guilty, but Sergeant VanLente says that there isn't enough evidence to prove it, and I agree with him. I just want to tell the suspect I know he's guilty and why I know and ask him out to the barn here to talk. VanLente or his minions would be in the barn waiting to overhear."

"Tell me why this isn't dangerous."

"Well, there are eight or nine people in the house—which is also why we can't talk there—and the barn is only fifty feet away, and the cops would be in the barn, and besides the guy is more treacherous than violent. He killed one person by indirection, you might say, and the second trusted him enough so he could hit him on the head. But he's not awfully physical. I definitely do *not* trust him, and I have backup."

"So I don't get it. What's the problem?"

"The problem is VanLente thinks that I'm doing this to

get a spiffy story. 'How I Lured the Killer to the Barn' in
three thousand words for the *Enquirer*."

"Oh, is *that* all? Well, put him on."

Great. I had succeeded in partly deceiving my best friend.
Now let's see if I could take away the father of an innocent
young girl.

I was trying to hide the weight of dread I was feeling. If
God's bulldozer a mile high had been heading for the
county, I could not have felt more horror. Nell had said,
hadn't she, that in the last ice age there had been a glacier
of ice two miles thick above this land? I felt as if it were
here and now.

I hadn't told VanLente the main reason why I wanted to
lure John out to the barn. I wanted them to arrest him out
of sight of Nell. This night was going to be hell for her either way, but at least she wouldn't have to have the ugly
picture in her memory of him being handcuffed. Would he
struggle? Would he scream? Whatever he did, let's have it
happen outside the house.

There was one other aspect of the case I did not tell
VanLente. It had to do with motive, though, and wouldn't
have helped him prove John's guilt.

I had promised to eat dessert, I told VanLente, so it
would be at least half an hour before I got John alone. It
could be longer, depending on what the family members
intended to do after dinner.

VanLente said, "I can't wait around all that time." Of
course—I should have realized that he was too important.

He agreed to leave immediately and noticeably and
send two men back to the barn on foot. They would be
warmly dressed and would wait in the dark. They would

carry a tape recorder and record what John said to me. They would also carry a radio on which one of them would call VanLente as soon as we got results.

So far so good.

I'd eat dessert and be pleasant. Then, like a Judas, I'd draw John out of the house.

· 28 ·

Peppermint stick ice cream with chocolate sauce. Usually one of my favorite taste combinations. I could hardly stand to smell it, hardly even to look at it. It was grotesquely pink, the melted slush slimy, and the chocolate reddish-brown color could have been old blood. I stirred it, making the whole mess worse.

Gran said, "I just didn't get around to making a pie. And I had all these wonderful Winesap apples—"

"Mom, don't apologize. You weren't feeling well," John said.

Marie said, "Stop worrying, Mom. This is delicious."

I felt lightheaded.

I couldn't take my eyes off John for more than three seconds at a stretch. My ears were playing tricks. Sometimes I heard everything, especially whatever John said, as if it were very loud and very piercing. At other times I missed whole gobbets of conversation.

Nell's face hovered over the ice cream, her fine, reddish blond hair moved slightly by the drifts of air that passed through the dining room. Her pale transparent skin looked so fragile, as if you could see the nerves and capillaries under the surface, capillaries just as thread-like as her hair, struggling to keep her alive. She maintained a chatter of talk, covering up the memory of the argument earlier.

"Don and I can bring up the lights, anyway, and get those on the tree," she said.

Marie said, "Sure. Always put the lights on first and get the cords out of the way as far as possible."

"And can I get a sheet, Gran, for under?"

"Yes, Pieternella."

"Great! Now?"

"Yes, Pieternella. But be sure to get one of the old sheets. Look at the hems for wear."

Marie rolled her eyes, as if her mother had said the same thing every Christmas for forty years.

Dan said, "Can I be excused, Gran?"

"Yes. Go and help Pieternella."

When the children had left, John said, gently, "Cat, we're not forgetting about Luis, you know. But this is traditionally the weekend we decorate the tree."

Was I wrong about him? He looked so untroubled, so much like a person should look who is a bit worried about a nasty event that only touches his family by happenstance. But if there is one thing I've learned in covering crime, it's that looking normal is the easiest thing for people to do. People always say with amazement, "How could she be such a wonderful actress? How could she look exactly like she was mourning her child, when all the time she had killed him!" It's not acting, exactly. Looking normal is normal for people.

Still, futilely wishing for a sign of guilt, some physical confirmation of the evil that was in him, I snatched glimpses of John as we cleared the table. No sign. He made no false moves.

Clara and Marie stayed in the kitchen to put the dishes in the dishwasher. I followed John and Hank into the living room, where the tree stood. Hank groaned theatrically and rubbed his stomach.

"Why do I eat so much? I don't dare sit down. I'll fall asleep."

"It's the holidays," John said.

"I'm gonna take a walk."

"Yeah, sure, go ahead."

Would this throw my plans off? Hank would be out there someplace, and John certainly wouldn't make guilty admissions at the barn if Hank was wandering around nearby.

Then Hank said, "I'm gonna walk down the creek. Maybe all the way to Pigeon Lake."

John said, "It's dark."

Be quiet, John; let him go as far away as he wants.

"No. There's a full moon."

"I guess."

"And I must've walked it ten thousand times already."

Hank went to the back door, just off the kitchen. He said, "Jenn, I'm gonna walk off some calories," and without waiting for her to answer, reached out—reached out to one of the pegs that once must have held his father's orange down vest—took a heavy coat, stuffed his arms into it, and went out the door. He gave not a flicker of a glance at the actual coat peg. There was no hesitation as he took down the coat. This was the real Hank, insensitive to human concerns.

Cal said, "I gotta go over to Ed's."

"You just don't want to decorate the tree," Nell said.

"So?"

From the kitchen, his mother called, "How're you going to get there?"

"Bicycle."

"Be back before nine. We can't wait here all night for you."

John and I were still standing in the living room door-

way with the open living room in front of us. But as if I
were in prison, I could feel another door clang shut behind me. We were closer and closer to the moment when
there would be no more choices at all, only defeat for John
and misery for Nell.

Don and Dan laid the strings of lights out on the floor and
plugged them in. Orange, red, blue, green—they spilled out
like flames across the floor. The two boys went along the
strings looking for burned-out bulbs to replace.

Nell opened one of the five or six boxes of ornaments.
"Oh, Cat, look. These are some of the old ones!"

John and I walked over. My legs felt stiff. Blown-glass
balls lay in a compartmented box. There were silver ones
with indented stars, red glass in the shapes of flames, and
several deep blue teardrops that looked very old, with
some of the metallic color worn off.

John said, "My grandfather bought those before World
War Two. They made most of the blown-glass ornaments
in Germany, then. I remember during the war how careful
we were not to break them. My mother kept saying, 'We
won't have any more of these for a long time to come.'"

"See this one, Cat!" Nell said. "It's got the face of an angel on it."

I felt tears start in my eyes. The face looked like Nell.
"It's beautiful."

Don said, "You got any extra bulbs in there?"

Fortunately he broke the spell, so that I could catch
John's eye and gesture toward the room at the end of the
hall that had been old Henry's office. He followed.

Last chance to back out.

I said, "We can't talk here. But John, I know what Luis
meant Friday night when he asked you to do the right
thing."

*   *   *

I walked quickly out to the barn. Were the deputies in place? It would be dangerous to speak to them, because John would be following any minute, but I glanced in the barn door. Although the interior was very dark, a trapezoid of light fell on the barn floor and for just a couple of seconds a man stepped into the dim light, cocked a thumb up at me, and then stepped back. The other deputy stayed out of sight.

Good. I walked a few feet away from the barn to the edge of the first field, the five-foot Scotch pines. From here I could see the front door of the house and the big door of the barn. The deputies could see me, and I would see John coming, so I could walk forward to meet him, and just naturally place us right in front of the barn door.

There were chickadees calling in the trees.

Absently, my eyes on the door, I reached over and tousled the head of the pine on my left.

The pine on my right exploded.

The human mind is so strange. I saw the needles of the tree fly apart in a cloud. In less than a second, as they whirled around in the vortex, I thought of tornadoes tearing up forests, of parsley whirling in a blender, of sand kicked up by bombs. At the same instant I was dropping to the ground. The trunk of the tree had flown away with the blast.

Then the sound of the blast hit.

A shotgun!

I was already lying on the damp sand. I rolled, trying to get away, but my ears were ringing and I knew my sense of where it had come from wasn't accurate. The chickadees fell silent. A shadow flicked across me. I scrabbled on hands and knees between two trees, then faster until I had put several trees between me and the shooter. Thank God these were pines, dense enough to hide me.

For the moment.

It had to be a large-bore shotgun. Probably that old twelve-gauge of theirs. The blast had torn the whole trunk out of the tree, leaving only the light needles whirling around in the afterdraft. And the sound was loud as a cannon.

Out of the corner of my eye as I had thrown myself to the ground, I had seen a deputy jump into the lozenge of light in the barn doorway. It seemed to me he had then made a sharp move sideways. I couldn't understand why he didn't do something now. Yell "Freeze!" Or even shoot John. What more proof did he need?

Out here it was darker than near the barn. But there was a full moon. The hunter's moon?

Bad thought. I shivered. By staying flat to the ground and looking under the tree, I could see back toward the barn. What I saw chilled me more.

The deputy was lying next to the barn door, his head cocked at an angle to his neck. Now what my eyes had seen, but not interpreted, made sense. He had jumped at the sound of the shot, leaped toward the door, tripped on the gasoline can, falling sideways, and hit his head on the doorframe. No way to tell how badly hurt he was. He was knocked out, and did not move.

There didn't seem to be any other deputy at all.

I crept quietly forward on hands and knees a little farther, then dodged fast from the shelter of one tree to another. Because the trees were laid out in regular rows, each time I dodged to another row I was exposed briefly to anybody who might be standing in the alley I crossed.

But I couldn't stay in one spot, either. For sure, John knew approximately where I was. He had seen me fall, then leap away. He would not know exactly which tree I hid behind, but he'd be damn close. He would have heard me scrabbling away, and he would know within a few trees one way or the other where I was. If he knew exactly, he would already have blasted right through the tree, like he had the first one, and I'd be dead.

The twelve-gauge John had used was a double-barreled shotgun, with side-by-side barrels. He would have one shot left, until he reloaded. Would that give me a chance? Could I draw his fire without getting hit, and then run like hell while he reloaded?

As the thought crossed my mind, I heard a telltale tick-click. Then almost instantly a click-chonk. He'd reloaded.

Judging by the sound, he was over to my right. And close. I tried to see through the branches. There were some small gaps, but when I tried to see through them, the light of the yard lamp got in my eyes. Once I thought I saw a movement, but no detail.

The bastard. He was intentionally keeping the light at his back, so that I was constantly confused when I tried to see what he was about to do. He was woods smart.

City mouse, country mouse. I was a city mouse. In Chicago I was street smart, and I knew how to use the land. Here I was a city mouse being hunted by a country hawk. Would somebody hear the shot and come out? More likely they would think it was a rabbit hunter.

I couldn't get up and run. I couldn't stay here.

"John!" I said.

A blast tore at the ground six inches from my head.

I rolled as the sound of the shot echoed, and now I tried to deflect my voice by blocking the left side of my mouth with my hand. Whether this would work or not I had no idea. He would have one shot left before he loaded again.

"John, this is nuts. They know you're out here. If I'm found dead, they'll know it was you who killed me."

"You think?" he called out. "Matter of fact, Hank is taking a walk. He won't be able to prove where he was. Cal left alone on his bike. Aunt Clara's asleep in the reclining chair. Gran's taking her five o'clock nap. Dead to the world. Nell's okay, of course. Nobody would suspect Nell. She's decorating the tree with Dan and Don. Alibi each other. I made sure of that."

I had been backing away while he was talking, as quietly, I hoped, as a mole tunneling underground. But then he stopped talking for two seconds, and when he spoke again, suddenly his voice was closer to me.

"Don't move!" he said, taunting. "I'm very near."

I shifted slightly and tried to deflect my voice again.

"The deputy saw you come out of the house." Oh-oh. I shouldn't have said that. If he finished me off, he might go back to the barn and kill the deputy, who I now supposed was alone. Too late to take the words back now.

"You think? Nope. I went out the back door and fired the first shot from behind your Bronco."

"The deputy is gonna wake up and go to the house and find that you're missing."

"He's dead to the world. He may even be dead. You're unconscious that long, you've got a concussion, minimum. Whatever testimony he came up with would be worthless."

"There'll be gunpowder residue on your hands."

"Gloves. L.L. Bean. The best."

He was crazy, of course, really, really crazy. There were a dozen places his plan could go wrong. Hank could come back to the house at any moment. Nell could decide to look for her father. VanLente might try to radio the deputy, and when he didn't raise him come in with his mars lights flashing.

The moon was slowly riding toward a patch of ragged clouds. If I could wait here until the moonlight went, I'd have a better chance. Time was on my side in a lot of ways. He couldn't stay out here forever. Hank would come back. But he'd know all that, and he wouldn't wait long. Knowing he was aiming the gun to fire again, knowing he had a good idea where I was, I took a necessary gamble. I turned and sprinted across the open space and into the five-foot trees in the next block. The gun boomed. There was a stinging in my ankle. One of the pellets must have hit there.

"Hold, it, Marsala. You can't get away."

I had run into the five-footers on purpose. I was five-one and he was five-ten or five-eleven. Just bending forward enough to run I was hidden. As long as I stayed behind trees. But unless he bent over a lot, I could see his head above the treetops. And if he stayed bent over very much for very long, he would tire.

It wasn't much advantage, but it was something.

Now I screamed as if I'd been hit, then ran flat out, as fast as I could, for the woods. John would be reloading as he ran after me. I hoped it would slow him down.

When I reached the edge of the woods, there was shadow. I didn't slow down. Briars scratched me, and then low beech branches hit my face. My feet caught in branches, but I bulled ahead. My only chance was to get close to the creek. The creek where Henry died. The creek would make small splashing sounds where it swept over stones or sucked past branches. I would find a place to hide, and the creek noises might cover the sounds of my breathing.

I ducked a thick branch at eye level and my feet tangled in old wood on the forest floor. I fell.

Behind me, John's thudding footsteps were getting close. If I got up, he would hear or see me, but if I stayed where I was, he would find me.

It was snowing. The moon was dimming, swallowed by

snow clouds. And I realized I was wearing a white sweater and white pants. If only I had white hair, he might not see me in moonlight, with woods shadows. My black hair would show against the snowy ground. I heard John swear as a branch snapped in his face.

I pulled the back of my sweater over my head and held still. As near as I could tell, I was lying in a tangle of fallen branches and leaves, all of it heavily dusted with snow. Suddenly, I panicked. What color were my boots? I couldn't even think! Brown, maybe. No, no—white. I remembered. What if the soles were dark? Silently, I burrowed them under some snowy leaves.

I held utterly, perfectly still. My reason for screaming had been to give him the idea I might be seriously hurt. Unfortunately, I had had no choice but to run at the same time—but people have run incredibly long distances with serious wounds and then died. There was a possibility he would think I was dead. I made no sound. Snow fell on my back. I couldn't see anything.

A stick snapped. John was very close.

My back was very cold. Under my body, snow was beginning to melt into my pants and sweater. But I didn't dare shiver. I tried not to breathe.

Leaves rustled. The sound of the creek was just audible. I heard John step past the place where my head lay, blinded under the sweater. I hoped the skin of my back was pale. If he saw me, he would aim the shotgun at my head and blow it apart. A twelve-gauge shotgun at two feet vaporizes a hole the size of a baseball.

Was the gun pointing at my head right now?

He walked past. I heard his feet circle past me, farther into the woods. But not very far.

Then he came back! He knew I was near, but he didn't know where. He stood, dead silent, not three feet away and I could hear him breathe. Could he hear me breathe? The creek whispered. I was willing to smother myself to keep silent, but if I held my breath, sooner or later I would gasp, so I forced myself to take in air very, very slowly, in long inhalations, in-in-in then out. Slowly, through the pores in the sweater, I saw the moonlight decrease.

His feet came closer again. He stood still, listening.

Far away at the house, a door slammed.

"Shit! Shit!" He snarled the words, as if he wanted to scream but didn't dare because somebody might hear him.

Softly, he said, "You'd better be dead, Marsala."

Then he walked away.

• 29 •

I lay in the dark, snow falling on my back, for a long time, blaming myself. I had done everything wrong. My plan had resulted in John raging around with a gun, more violent than he had ever been before, and now he was headed back toward the house, angrier and crazier than when he left.

My ankle throbbed where a shotgun pellet had embedded itself. Several places on my head hurt. Lashes from the branches I had crashed through. Something was trickling into my right eye, and it was probably blood. But lying perfectly still meant survival. I started to shiver. Finally, I began to shiver so hard that I knew anyone within ten feet would have heard the leaves rustling. So I looked out from under the sweater, then sat up. It was totally dark. I stood, pulling down my sweater, but it was coated with snow inside and didn't give me any warmth. I was chilled through.

Should I go to the DeGraafs or cut overland and try to find a neighbor's house? Somebody named Van't Hof lived to the east, but I didn't know exactly where.

Feet dragging, I struck out toward the east, which would take me through the pine fields and across the DeGraafs' driveway, but near the road, not the house. I trembled and shivered, and kept telling myself that was good. When you started feeling warm and stopped shivering, that meant you were sinking into hypothermia, didn't it?

The lights from the DeGraafs' windows glowed up onto snowflakes in the sky as I crossed the driveway. I could not see the house itself. Otherwise the night was dark. If John was waiting for me someplace, I wouldn't see him. Maybe he wouldn't see me, either. But he'd hear me. I tried to walk softly, but there was no strength in my legs now. They scuffed the leaves and dragged on the ground.

I fell again, just to the side of the driveway. It would be very nice just to lie down and sleep here a little while. A person would gain strength with a little rest. Ten minutes would be a nice nap.

No. Get up. I rocked forward onto my hands and knees. There was a light in my eyes. Hallucination?

Flashing lights. Mars lights.

VanLente carried me into his squad car.

"I knew this was a terrible idea," he said. "Now I got a cop injured and you, too."

"The idea was just fine. You told me you'd leave two guys and you left one."

"I should never have got a civilian involved."

"Damn you, VanLente, *you* messed up! Not me! If you hadn't broken your promise, you'd have John in custody and Nell wouldn't have to see whatever happens next! Stupid cop, you can't even keep your goddamn word—" I was trying not to break into tears.

"Screw you, Marsala!"

"Hey, you've already achieved that pretty well, haven't you?"

"Be quiet! We're here."

"And as far as me being hurt, I wouldn't think of telling

anybody around here or going to any goddamn hospital where they might connect me with you. I wouldn't think of getting you into trouble, just because you screwed up!"

"Quiet!"

We pulled up in the front of the DeGraaf house and braked fast. All the lights were blazing, and we had no sooner rocked to a halt than I heard sirens. Flashing lights hit the back of our car. The ambulance. VanLente leaped out, leaving me to fend for myself.

Which I preferred. The hell with him, anyway.

Nell, Marie, and Aunt Clara were bending over the deputy, who lay unmoving, covered up to the neck with a blanket, while Hank and John and the boys stood around. Presumably Jennifer and Gran were inside.

John saw me the instant I emerged from the car. His mouth opened, then closed again grimly. He clearly had hoped I had been shot and was lying dead out there in the snow.

Clara spoke to one of the paramedics as the other knelt near the deputy. All I heard her say was "Confused, but semiconscious."

VanLente stood rigid as a tree while the EMTs assessed the deputy. None of the rest of us moved much either. After three minutes they got a gurney, loaded the man into it, and trundled it with difficulty to the ambulance, the small wheels bogging down in the sandy driveway.

"All right, everybody. Let's go in the house."

VanLente was at his most dictatorial, but I was shivering violently and eager to get out of the cold.

Cal picked this moment to ride up on his bike, yelling,

"What happened now? What's going on?" Nobody answered him. He dropped the bike where he stood and followed us into the house.

As soon as we got inside in the light, Nell and Clara noticed I was shivering and bleeding. Nell said, "Cat! You're hurt!"

"I'm scratched by branches. It's nothing much." I swiped my hand across my face, though, and it came away bloody.

Aunt Clara eyed me closer. "Cat, sit!" I sat, picking the dark chair because I was wet. "Nell, get hot coffee or hot cocoa. Ruth, get a cloth with warm water. Cal, run upstairs and get a blanket and two pairs of socks. Cat, get those shoes off your feet."

"Y-yes, okay." My teeth were chattering.

"I'd like to take you upstairs and get those wet clothes off you right now, but I suppose you'd pitch a fit, under the circumstances."

"Yes, I'd p-p-pitch a f-fit."

"Don, ask your grandmother where to find a hot water bottle. Put hot water in it and bring it back."

He went instantly.

Now Nell was back with cocoa. I took it from her, looking into her eyes for just a second before guilt or pity forced me to look away. We were at the end of everything. It might be possible even now to back away, say I didn't know who had chased me, tell VanLente I wasn't sure it was John. But it wouldn't be easy.

Gran had come in with a clean cloth dampened with soapy water. Clara wiped my forehead and chin, while Nell looked on, wringing her hands.

"Are you all right?" she asked.

"Yes, really."

"Poor Cat. What happened to you?"

"Honestly, child," Clara said. "Cat will survive." Cal and Don provided blankets, hot water bottle, and socks, and Nell helped me pull the socks on. Clara put the hot water bottle in my lap. I felt like hell. People sometimes say they wished the floor would open up and swallow them. I wished it now.

"If you're finished with Ms. Marsala," VanLente said, "I have some work to do here."

Silence came over the room. Everybody sat, except VanLente, John, and Hank. John and Hank stood near the fireplace facing VanLente, about ten feet away from him, as if they were British lords, waiting to hear what the constable had to say. I looked John in the eye, and he tried to stare me down.

Let's not do this. I'll go home now.

I wasn't ready for VanLente to say immediately, "Ms. Marsala, who attacked you and my deputy?"

Oh, lord.

I still locked eyes with John. Deep in my throat, I heard myself whimper. Nell—I couldn't think of looking at Nell.

I said, "John DeGraaf."

Nell said, "No," in a small voice. Gran gasped and closed her eyes. Her mouth moved. She was praying.

"He came out of the house with a shotgun. When he fired at me, the deputy jumped up and fell against the door. I ran. John stalked me through the field down to the woods. He fired—he must have fired at me five or six times. He reloaded as he chased me."

John took one step toward me. "I haven't been out farther than the garage. See—my feet are dry. I couldn't have chased anybody through the woods in these pants."

It was true. His hair was slightly damp, but he had changed his boots and pants. Jennifer whispered tensely to Dan.

John said, "She's been hurt, not by me, and she's raving. Anyway, it's dark out. She couldn't have seen who chased her—if anybody did. I heard shots, but I don't know who it was. Maybe somebody was just hunting rabbits and Cat panicked and ran into the trees."

"The deputy saw the effect of the first shot," I said to VanLente. "Is he conscious?"

"Partly. He'll be able to tell us what he saw tomorrow."

But of course John knew the deputy hadn't seen enough. Still not looking at Nell, I said, "Then you'll know that I was shot at deliberately."

John said, "If so, it wasn't me. But Hank was out for a long time."

For a second, Hank didn't understand. When he realized what John was implying, he was stunned. He said, "What! What do you mean?"

"And then there's Cal," John said. "He went out. Nobody really knows where. Look at their feet. *They're* the ones with the wet feet and pants legs. Cal's a screwup. He didn't like Luis, either, you know."

As he spoke, everybody else in the room became quiet. They stared disbelievingly at John. Dead silence. Even Nell stared at him, astonished at this easy blaming of his own family.

I said, "Sergeant, I think there's a way you can verify this."

"What?"

"Look to see whether John has a bruised shoulder. A twelve-gauge shotgun has quite a kick. The person who fired it should show the impact."

John said nothing.

"Come to think of it," VanLente said, "shotguns throw a fair amount of gases and particles. His hands—"

"He wore gloves," I said.

"All right. His neck and cheek. A shotgun will shoot nitrates into his cheek if he fired from his shoulder."

John cocked his head sideways and eyed us. A bemused look came over his face, as if he thought we were trying to trick him. Then it changed to repugnance. We had offended his sense of right.

"You're evil people," he said. "I'm entitled to protect my child. My father was going to give away the money she needed to survive. Just for some old family sentiment. What did he think he was, landed gentry? Now that he's gone you can't hurt Nell so much. Unless my mother chooses—she's so judgmental—unless she disinherits Nell for my deeds."

"John, what are you talking about?" Gran said. She was gasping for breath and pale.

"If you knew I'd killed Dad, you'd punish me unto the last generation. My descendants. You'd punish Nell by disowning her."

Trembling, Gran said, "John, I would not. That would be un-Christian."

Her composure broke. She started to cry. It was the first genuine emotion I had ever seen on Gran's face, and it appalled Marie and Hank. Marie just stared. Clara got up and went to Gran. She took her in her arms and rocked her—two elderly women, rocking back and forth. Hank turned and strode to the hall. "I'm calling Dr. Brink," he said.

John spoke directly to Nell. "Luis was trying to blackmail me. He realized I'd hidden the vest. He thought he could get money out of me. He wasn't as wonderful as you thought. I told him I'd meet him at the barn for a talk as soon as I could get away."

Nell shook her head, eyes wide. She looked like a deer caught in headlights.

"But then, when I got to the barn, he didn't want money at all. I don't know why that was, but I knew what he really wanted was for me to be destroyed. And then you would be destroyed, too. He said I had to turn myself in, or else. How could he be so silly?"

Nell couldn't speak. VanLente said nothing, either, but waved his finger at his deputy. The deputy walked slowly to John, took the handcuffs off his belt, slipped one around John's left wrist, closed it with a click, brought the hand behind his back, palm out, pulled the right hand behind, and clicked the other handcuff over it. He clamped his big fist over John's elbow. "C'mon, pal," he said. He walked John toward the door. It wasn't until they got out on the porch that I heard him start to read John his rights.

For three seconds we all sat like statues. I didn't dare look at Nell. Marie broke the tableau first and reached to the child, but she jumped up.

Nell took two steps to stand directly in front of me and said, "I hate you, Cat. I hate you!"

Nell ran out of the room and up the stairs. Marie ran after her, but she was back in a minute. "She's locked her door," Marie said.

Hank said, "Dr. Brink will be here in twenty minutes."

I got myself together enough to shed the blanket. It was a good thing that Nell was gone. They could talk as much as they wanted. "I'd better leave now," I said.

Marie said, "Oh, no you don't. Not yet. You seem to know more about us than we do. What's all this about Luis blackmailing John?"

"Luis didn't try to blackmail John. John just thought he

had. I heard part of the conversation. What Luis actually said was 'Do the right thing.' "

"That doesn't sound like 'pay me money.' "

"No, but John thought it did. He thought Luis was saying 'Do the right thing by me.' At that point, several months after killing his father, John probably saw everybody as just as venal as he was. He knew then that Luis held his life in his hands. John was terrified. It was a case of the wicked fleeing where no man pursueth."

Gran, with Clara's arm still around her shoulders, said, "How could John kill Luis that horrible way?"

"Mother," Marie said, "you ought to go to bed. We'll send Dr. Brink up to you."

"Marie! This is my house, and I'll ask what I choose to ask."

"All right, Mother, if you insist on it. I think John must have been furious already at Luis because he thought Luis was seducing Nell."

I said, "I'm not so sure. He may have been afraid that might happen some day and he may have been thinking in the back of his mind that by killing Luis he'd take care of that, too. I mean, that may have added fuel to the fire, but I doubt that was the main reason why he was so vicious."

"What was?"

"Well, I think John, underneath, was a fanatic." Briefly, I wondered whether John might take after Gran in that way, but I wasn't going to say so. Everybody here was hurt enough already. "We think of violent people as ones who flare up all the time, but there's also the quiet fanatic who has a potential for a breakout."

"I can see him lashing out at somebody who threatened Nell. But the viciousness of it—"

"He felt justified. It's often that way for people who think of themselves as good, law-abiding people. When they're pushed to the point of killing, or decide for some reason that they *have* to kill, they think they're right about that, too. To him he was killing for a good reason—to protect his child. But he believed *he shouldn't have to.* He was absolutely furious at Luis for *making* him kill him."

Hank had been rocking back and forth from foot to foot, obviously agonized. "It just doesn't make sense. Look, John had a decent job. He didn't need money for Nell *that* badly."

"That's true," Marie said. "He has a good job."

"He'll have a good income for the next twenty years," Hank said, "and then he'd have a pension and by then Nell would be set up in whatever work she chose to do anyhow."

"What if he quit work now?"

"Then he wouldn't have much. He's only been there fourteen years. He can retire after twenty years."

"What difference does that make?" Marie said. "He's *got* the income. He shouldn't have needed the money so, so desperately! Why was he so desperate?"

"John is dying," I said.

Marie and Hank shook their heads. Marie said, "No, that's not true."

"He is, though. You know that chunk missing out of his shoulder? I thought it was a chain-saw cut. But it wasn't shaped like a chain-saw cut; it was more like a small crater. I think he had a melanoma removed, probably last spring. From the size, they probably told him it had already metasticized. That's why he went to the University of Michigan this summer. Not for a six-week graduate course, but for chemo, which didn't cure it. It just beat it back a bit. That's why he came back so thin and tired, not because he'd been working too hard. John inherited lots of good things from the DeGraaf ancestors, but also that vulnerable pale pink skin, and he's worked long hours in the fields in the sun all his life."

"Oh, my God," Clara said. "I think you're right. My sister Helen died of it seven years ago."

I went upstairs, picked up LJ's cage, and tiptoed down to my car. For once the damn bird had the sense to keep his beak shut, so I passed through the house without anybody seeing or hearing me. I put LJ in the car and belted his cage into its own special child seat.

Back in my room, I stuffed the last items of clothing into my duffel bag, picked up my laptop, turned out the lights, and left. On the table I left a note:

> *Dear Mrs. DeGraaf, Hank, Marie, Clara,*
> *and Nell,*
>
> *You've all been very hospitable to me. I'm sorry about everything that has happened. I wish I'd met you all some other way, some other time. You deserve many years of peace and happiness.*
>
> *Cat*

I tiptoed out of the room, the duffel bag slung over my shoulder. At the end of the hall, where the old wing went into the new wing, Marie was just opening a door. Nell's door. She heard me and turned, first closing the door. She came partway toward me.

"You're leaving?" she said.

"Yes."

"Good."

"Take care of Nell."

"If anybody can."

She turned her back on me. She was angry, angry at me and probably annoyed with herself because she knew I hadn't set the avalanche of events in motion.

On the first floor, I could see Hank at the kitchen table, his head in his hands. Dr. Brink was hovering over him, talking. Gran stood next to them both, pouring coffee. They caught sight of me and my duffel bag. Hank turned his back to me.

Gran came out to meet me.

To my amazement, she held out her hand.

"I'm sorry," I said, taking it.

"You have nothing to be sorry for."

"I haven't?"

"No."

"But John is your son."

"Henry was my husband."

I could still feel her handshake as I drove down the two-track sandy driveway. Gran was doing what she had always done, no doubt done all her life, going forward, making the family run, making sure that the house was warm and the food was ready for dinner. If she survived, she would be there, making a home for Nell.

• 30 •

Tonight is Christmas Eve. I have been working these last three weeks on a new project. It is a long article titled "The Uprooting," and it has to do with the destruction of small family farms. George at *The Insider* has agreed to buy it, for a sum that will pay my rent for December and January. It was hard to write, though, because it was so sad.

My trauma surgeon buddy and semisignificant other, Sam Davidian, took the shotgun pellet out of my ankle. Since doctors are supposed to report gunshot wounds, I tried telling him that one of my nephews was playing with a BB gun and winged me, but I don't lie well, especially to people I like. He got me to admit that I wasn't going to explain what happened. Like a good guy, he accepted it.

I finished the article on Christmas trees, meeting the shipment in Chicago and watching the lot owner and his "woodchucks," as they are called, set up the retail lot. I watched people come to the lot, most of them with children. The kids ran around making "This one! No, this one!" squeals, giggling, having a wonderful time. Some of the kids were very solemn, studying each tree, assessing, though they didn't know it, whether it was "two sides good" or "three sides good" or the premium "four sides good." I personalized the trees more than was truly sane, thinking of the fields they had grown in, the winters, the dry summers, thinking as if it were human of how a tree would feel to be decorated with tinsel and glass globes in a warm home, the center of attention.

And then cast out? And the cycle starts over.

Forget it. The children's delight made me happy.

I had not felt quite as happy watching the tree-lot employees cut the baler netting from the trees before they moved them onto the lot. That netting made me sick.

Long John Silver was ecstatic to be home, but he expressed it with his usual ill temper at having had to put up with adversity. He bit my ear lobe and then flew up and sat all night on the curtain rod, where I can't reach him without getting on a chair. And if I get up on the chair, he always flies to the other curtain rod. I know better than to get involved in his games.

So it's Christmas Eve, and Long John Silver and I are sitting here alone. Sam has gone to Boston to spend Christmas with his ailing ninety-two-year-old grandfather. He left a present, which I will open tomorrow. I'm reflecting on which is more important—do we owe our parents more because they raised us, or do we owe our children more because we are responsible for their existence and they are the next generation, the future? John DeGraaf, and Hendrik too, certainly believed the second.

I open a very tiny bottle of champagne, the size that wine lovers tell you is too small and bad for the champagne and won't taste right. Doesn't matter to me.

I have a banana for Long John, which he thinks is a special treat, and crackers for me, my Polly not wanting crackers but bananas, and with my crackers I have a nice ripe Danish Brie.

Long John flies down, cocks his head at the Brie, and says, "Something is rotten in the state of Denmark."

I throw a cracker at him, but miss.

And, of course, I think about Nell. Once, about a week ago, I phoned Marie, but her number had been disconnected, so I called the radiology department at the hospital. She was there.

"I've gone to live at Mother's," she told me.

"You said you never would."

"Well, I had to. To take care of Nell."

Her voice was neither cold nor especially welcoming, either. I said, "How is Nell?"

"Sad. All the more so because she realizes he did it for her."

"He did it for his *idea* of her. Nell is bright and sensible and could have lived into the future very capably without help."

"That's true. I've become somewhat closer to my mother. No, maybe she's become closer to me. She realizes you can't make the world work just by a set of rules."

"Good. Good for both of you."

"Families shouldn't have to go through this," she said. "Fighting over land. Hank still wants to sell. I want to keep the land."

"Will you be able to keep it?"

"I don't see how."

There was a silence. After half a minute or so, she said, "Cat, I know you had to do what you did. And I know John has to pay for what he did. What he did was wrong. No, it wasn't just wrong, it was hideous. He killed *my father,* too, and I know that. I loved my father. We would *not* have been better off if the murders had never been solved. We would have had a killer among us for however long he lived, and then doubt in our minds for the rest of our lives. Even if he had confessed later, at death's door, it wouldn't have helped. People would have thought he was just getting the rest of us off the hook."

"Thank you for saying that."

"But I don't think Nell feels that way. She's very young, you know, even though her thinking is often mature. She's very angry at you."

"I suppose. Well, she has you, Marie, and you may be exactly what she needs."

"We need each other."

So here I sit, alone except for LJ. In my hand is a small box. It came this morning. There is a crumple of tissue paper inside, and a card. The card says, "I'm mad at you, but I know it wasn't your fault. Nell."

Lying in the nest of tissue paper is a Christmas ornament, one of the old ones with the face of an angel, from the DeGraaf family tree.

ABOUT THE AUTHOR

Barbara D'Amato won both the Anthony and the Agatha in 1992 for *The Doctor, the Murder, the Mystery: The True Story of the Dr. John Branion Murder Case*. Her mystery novels include *On My Honor*, which was nominated for an Anthony in 1990. Her musical comedies have been produced in London and Chicago. She has worked as a carpenter for stage-magic illusions, an investigator in criminal cases, and a teacher of mystery writing to Chicago police officers. Her Cat Marsala mysteries are *Hardball, Hard Tack, Hard Luck, Hard Women*, and *Hard Case*.